# *A Precarious Kiss*

Afterward, she remembered that it was as though she had power to do no else but accept his kiss. If it was meant to be comforting, perhaps it was—at first. Then something seemed to take flame between them and she melted against him. She was enfolded in his strong arms and kissed nearly endlessly. The kiss was infinitely better than her first—the one in the barn.

At last she withdrew, giving him a tentative and misty smile. Then the memory of what had happened before popped into her mind and she gasped.

"What is it? You look as though someone just stabbed you!"

"And well they might. That ivory dragon has gone missing. We still have the little carved box, but that scarcely compensates for the ivory dragon that ought to be inside. How do we explain that to the baron, pray tell?"

# The
# Ivory Dragon

*Emily Hendrickson*

A SIGNET BOOK

SIGNET
Published by New American Library, a division of
Penguin Putnam Inc., 375 Hudson Street,
New York, New York 10014, U.S.A.
Penguin Books Ltd, 80 Strand,
London WC2R 0RL, England
Penguin Books Australia Ltd, Ringwood,
Victoria, Australia
Penguin Books Canada Ltd, 10 Alcorn Avenue,
Toronto, Ontario, Canada M4V 3B2
Penguin Books (N.Z.) Ltd, 182–190 Wairau Road,
Auckland 10, New Zealand

Penguin Books Ltd, Registered Offices:
Harmondsworth, Middlesex, England

First published by Signet, an imprint of New American Library,
a division of Penguin Putnam Inc.

First Printing, January 2002
10  9  8  7  6  5  4  3  2  1

PUBLISHER'S NOTE
This is a work of fiction. Names, characters, places, and incidents either
are the product of the author's imagination or are used fictitiously,
and any resemblance to actual persons, living or dead, business
establishments, events, or locales is entirely coincidental.

# Chapter One

"Drat," Harriet murmured as a cloud drifted to obscure the bright, early-summer sun. She glanced upward, absently taking note that the cloud was rather dark and most likely promised rain.

Turning back to the project at hand, she forgot about a possible wetting to concentrate on the lovely example of a blue gentian. The least she could do for her dearest aunt was to make her watercolor rendition of the bloom as accurate as could be. Aunt Cornelia wished her collection of wildflower paintings to be as complete as possible. As she said, she could identify any plant, she simply couldn't paint a blue gentian—or anything else—to save her life.

When dearest Aunt Cornelia offered a home and warm welcome, Harriet had eagerly accepted and had not had even one sorry moment. Except . . . there had been a dearth of gentlemen her age in the area. Either the men were too old or too young, or like the lanky, bespectacled fellow who had a tendency to tag along when least wanted. He had desired to go with her today. After catching a glimpse of Harriet's momentary expression, Aunt Cornelia firmly banned such a notion, saying, "Harriet does not like to be distracted from her painting."

Pleased that he might be considered a distraction by anyone, the poor fellow went, at least for the present. That sort never gave up.

It had been kind of her aunt to extend an invitation to stay with her while Harriet's sister Charis and her new husband sailed off on their honeymoon. Marcus issued her an invitation to join them, but Harriet didn't think she could stand their mooning about all hours of the day. If ever she fell in love with a gentleman, *she* would be more circumspect for certain.

Mama was available, of course, but Harriet didn't have the heart or inclination to impose herself on her newly wed mother. That dear lady was deeply involved in redecorating her new home, to the general's delight. Harriet was so overjoyed to see her mother alert and interested in life again after the death of Harriet's father that she felt her own presence quite unnecessary.

The first drop of rain fell just as Harriet applied the final touch of shadow to a fringed blue petal. Hastily gathering up her painting equipment and the still-wet completed blue gentian, she dashed madly for the nearest structure, a storage barn.

Inside, it was dry and clean. The hay from last year was almost gone, and the barn awaited another crop. Dust motes floated in the air, bits of hay littered the rough wood floor, and the structure had the air of waiting . . . for something. It was rather removed from the main house and outbuildings. The estate manager said it was useful, being so handy to the road and all.

Harriet spotted a small wooden shelf upon which she could safely place her materials. She knocked something to the floor as she did. Curious, she picked it up, examining the object with a frown. It was a pretty little thing made of wood, and elegantly carved. She held it while brushing raindrops from her old percale dress.

Suddenly she heard a sound, the soft mewling of a kitten. So this was where the kitchen cat had gone to produce her litter! Scrambling up a ladder providentially leaning against the loft, Harriet was entranced to see three balls of gray fluff nestled close to the mother cat. The cat gave Harriet a superior look, as though demanding admiration for her offspring.

Harriet tucked the little carved box inside her bodice, then crouched down to examine her discovery. How very dear the little ones were—blue eyes peering at her with trust.

"Katy-cat, I'll be most careful of your children," she confided to the concerned mother. She suited her words with actions, scooping up one kitten with gentle hands to admire the little one, murmuring soothing words to mama cat all the while. Was there anything so precious as a tiny kitten?

Cuddling the ball of gray to her bosom, she lightly ran a finger over it before she heard the noise. Someone was coming.

Harriet froze in place. A horse and carriage dashed along the narrow lane. They slowed, stopped at the open barn door. Within moments, someone led that horse and carriage right into the barn! Who?

Doubtless the driver wanted shelter from the rain. But since this was a lane that went nowhere—other than Aunt Cornelia's house—who could it be? Harriet edged forward to peer down from the loft, moving silently on the hay.

A man. A gentleman from his appearance. He saw to his horse first, then he removed his hat, knocking it to remove the raindrops. Dark hair curled attractively about a well-shaped head. But then, Harriet was some distance away. He probably was nothing to admire when close.

Looking about him, he brushed off his coat much as Harriet had done her dress. Only those broad shoulders offered a firmer foundation for his coat than did Harriet's slim frame for her dress. He began to walk about, and she followed his progress with increasing curiosity.

To her surprise, he prowled around the barn as though hunting for something. She knew when he spotted her painting paraphernalia. He had the nerve to study her painting, too. What a nosy snoop!

He continued his prowl after setting her painting aside. She wondered what he thought of her work. Most likely he considered her work amateurish, and deservedly so. But she thought herself a decent amateur and had received many kind words on her watercolors. Harriet frowned, wondering what on earth he expected to find in a dusty old barn. She did not recognize him in the least. Aunt Cornelia had invited quite a number of local gentry to meet her, and Harriet knew that no one of this man's stature had been among them.

When he disappeared from her view, she—still clutching the kitten—leaned forward to see if he chanced to find whatever it was he sought. What that might be puzzled her greatly. A trustworthy stranger would know of nothing concealed in an unfamiliar barn. Surely he did not think there was anything remarkable about this building!

Her unfortunate move had a disastrous effect. In one fell swoop and with a cry of alarm, she and the kitten, along with a generous bunch of hay, slithered to the floor below to land not far from the horse that had been munching on a convenient pile of hay. Clearly affronted, the poor horse backed away, giving Harriet a baleful stare.

The stranger whirled about to stare at Harriet as though she was some manner of ghost. "What the . . . ?"

His rush to her side to assist her to her feet brought mixed emotions. He asked, "Are you all right?" On one hand it was comforting to have someone so concerned for her well-being. On the other hand, it was most embarrassing to discover a very handsome gentleman gazing at her as though she was an unwelcome apparition.

"Only my dignity," Harriet replied dryly. "Amazing how hay provides ample cushioning in a fall." She brushed bits of hay from the skirt of her gown, turning her gaze to the kitten rather than the man. What would she find in his eyes? Contempt for such a hoyden as a girl who climbed to a loft? Or possibly concern? Or perhaps total disinterest such as she assuredly deserved. It was difficult to imagine how she could be at a worse disadvantage. Between her wretched dress and bits of hay everywhere, she must look an absolute disaster.

"I see."

His abrupt remark, uttered in such a bland tone, brought her curious gaze to his face at last. What she found there sent her heart to her toes. Here was a man as might frequent any maiden's dreams. Handsome did not begin to cover his qualities. Double drat! Those dark brown eyes, so rich and lively, held vast amusement. His firm lips curved in an engaging smile, while she could not fail to observe there was nothing the least displeasing in his entire appearance. Confound it!

"Well, I am pleased to offer you entertainment. Usually a downpour is so dreary," Harriet snapped.

Her annoyance only served to make him laugh. He extended a beautifully gloved hand to her bare and somewhat paint-stained one, offering belated assistance.

Giving her hay-bedecked, rumpled dress a rueful glance, Harriet brushed off what she could, then faced the man with her backbone firmly in place. Wouldn't you know, the stranger had to be the most attractive man she had seen since she left London? But she must remember his suspicious behavior. Sensible, well-mannered people didn't snoop about strange barns. Holding the kitten close to her bosom, she said with as much calm as she could manage, "Precisely what are you doing here?"

"Retreating from the elements. In case you had not noticed, it is raining buckets out there."

Blast it, why did he have such an appealing grin? And was it solely because of her dishevelment or did he simply find her query amusing?

"I am aware of the rain; I could scarce not be as I sought refuge in here as well. You are a stranger hereabouts. I am curious what you are doing traversing this lane, since it goes nowhere other than to my aunt's house." There, she had put him on the spot. How would he wiggle his way out of this?

"Is it, now?"

What he might have added was not to be known, as the rain ceased as abruptly as it had began. Water could be seen and heard dripping from the eave and a nearby tree. The deluge appeared gone.

"The shower is over."

"So it is," Harriet allowed. She bestowed a helpless look on the kitten. Should she climb up the ladder to replace it where it belonged, thus affording the stranger an improper glimpse—or worse—of her ankles while doing so? If she deposited the kitten on the hay, it would make much work for Katy-cat to fetch it. With a small sigh of resignation, Harriet walked to the bottom of the ladder and gingerly placed one foot on the first rung. She turned to cast a disgruntled look at the stranger. "If you had any manners, you would leave now."

He chuckled. It was one of those rich sounds that delighted the ear. "Why do not *I* restore the kit to its mama? That would solve your dilemma, would it not?"

"It would be a help," she admitted gruffly, and then castigated herself when he gently took the kitten from her outstretched hand and made short work of climbing to the loft to leave the kit with its mother.

After offering polite thanks, she walked to the shelf to retrieve her belongings, wishing that she had thought to wear a decent bonnet instead of this ancient wreck she wore when out painting. "Good day, sir. It was interesting."

She could scarce say they had met. As was proper he had not offered his name, nor had she given hers. Although as nosy as he was, he might have seen her name written on her paint box. He gave no indication he knew who she was, nor did he ask. What a lowering reflection that was.

"It could start raining again, you know," the stranger offered, his manner civil, but no more.

Clearly, he had not the slightest interest in her! Not that she wanted to further her acquaintanceship with him, mind you. Sometimes being proper was a dratted nuisance.

His behavior was dashed smoky. She glanced around the barn, trying to see it from his point of view. There was not one thing that could be labeled unusual or worthy of investigation. So why had he peered at every corner as though expecting to find a treasure? Exceedingly peculiar behavior, to her way of thinking.

"What I mean to say is that it could commence raining again whilst you are on your way to the house, wherever that is. I would hate to see you drenched and possibly catch cold."

"You would know nothing about it if I did," she pointed out logically.

"Allow me to escort you to you destination," he insisted. Looking at the painting she held so carefully, he added, "I would not like to think that your lovely watercolor was ruined because you were afraid of me. I promise I am quite trustworthy." His persuasive manner was the sort that could likely charm the paper from the wall. "Do join me."

"Said the spider to the fly," Harriet muttered. He was right, however. She was quite pleased with her painting, and it would be a shame to lose it because she was too cowardly to chance a ride with the stranger for the short distance to her aunt's house.

Giving him a look that promised she could bonk him over the head with her paint box if necessary, Harriet nodded ever so briefly. "Very well, I accept your offer. But only because I would not wish to have my painting ruined. That was a particularly fine specimen of blue gentian. My aunt wished to add it to her collection."

"So," he continued quite as though she went with him happily, "your aunt has an interest in wildflowers?"

Settling on the seat after he had helped her into the smart curricle, Harriet merely nodded. Since he had turned away, she decided to add, "Indeed, she does. She grows them as well."

He managed to guide the horse and curricle from the barn, then swung up to join Harriet on the seat. It seemed to her that the curricle had shrunk. Was it necessary to be so close? She inched sideways and missed the little smile that crossed her companion's lips.

"Only a clever gardener manages to successfully transplant wildflowers to a garden." He gestured to the right, and Harriet nodded in reply. They set off at a prudent pace.

"As to that," Harriet replied honestly, "she has a marvelous gardener who can do about anything. She just tells him what she wants. But I believe she could do it if she wished, for she is a very determined woman."

"As are you?"

"A gardener?" Harriet asked, deliberately misunderstanding him.

He chuckled again, and she felt the warmth of it clear over to where she so uneasily perched. "No, determined. I believe you are one of those people who know precisely what you want from life, and seek after it. Am I wrong?"

Harriet nibbled at her lower lip. "I've not considered the matter. However could you reach that conclusion, anyway? You have barely spoken with me." She ought not have asked such a question, she knew that. But she also thought his conclusion an intriguing deduction.

The horse trotted along at a gentle pace. It wasn't the dashing clip she fancied he usually went. The thought improved her view of the situation a bit. At least he wasn't risking their necks to be rid of her company.

"Your painting is decisive. Your manner is such that I feel you are sure of yourself—that you know what you want in life. As to what that might be, I can only hazard a guess."

He drove with a sureness and skill Harriet could not but appreciate. She knew of drivers who were so inept they shouldn't be allowed out on their own. She considered his words while admiring his expertise with the reins.

"I really am not sure," she admitted to her surprise. "I suppose a young woman is to want a husband, a home, and children."

He glanced at her, a slight frown on his forehead. She turned her head so she could no longer see even a bit of his face. She found the sight disconcerting.

Continuing, she added, "I feel certain this is an exceedingly strange conversation for us to have. I cannot recall exchanging views on the matter with anyone before."

"I suppose gently bred young ladies do not admit to deeper thinking."

At this remark Harriet did look at him. "What a dreadful thing to say. You must know full well that a girl must not be considered a bluestocking sort. Rest assured that were I truly seeking your interest and approval, I would be very demure and not venture an opinion on anything." She folded her hands in her lap and tried to appear as prim as she might.

He laughed. "I don't know whether to be insulted or relieved." He sought her eyes and smiled when she didn't reply.

"There, ahead, the gates to my Aunt Cornelia's house." She shifted as though she was about to leave the curricle as soon as possible and found his hand restraining her. She gave him an inquiring look.

"If you think I shall deposit you like so much baggage and allow you to walk up the avenue to the house, you are sadly mistaken. I would like to meet your aunt."

"Oh?" Harriet wondered why.

"Besides, it is only proper, you know."

"Hmm," she replied, wondering what her aunt would think of the stranger and his nosing about the storage barn.

"In spite of the situation, I imagine you are a proper young miss."

Harriet thought back on some of her escapades and decided not to answer that remark. Prevarication always found one out, she had discovered over the years.

They drew up before the front of the neat Georgian structure. Harriet gave an admiring look at the pretty place her aunt had acquired. How obliging of her father to give her this refined gem of a house after her fiancé had been killed in an accident and Aunt Cornelia decided not to wed anyone else. She had decorated it with her elegant, simple taste, and Harriet thought it quite the loveliest house she had seen. That it was also extremely comfortable was an added plus.

"Very nice," the gentleman at her side commented quietly. "I have always thought that this style was attractive, particularly with the columned portico."

"Wait until you see the interior. My aunt is possessed of a delicate sense of beauty."

Carefully holding her watercolor and paint box, Harriet allowed her escort to assist her from the curricle.

A young groom whisked around the corner of the house,

evidence that their approach had been noted. He took the reins in hand and slowly began to walk the horse.

Harriet concealed a smile. The servants had calculated the guest's intentions to a nicety. They left the carriage in capable hands and crossed to the front entry.

Her aunt's dignified housekeeper opened the door, giving Harriet a wary look before turning an approving gaze on the stranger. "Your aunt is in the drawing room, Lady Harriet."

Noting the gentleman's quick expression of surprise, Harriet went to the drawing room that was on the ground floor, as was customary in many of the newer country houses.

Aunt Cornelia rose from where she was seated, reading by a window. She was an older version of her niece, auburn hair peeking from a white cap and astute blue eyes. She hurried to Harriet exclaiming, "My dear, what has happened? Your dress . . . ?" That she doubtlessly noticed the bits of hay and Harriet's disheveled look without additional comment was a blessing.

"Blame it on the rain. I sought refuge in that storage barn by the lane and couldn't resist finding Katy-cat's latest litter. That accounts for the hay and my rumpled appearance—and this gallant gentleman at my side."

Aunt Cornelia rightly assuming that the gentleman had not introduced himself, turned to him and offered a dainty hand. "Lord Stanhope, how pleasant to see you again. I fancy you are just recently returned from London? Allow me to present my dearest niece, Lady Harriet Dane. She is my sister's child and staying with me for an extended visit while her sister and mother settle into new houses." At his look of inquiry, she added, "Both married recently."

"I am charmed to meet Lady Harriet. It was a lucky thing that I chanced on that barn. I'd have been soaked otherwise. And I enjoyed meeting your niece, even under such unusual circumstances. Fancy two painters caught in the rain and seeking shelter in the same barn."

"You are a painter, sir?" Harriet couldn't resist asking. He didn't look like one.

He replied with a modest bow, "I am a painter of sorts. That is why I was out and about, looking for a picturesque place to paint."

Harriet shot him a look of disbelief. He wasn't the least like any of those *artistes* she had met who ambled off in what they claimed was a "search for picturesque" beauty that deserved preservation. And why did he prowl about once in the barn? It was scarcely worthy of notice.

"The barn is old, but solid, I believe," Aunt Cornelia inserted, likely to cover Harriet's silence.

"So it seemed," he said with absentminded politeness. "Your niece is talented with her paintbrush. She said you have collected her paintings?"

"Indeed, you may see them sometime if you wish."

"Aunt Cornelia," Harriet said in a warning tone, "I doubt if Lord Stanhope is the least interested in my paltry daubs." She smoothed down the skirt of her dress, wondering if it would ever be wearable again, for it seemed hopelessly crushed to her eyes. Perhaps her maid could do something with it?

"You are too modest, my dear girl," her aunt protested. "I feel certain that the earl will find them delightful. I do not recall seeing any of your paintings, my lord. I trust you brought a few with you when you came from London? Your dear mother said you intended to be there for an extended stay."

"Something came up that needed my attention here."

Harriet had the oddest feeling that he had not wished to confess to that last bit of information. Why not? Had he been summoned home for some reason? Of course it was none of their business, whatever the reason be. But it added to his sense of mystery.

"I am indebted to Lord Stanhope for his courtesy in bringing me home." Harriet spoke with the same sort of civility he had exhibited earlier.

"I would expect nothing less from the gentleman." Aunt Cornelia smiled at him, and Harriet thought it somewhat fatuous.

"She is now safe, and I may return home in good conscience. Dare I hope that you would both join us for dinner one evening soon? I know Mother would be delighted to see you. She mentions you often."

"Indeed, we would." Aunt Cornelia walked with him to the entry hall and lingered as he let himself out to where the groom waited. Harriet followed her.

Closing the door, she turned to cast a reproving eye on her niece. "Harriet, I cannot believe you met Lord Stanhope looking like that! That must be your worst dress, and if I ever see that bonnet again, I shall do violence to it. Naughty child, to be so neglectful of your appearance."

"I cannot see wearing something good to prowl about the estate while painting flowers. Normally I do not see anyone—save for a worker in the distance. My budget is improved, thanks to Marcus giving me such a generous allowance, but I'll not squander it on gowns to be ruined while sitting on a rock!"

"Your new brother-in-law is to be commended, my dear. However, I doubt he would wish you to be badly garbed."

Tired of the subject, Harriet turned to one more interesting. "Where does Lord Stanhope live? Close by?"

"I've not been to visit his mother since you came here." An amused gleam entered her eyes, and she continued, "I cannot wait for you to meet her. He has a, er, rather unusual family."

Now definitely intrigued, Harriet led her aunt back to the drawing room, where a small fire burned to remove any chill from the damp air. "Do tell me all."

Settling herself into a comfortable armchair, Aunt Cornelia smiled. "Well, as to his mother I shall let you judge for yourself. His brother, Lord Nicholas, is golf mad. I am told he is creating his own golfing course somewhere on their property. The marquess is nutty about birds. I shall say no more on that matter, either, less I spoil the acquaintance for you. His aunt and uncle Plum reside there at present, and both are collectors of a sort."

"They sound a trifle eccentric to me."

"A trifle? I suppose you might put it that way. Everyone has a different reaction to them. The Marquess of

Lanstone is a compelling person, fascinating, to say the least. His wife is also, in her own way."

"And Lord Nicholas? I should think someone who is 'mad' about something as unusual as golf would be considered a bit peculiar. I have met gentlemen who have mentioned they play an occasional round, I think they call it. But to be mad over it? How strange." Harriet held her hands to the fire, realizing she was more than a little chilled. Heaven only knew if she might have caught a cold wending her way back to the house. "I think Lord Stanhope seems fairly normal at any rate. But he was prowling about the barn before I fell off the loft."

That statement was ignored in her aunt's horror at Harriet's fall. She had to be told all the details, and shook her head over them. "Harriet, dear, I hope I do not have to admonish you. I should dislike that very much. Of course you could not have imagined that Lord Stanhope would take refuge from the rain while you were there. But dearest, the sensible woman is always prepared. Try to remember that, will you?"

Harriet nodded. How could she disagree with such common sense? She rose, murmuring something about changing from the ruined dress into something more presentable, and left the drawing room.

In her bedroom her maid fussed over the dress, commenting she doubted she could repair it. Harriet put the little wooden box into a dresser drawer, and turned to be helped into a clean gown.

"I suppose it is beyond all hope," Harriet remarked while slipping into a simple cream gown that went well with her auburn hair. A blue riband accented the front of the gown, just below her bust. It matched her eyes, so she was told by a few of the doltish swains she had met in London. Perhaps she had been too particular? But her brother-in-law was such a fine example of manhood, she had held him up as a pattern the others would have to follow.

"Well, now, I guess I could do something with it." The maid gave the crumpled dress an assessing look, then left the room once satisfied that Harriet had no need for her ministrations. The bonnet was to be burned—even Abby didn't want it!

Gathering her needlework in hand, Harriet went down the stairs to join her aunt. The day was not so dark that she couldn't set a few stitches without a work candle. She accepted her aunt's admiration for her improved looks, then plunged her needle into the delicate lawn to embroider while she considered the stranger.

Why had she never seen Lord Stanhope while in the City? Obviously he must be of the highest *ton*. Yet, not even in Almack's had she caught sight of his impressive form, nor had she heard a word of gossip about him. That was distinctly odd. It was a pity Aunt Cornelia wouldn't know, because she rarely went to Town—only when she desired to select a new gown or a piece of furniture for her home.

Immersed in her consideration of the stranger, she failed to take note of her aunt's speculative watch.

# Chapter Two

Philip took one look at the untrustworthy sky and decided he had better raise the hood on the curricle. The Quince groom assisted. Within minutes Philip left the interesting residence of Miss Cornelia Quince and her oh-so-charming niece Lady Harriet Dane. As he bowled down the lane for the Stanhope estate, his expression turned wry. Home.

Could there be a place less like a home? He wondered if it might be a madhouse. Assuredly, the collection of people gathered under his roof were unusual, to say the least.

Turning his thoughts in a more pleasant direction, he smiled at the memory of Lady Harriet. Now, there was someone who was unusual, but in a delightful way. She was certainly not the customary young woman, the milk and water sort who couldn't say boo to a goose. It was almost lowering to think she was not interested in him in the slightest. It had been a first for him when she stated that *were* she interested in securing his notice, she would behave differently. Philip supposed it was true. Women simply did not reveal their genuine selves when pursuing a husband. They might not want to admit they were in pursuit— nevertheless, they were. He had been the recipient of simpering giggles, near compromises, and downright attacks too many times not to recognize the signals. Lady Harriet merely stared at him as though he were a slug in her garden.

It would be a simple matter to persuade his mother to invite Miss Quince and Lady Harriet to dine. With his Aunt Victoria and Uncle Melrose in the house, they would be a fine group, likely a dozen before she was done.

Well, it was a good thing that Lady Harriet was not attracted to him. His relatives would surely put her off once she met them! His bark of laughter failed to startle his horse, far too accustomed to such things to pay the slightest attention.

The summer rain returned just as Philip feared it would. How providential he had put up the hood. It didn't prevent his getting a bit damp, but he avoided a soaking when he pulled up the waterproof covering over his legs. When in the country he always kept a waterproof by his feet for easy unfolding so he could simply give it a tug and up it would come. While he could take the family carriage if he wished, he preferred to drive himself about. It wasn't merely the pleasure of the drive, it was the need to be able to halt quickly when he wanted, and the maneuverability as well. If he was going to get to the bottom of the mystery, he wanted no coachman to report his doings to the grooms and household staff. He had no illusions that anyone would keep his mouth shut if another of the Stanhope family took to odd behavior.

His thoughts returned to Lady Harriet in that utterly dreadful dress, looking confused and a bit angry, not to mention suspicious. What did she think he was doing in the barn? She couldn't guess the truth. It had been a wild notion at best and obviously wrong, but he hadn't known where else to begin his hunt. She had been a delight, clutching that tiny kitten as though it could defend her from his attentions—if he'd had any. Which he hadn't. Not at that moment, at any rate.

She possessed a lovely face, her figure—revealed more than was proper in that damp, faded, elderly painting dress—was superb, and he considered himself to be an excellent judge. Auburn curls had vitality even in the dull light of the barn, and her blue eyes flashing with scorn had been a wonder to him. Why did the sparks from them not ignite the hay into which she tumbled? Never had he been so startled as when she came swooshing down from the loft. He'd had to stifle an alarming desire to pull her up and into his arms! He shook his head. No complications of any sort were wanted just now. He had quite enough on his plate as it was.

A groom dashed out into the light rain to meet him. Philip handed over the reins to the lad, then hurried to the main house.

His mother was the first person he found. Her orange gown striped with puce and lime hurt his eyes just to look at. He bowed politely. "Mother, I chanced to meet the niece of Miss Cornelia Quince while out, and I think it would be good to invite them to dine with us. Miss Quince lives very quietly, and it must be a trifle dreary for a girl accustomed to the City." He paused. "Nick might fancy her."

That cinched the invitation. The current aim of the Marchioness of Lanstone was to marry off her younger son, Lord Nicholas. That he was indifferent to every young chit she had paraded before him didn't discourage her. She firmly believed that if she tried hard and long enough, she would succeed.

"The very thing. I've not seen Miss Quince for far too long a time. Her niece . . . she is presentable?" Lady Lanstone gave her older son a shrewd look, as though she wondered what his motive might be.

"Auburn curls and blue eyes that sparkle, medium height, slender as a reed, and she paints quite well I believe, from what I saw." Philip observed his mother with amused eyes. She was patently obvious in her ploys, but so delighted with her efforts that no one truly minded.

"Hmm, best invite one of the girls from the rectory to help even numbers. You do not mind, do you?"

"Ask any one of them. There are four left, are there not?" The eldest of the five Herbert girls had wed not long ago, leaving the other four and the son, Adam, still at home. All the girls were charming. He always enjoyed their company.

"It shall be Nympha, for she is the most sprightly of them all and she is such a good listener. Why, she can listen to Nicholas for an hour without her eyes glazing over!" Lady Lanstone beamed a smile at the memory.

"Amazing," Philip replied, his voice dry. "What about another older gentleman for Miss Quince?"

"She will never marry, you know. I think she is so content with her single life she wants nothing to do with a husband. Strange woman!" Lady Lanstone shook her head, turning as she added, "The major—he will be just the one. Swears he will never be caught in the parson's mousetrap. They ought to suit each other very well. Very well, indeed."

"Mother," Philip cautioned. It amused him to hear his mother call the very proper Miss Quince strange. It was little use to admonish his mother, she had sailed forth to find the housekeeper to begin her planning. First the menu, then the invitations, which was in reverse order, but that didn't bother her ladyship. That she had another spot of matchmaking to muddle up made her eyes light up and her smile wider.

Well, Major William Birch could jolly well take care of himself. A most capable man, he had avoided every woman who tried to tempt him into matrimony. That he was considered handsome by some, had bought a fine home, and had enough money to make his life comfortable made him a good catch. Pity he didn't want to be captured. But then, neither did Philip.

Oh, Philip knew he'd have to wed someday. He wondered where he could find a woman who could tolerate, or possibly like, his family. They needed someone to manage things, for a more helpless collection of individuals he had never encountered. And even with the help of Figg, his father's secretary and man of affairs, the job seemed to fall on Philip's shoulders. With a sigh, he strode off to hunt up his father. Wherever he was to be found, Figg was likely nearby.

"There you are!" Philip rounded the corner of the library, where his father was usually perusing something to do with his blasted birds. Figg sat close by him, ready to take notes.

"You want me, my boy?" Lord Lanstone glanced up from his latest purchase, an immense volume illustrated with fine renderings of birds. The room was full of them—birds, that is. His collection having to do with all things avian grew by the month. Philip rather thought it had all begun when his father had found an unusual bird nest and sought the creature that had built it.

Philip idly wondered what could be done when the room became too full to house the collection. They could probably add space. This was a corner room and would not be impossible to achieve an addition.

"Actually, I wanted Figg. Mother is going to give a dinner, and if the guests are to plan in advance, you had best likely do the invitations. Otherwise, she will forget the date or time. It will include Miss Quince, her niece Lady Harriet Dane, Miss Nympha Herbert, and Major William Birch. With Aunt Victoria and Uncle Melrose together with Nick and myself, father and mother, it will be a goodly group. What say you to inviting Miss Cherry, Figg? I have observed that lady smiling at you after church of late."

Figg colored rosily. "A very nice lady, indeed, and it would be most kind to invite her. I doubt she is asked out to dine very often. Her mother, you see."

"Ah, yes. Life is full of complications, isn't it, Figg."

"Indeed, sir." He looked to his employer. "If I may go, I shall discuss a date with her ladyship at once." At a nod from Lord Lanstone, Figg bustled from the room, his habitual worried expression on his thin face.

"You plotting something? I recognize the look, you understand. Always had it when you were a boy and up to something clever."

"As to plotting, Father, I am not very good at that anymore. Nick is the one who likes to plot."

"Didn't answer my question." Lord Lanstone frowned, twitched his elegant, mustache, and picked up his latest acquisition. "Fine book."

"It is a magnificent book. Thank goodness our income is sufficient to allow you to buy it." Philip leaned against the desk to study his parent. Would he ever cease collecting? Probably not. The best thing to do was to consult an architect to see how best to extend this room.

"Trouble with finances? Figg hasn't said a word to me about it. Do whatever must be done, my boy. Trust you completely."

Philip knew better than to suggest that his father assume his rightful place as head of the Stanhope fortune. All he wanted was his dratted birds.

"Your mother wants a Venetian window put into the dining room," Lord Lanstone said, looking expectant. "Says it is too dark in there. I suppose it would cut down on candle usage." He gave his son a hopeful look Although he rarely paid attention to his wife, he likely cared something for her.

"Actually, I had thought about consulting an architect regarding something else. I could see to the window at the same time. Late summer would be a good season to make the alteration." Philip wandered to the window, staring across the land in the direction of the Quince house. If he ever married, what would his father do without him? Figg wouldn't be able to manage him or the estate on his own.

"Knew you could tend to it. Can't be bothered myself." Lord Lanstone placed his new book on a special stand so he could better admire it.

"What would you do if I chanced to marry? I doubt Figg can handle everything around here. He has enough just coping with your stuffing birds and hunting for books."

"Bah! Find you a gel and bring her here. Bound to get along with all of us. You'd not choose a numskull."

Just the prospect of bringing any gently bred woman into this house was daunting. It would take someone utterly unflappable! The image of Lady Harriet popped into his mind, only to be dismissed. Her mode of dress was even worse than his mother's, even if she did have shining auburn curls and sparkling blue eyes. She also declared she was quite uninterested in him. Not attracted in the least. Well, that made two of them. He wasn't much captivated by her, either.

"There you are!" Nick popped around the door, quite as though Philip had been hiding from him. "Need to see you a minute or two, Philip." A little brown-and-white terrier stood at his side, wagging its tail.

Philip exchanged a look with his father, then left the room, knowing that Nick was as uninterested in birds as his father was in a golf course. "What is it now?"

"First of all, I must thank you for suggesting I get a terrier to take with me. First-rate little dog and a better one to get the vermin on the land I've never seen. He can dig into any hole and come up with the critter like anything." Nick nodded in admiration.

"I'm glad you find the dog of use. You said first?" Philip gently reminded.

"I need you to sketch one of my holes. If you would come along this afternoon, I could show you the terrain and what I want. It's a fair piece of meadowland, with sandy soil and a bit of gorse here and there to create good hazards. I want to plot out where the other bunker should be, and I need to calculate the size of the putting green. If you could just sketch it for me, I could better envision it." He gave his usually busy brother a hopeful look.

"Of course. Be glad to help," Philip said, walking along the hall to where his drawing and painting equipment was stored, Nick tagging after him. The cupboard was handy, and he never had to bother anyone if he wished to get it.

"Philip," commanded a voice from the stairs.

He halted and looked up. "Yes, Aunt Victoria?"

"The post brought another cupid for me, and I need a pretty shelf upon which to place it. Do something."

"I shall mention it to the carpenter on my way to the stables."

"Good. And Melrose wants a shelf for his latest acquisition, a lovely chess set from Portugal. You must see it to appreciate its beauty." Her high, fluting voice soared down the stairs to pierce his ears.

"Yes, Aunt Victoria." He hastily grabbed his equipment, then nudged Nick before him until they managed to escape the house.

"Why do you allow her to do that?" Nick demanded as they strode to the stables and their horses. Nick's dog pranced along at his side, having no trouble keeping up.

"You all demand of me," Philip finally replied. "If it isn't you wanting a sketch, it is Father wanting a bird stuffed, or Aunt Victoria, or Uncle Melrose wanting something done. Mother never asks for anything, but I end up doing what she wants anyway. I do not mind, but I sometimes wonder what you would all do if I disappeared. Or married."

*Where did that come from?*

"You? Married? That's a laugh. Who would you bring into this house? You don't know any saints." Nick guffawed at his humor.

As they neared the stable, a footman intercepted them. "Sir, this package just came in the post. The groom brought it from the mail a few minutes ago."

Philip glanced at the box. "The taxidermist. Must be that bird Father shot and wanted stuffed. Take it on up to the house at once, James. I imagine he is eagerly awaiting it. Oh, and instruct Parrot that his carpenter services are required by Mrs. Plum."

"Moldy old birds." Nick grimaced. "Don't see what he finds of interest in them. Keeps him inside most of the time. He needs to be outside more." Nick watched as his horse was saddled, accepting his reins when it was ready.

Rather than wait around, Philip tossed a saddle on his roan and was ready to leave at the same time. He slipped the case with his paints and pencils and the pad of paper into a loop so it could hang from his saddle.

"I suppose you think he would benefit by learning how to play golf." Philip gave Nick an oblique look. "When you told him the object of the game was to drive a ball as far toward the next hole as he can, he pronounced you daft. I must say, the idea of spending hours knocking a ball from one hole to the next seems pretty silly."

"You have to try it, brother. Why, the chaps I've talked with who play up in Scotland say there isn't anything finer. I want to make a course down here that will draw fellows from London for a day or more of the sport. I can't be dependent on you forever, you know."

"You fancy you can make a living out of a golf course? I give leave to doubt it, but if it is what you want and you believe in it, who am I to say nay?" Philip followed his brother over a rise in the outlying meadowland to where he had staked out his future course. Nick was welcome to the land Father had given him.

The land wasn't good for much. As Nick had said, the soil was sandy and gorse littered the landscape, dark green ragged shapes against the short, crisp grass. One bunker, or sand holes as Nympha called them, had been dug. It had assumed the shape of a kidney bean, and Philip wondered if that had any significance.

"I sent off to St. Andrews for the rules of the game. They call it *The Royal and Ancient Game of Golf.* My, that does sound impressive, doesn't it? Do you know it goes way back? James the Sixth played it, they say."

Philip looked over the area, studying every aspect of it. "Amazing," he murmured. "Well, one has to have a lot of idle time on his hands to play golf."

"Nympha Herbert says women could play as well, but I doubt it. The game requires strength and a certain amount of calculating."

"It ought to be a snap for women if that is the case. A more calculating bunch I can't imagine. By the way, Miss Herbert will be dining with us one of these days. Mother is planning to invite Miss Nympha Herbert and Miss Quince as well as Lady Harriet Dane. She is Miss Quince's niece and residing with her at present. Figg is to ask Miss Cherry from the village as his partner. I do not hold with omitting that good man from company."

"What's got into you, Philip? You sound, oh, I don't know, almost bitter. T'aint like you at all."

"What do you know?" Philip rode forward a bit, then turned to face Nick. "Now, show me where it is you want the sketch done and how."

Recognizing his brother was not about to reveal anything of himself, Nick obligingly described what he wanted, concluding, "I think this hole ought to be about a hundred yards along the ground. They vary in distance, you know."

"Indeed, you have made me aware of that," Philip said with more than a touch of dryness in his voice. "You do not think that later parts will be too close to the sea?"

"No, for the ones up in Scotland are right on the sea, and there is even a rule covering the accidental hitting of a ball into the water."

Philip shrugged and went to work with his pencil and pad. Within moments he was totally engrossed.

The terrier, name of Rags, went to work as well, snuffing out a rabbit and probably terrorizing it into the next county.

"Isn't he a great little fella?"

"Umm hmm," Philip murmured, just wanting to get his job over and done with, although he had to admit it was rather nice out in the sun with a gentle breeze ruffling his hair now that the rain was over. Perhaps this golf thing might not be too bad. "Oh, Nick, I forgot to mention that Mother wants a Venetian window in the dining room, and I expect I shall have to have a room added to the library, making it a sort of double room, if you know what I mean—an archway or something joining the two. Father's bird collection will demand it sooner or later. I thought I'd find an architect to do the job."

"There's no end of work for you, is there?"

Philip glanced at his brother. For once Nick almost sounded sorry for him.

At Quince House Aunt Cornelia stood in the entryway to peruse the crisp paper just delivered by a Stanhope footman.

"What is it, Aunt Cornelia?" Harriet paused on the bottom step of the stairs to survey her bemused aunt.

"Well, I must say, when he says there will be a dinner party, he means what he says."

"Dinner party? He says? What are you talking about?"

"Lord Stanhope said he wanted us to join them for dinner before long, and here is an invitation for next week."

"You will accept, of course." Harriet smiled at her aunt, taking the last step to join her. "I must see that motley collection of creatures you have teased me about."

"Heavens, do not permit anyone else to hear you call them a motley collection, even if they are," Aunt Cornelia declared firmly. Then she smiled. "Although, motley does apply very nicely. I suppose I should explain the others. There will likely be his brother Nicholas, Lord and Lady Lanstone, of course. Then her sister Victoria Plum and her husband Melrose, who live with them for the time being. Melrose Plum is temporarily out of funds, and they find it most convenient to live at Stanhope Hall. I imagine Figg will be there as well, with some lady from the local area as his partner."

"Figg? What an odd name."

"He is secretary to the marquess, mostly tabulating his bird collection and his books on birds."

"Gracious. Lord Nicholas is the one you called golf mad?"

"Yes, he is the one." Cornelia smiled a bit.

"I have heard a little about it, and it sounds ridiculous—chasing a little feather-stuffed ball around with a long club in hand. What about his aunt and uncle?"

"Victoria collects cupids. Melrose Plum collects sets of chess. As I cautioned, it is a rather unusual family."

"And what does Lord Stanhope collect?" Harriet led her aunt into the drawing room, pausing to send the maid for a tray of tea.

"Nothing, at least from what I have heard. Poor man, I expect he spends his time seeing to the members of his family."

"Then he is the normal one?" Harriet persisted. If he was the normal one, poking about strange barns where he had no business in being, the others must be utterly mad.

"I should suppose so. I must say he has enormous

patience with the lot of them. I wonder if he will ever marry? There aren't many women who could tolerate that group, and I doubt he can leave them on their own. They depend on him, you see."

"Like a lot of infants yet to be weaned."

Cornelia laughed. "How well you put it. What do you suppose would come to pass if he left them all to their own devices?"

"Maybe they would have to grow up and become responsible adults."

Sobering, Cornelia gave her niece a concerned look. "You hold some rather stern ideas regarding people you have yet to meet."

"I've met other pampered people in London. Spoiled, yet nice enough. As long as someone is willing to indulge him or her and all their desires, why should they grow up? It is a lot more fun to merely do as one pleases."

"There are some people who are genuinely helpless. Few women have been taught how to cope with the problems life can present." Cornelia gave her niece a sage look, as though to remind her that oftentimes a woman had little choice in what life offered.

Harriet smiled. "Yet you manage beautifully. Your house is perfect and the housekeeper knows just what to do, because you have trained her well. It is a pleasure to be here with you."

"What a lovely thing to say, my dear. Had I already not been delighted to have you with me, I would assuredly be so now." She turned to see the maid bringing in a large tray upon which was all needed to make a splendid tea.

"Plum cake and lemon biscuits," Harriet cried with pleasure. "Your cook will utterly spoil me, dearest aunt. You must have told her I dote on plum cake, not to mention lemon biscuits." They found chairs by the fireplace, and Harriet poured for both. "I wonder if poor Lord Stanhope gets anything half as delicious as plum cake for his tea?"

"Poor Lord Stanhope, indeed. You should know he is

one of the wealthier men in the country. He can afford
to indulge his relatives."

"And well they know it," Harriet murmured darkly,
guessing how it must be.

It was late by the time they arrived back at the Hall.
Philip strode from the stables, leaving Nick to take care
of matters there. Philip figured he might as well send off
for the architect he had in mind. The chap came well
recommended, and it might be difficult to obtain his services. He was a younger son of Lord Heron—Pericles
was the name if Philip recalled correctly. Figg would
know his address. Figg could find anything.

Briefly he wondered if Pericles Heron would suit Lady
Harriet. Then he smiled at that silly thought. Harriet
Heron? Never.

"All is set, dear boy." Lady Lanstone bustled along
the hall, intent on cornering her older son before he
could slip away from her. "The dinner will be next week.
Cook has devised an elegant menu that should please
the most delicate of tastes. I can scarce wait."

"I hope you will not be disappointed, madam. You
have seen before that your matchmaking efforts are not
received the way you planned." Philip held a neutral
expression with difficulty. His mother might be exasper-
ating and have the most abominable dress sense in the
world, but she was a constant delight, at least, to him. It
seemed her esteemed husband didn't care a jot one way
or the other.

"This time I cannot fail. If what you have told me
about Lady Harriet is true, she is bound to be enchanted
by Nicholas. How could she not find him delightful?"

"By the way, Father said you desire a Venetian window for the dining room. I intend to hire an architect to
see about another project, and I shall consult him regarding the window as well. Actually, I think it a very good
idea. As Father said, it might save on candles." He didn't
mention that it would take years to make up the difference between the sum required for the elaborate window

versus the candles. If his mother wanted it, she would have it. "Mind you, it may not be possible, given the wall in there and all. Do not get your hopes up until it is a done deed."

"Rubbish! I know you will manage it, Philip."

He raised his brows in reply, then marched along the hall until he found Figg. "See if you can locate an address for Pericles Heron. He is the younger son of Lord Heron, so that direction might do. It ought to be in one of those peerages or somewhere."

"The window, my lord?" Figg looked hopeful.

"And a good-sized room to add onto this one as well."

"Your father will be very pleased."

"So I imagine," Philip said, his expression sardonic.

# Chapter Three

"It is an imposing house, Aunt Cornelia." Harriet gazed from the carriage with judicious eyes. "Yet it looks comfortable. There is no elaborate staircase rising to impress one with a grand main floor, yet the stateliness is evident in the presentation and those substantial wings to either side of the central block. It is a fine example of eighteenth-century architecture, I think. I admire that rose-color brick."

"I understand there are to be a few changes."

"However did you learn that? Lord Stanhope said nothing about such a plan when he was with us. Not that I would expect him to talk about changes with a chance-met stranger, that is."

Aunt Cornelia smiled. "One of our maids is walking out with a footman from the Hall. She mentioned it to Mrs. Twig, who informed me."

Harriet suspected there was little the housekeeper didn't learn, one way or another. Any development touching upon the life of a household was bound to be shared by all affected. "Of course," she murmured while admiring the fine front door. It was massive and of fine oak. There were windows above as well as a window to one side of the door, evidence that the interior would be well lit. It also assured those inside that no one would approach the house without being observed. She shuddered at the thought of the window tax they must pay.

The front door opened as soon as the carriage drew to a halt before the house. The pair left the carriage promptly, all Harriet's thoughts of examining the house dismissed by the expectation of meeting Lord Stanhope again, not to mention his family.

"Do I look presentable?" Harriet whispered as she shook out the folds of her best primrose sarcenet gown trimmed with rich cream lace and a riband of black velvet. She chose not to wear an evening hat, but had instead tucked a delicate arrangement of silk flowers in her hair. It peeked from her curls with what she hoped was a touch of elegance.

"Indeed. You look utterly divine, my dear. In fact, I shouldn't wonder . . ." Whatever Aunt Cornelia intended to whisper in reply was cut short as they crossed to the door. It would never do for the servants to overhear a personal comment.

Harriet and Miss Quince were welcomed into the house by the dignified butler whose name, according to her aunt, was Peel. Of course such an establishment would have such a man. It was not the modest house Aunt Cornelia possessed, presided over by the venerable Mrs. Twig. That he knew her aunt was evident when he addressed her by name.

"Good evening, Miss Quince."

"Hello, Peel. This is Lady Harriet Dane, my niece." Aunt smiled at Harriet as she spoke, hinting at the fondness they felt for each other and indicating that her relative was a welcome addition to her home.

He nodded politely, then took Aunt Cornelia's lavender velvet cape, handing it to a footman before escorting the women the length of the large entrance hall to the rear of the house.

Harriet quickly glanced about her, admiring the beautiful staircase that wound around three sides of the hall to the first floor. It was graceful, brilliantly lit by those windows she had noted as they drove up. Since it was early evening, the splendid chandelier overhead had not yet been lit, but there were sconces with tall candles adding light to the area. Perhaps that chandelier wasn't necessary except for grand occasions?

"The library is off to that side." Cornelia spoke softly with a nod to the left of them. "It is one thing that is to change. I believe Lord Lanstone requires more space for his collection."

"That might be interesting," Harriet replied with equal care. "You imply there is to be more."

"Later," Aunt Cornelia murmured as the butler ushered them into the drawing room. It overlooked the park that extended from the rear of the house, and the view was magnificent, even in the fading light. It merited more than the hasty perusal it received from Harriet before she properly turned her attention to her hostess.

"Dear Miss Quince. And this must be your niece, Lady Harriet Dane. How delightful you could join our little group. Allow me to make you known to the others with us this evening."

It took Harriet a few moments to adjust to the amazing gown worn by Lady Lanstone. Hadn't she seen something of the sort at Astley's Amphitheater? The figured silk was a violent pink shot with silver and the gown had spotted lace sleeves and bodice. On her head she wore a turban a-al-Turque of the same figured pink silk bedecked with pearls, two rows of which went straight across her forehead. In the center of the turban sparkled a fair-sized diamond crescent. The total effect was somewhat overwhelming.

"Come, my dear, you must meet my sister." She grasped Harriet by her arm to lead her to an imposing woman garbed in puce satin. A sweet-looking girl simply dressed in white muslin was at her side.

"Lady Harriet Dane, this is my sister Mrs. Melrose Plum. Her husband is over there talking to my son, Nicholas. And, perhaps you have met Miss Nympha Herbert? She is one of the rector's daughters, I forget which one."

"We haven't met and I am the fourth girl, Lady Lanstone. How lovely to have another woman my age, Lady Harriet. That is to say, well . . ." She glanced at all the older women in the room, then turned a delicate rose.

"Yes, I have observed that there is a dearth of young ladies in this vicinity," Harriet quickly inserted to help out the poor girl. "I shall welcome your company."

Lady Lanstone pulled Harriet along with her to introduce her husband and son Nicholas, ignoring Mr. Plum. Or perhaps she might have introduced him had it not been the intrusion of the butler with another gentleman at his side.

"Major William Birch." Peel stood slightly behind the major, appearing highly satisfied with the latest guest to arrive.

A distinguished gentleman garbed neatly in a wine velvet coat over black breeches stood surveying the assembled group. His stylish white waistcoat showed off a trim figure. Only the threads of white in his dark hair gave a hint that he was among the older men. Harriet guessed him to be near her aunt's age. His only fault, if it be one, was that he possessed a decided limp.

There was not a hint of the dandy about the major, nor in Lord Nicholas, who wore a sharp black coat over a dashing white waistcoat and black pantaloons. A large emerald pin gleamed from his neck cloth. His languid air must conceal a temperament that was all activity, if what Aunt Cornelia said about him was true. No one interested in building a golfing course could be as indolent as he presently looked.

Lord Lanstone moved forward to welcome the major, while at Harriet's side Aunt Cornelia gave an audible sniff. She said nothing, but Harriet wondered at her reaction. Surely Aunt must have met the man before, as this was not an especially large community. Did she disapprove of him? And if so, why? How intriguing!

It seemed the gentleman wasn't pleased to see her aunt, either, for he bestowed a cool, if polite, glance on her before being introduced to Harriet.

She said all that was proper, then eased her way back to where Nympha Herbert stood in silence as Mrs. Plum held forth on the upcoming village fair. She seemed to take it for granted that Nympha would not only attend, but contribute much energy to the organization of the fair.

Most likely noticing Harriet's wondering expression, the girl smiled. "Rector's daughters are expected to take part in all village functions. It goes along with being in the rectory, you see."

Harriet didn't actually see why it ought to be so, for after all, simply because they had been born there did not mean they were to serve the community. That job was their father's responsibility. Or perhaps the squire's? Every village of any size appeared to have a squire to oversee things of this sort.

"Is it to be very soon? I do enjoy a country celebration." Harriet looked at Mrs. Plum, who for once remained silent.

"About three weeks. It is too early for a harvest fair, but I think it has something to do with the person who founded the village. Do you know what it is, Mrs. Plum?" Miss Herbert had respectfully turned to address Mrs. Plum, who in turn shrugged and wandered away.

"What a strange way to answer a query," Harriet observed.

"Oh, you mustn't mind Mrs. Plum. I suspect she does not hear well and does not like to admit it." Miss Herbert looked directly at Harriet, a twinkle lighting a pair of very fine blue eyes.

"I understand they live here? That must be agreeable for Lady Lanstone."

Nympha gave Harriet a hesitant smile. "I rather doubt it. It has been my experience that relatives can often cause problems, and they have been here for a long while. I should think Mr. Plum would have repaired his fortunes by this time."

"Not everyone is clever at managing money, or so I have observed." Harriet took note of Lord Stanhope at that point. From where he stood across the room he stared at her as though she had grown two heads since he last saw her. "Please, do tell me that something is not amiss with my hair or gown. Aunt seemed to think all was well when we arrived, but Lord Stanhope appears to be staring at me."

Miss Herbert joined Harriet in bestowing a puzzled look on his lordship. "I wish I might look half as good,"

Nympha responded softly. "I am all admiration for your gown, and the added touch of flowers in your hair lends a fresh look to you. Such simplicity is so modish."

On the far side of the room, Philip stared at Lady Harriet before he recalled that it was most ill mannered to do so. Egad, the badly dressed girl of a week ago had transformed into a stylish young woman of the *ton*. It was amazing what a bath, proper clothes, and modishly dressed hair could do. He had judged her by her appearance while out sketching and painting. He ought to have known better.

"Well, Stanhope," Major Birch inserted into Philip's reflections, "how do your plans progress? Have you had any reply from Heron as yet? I warn you, he is a devilishly clever chap—brilliant, actually. Don't be surprised if he overturns all your thoughts on what you want to accomplish with the house." Birch glanced at Lady Harriet and back to Philip. "I see you find your guest of great interest. Let us hope she does not take after her aunt."

"Miss Quince seems all that is amiable." Philip scolded himself for appearing so obvious in his examination of Lady Harriet. But, dash it all, she hardly seemed the same person!

"Seems is the word. Has a tongue tougher than leather, that one."

"Never say so," Philip said with a frown. "I cannot believe such a thing." He gave his friend a sharp look. "What on earth brought that on?"

"A little disagreement. I would rather not speak of it."

Totally mystified and wondering why Birch had bothered to mention it at all, Philip nodded acquiescence.

"Lady Harriet is a young lady of curious disposition. I encountered her while she was out painting a flower for Miss Quince. Happened to rain, and we both took shelter in that storage barn along the lane to Miss Quince's house.

Major Birch grimaced. "I am surprised Miss Quince is still absorbed in her flowers. But then, everyone around in these parts seems to adopt an avocation of some kind. Perhaps it has something to do with the water? Or something catching?"

Philip gave Birch an amused look. "Never say *you* have taken to the tendency to collect?"

His friend nodded.

"What? I must know."

"Actually, I found several old snuffboxes when I was prowling about in the attic of my new house. Intrigued me, don't you know. Decided I would hunt for a few more. And there you are, a full-blown collector before you know it!"

"Indeed. I quite see how it can happen." Philip gave the major a smile while keeping an eye on Lady Harriet. She walked with such grace and charm. How had he missed that before? And her voice. When not angry, it had a lilting quality to it he found utterly delightful.

"At any rate, it is lucky no one happened on you in that incident with Lady Harriet. You would have been compromised for certain, and we would now most likely be celebrating a betrothal."

"Good heavens!" Philip's head reeled with the implications. "I merely paused to get out of the rain. Lady Harriet had done the same."

"Who is to know that? Never fear, I will not say a word to anyone. But may I suggest you keep that meeting under your hat?" The major gave Philip a sapient look full of meaning.

"By all means. It isn't as though Lady Harriet were not an acceptable *parti,* I am just not . . ."

"Not ready to settle down yet? I doubt *I* ever will." He glanced in the direction where Miss Quince stood, her back to him while conversing with Miss Cherry from the village.

At that point Peel paused in the doorway to announce that dinner was served.

Harriet dared to look to where Lord Stanhope talked with Major Birch and was relieved to note that they appeared deep in discussion, and his gaze was no longer upon her. "I wonder whom we are to partner?" She spoke in an undertone to Miss Herbert, not wishing to be overheard.

"Let me guess. I will be with Lord Stanhope, you will partner Lord Nicholas, while Mr. Figg will have Miss Cherry. The Plums will fit in where needed, which leaves your aunt with Major Birch."

"I wonder how she will like that?" At Miss Herbert's look of query, Harriet added, "I have the feeling that all is not roses between those two."

"I know what you mean, but I've heard nothing of any argument between them. In a small community like this, word travels quickly if something is amiss. Whatever it is, it is exceedingly private or of long-standing duration."

Harriet gave her new acquaintance a look of respect. Then she turned slightly as Lord Nicholas approached. He bowed most elegantly, then offered his arm to Harriet.

"Mother said we are to be partners. I trust you won't find me too onerous." There was a sparkle of something in his eyes. Mischief, most likely.

She laughed. "I shall be pleased to go in with you."

Right behind him, Lord Stanhope came to gather Miss Herbert for the walk to the dining room. Precedence was abandoned this evening, that much was evident. Else she would have been with Lord Stanhope, and Miss Herbert would have found herself with someone else. Probably she would have paired with Lord Nicholas as she was on equal footing with Aunt Cornelia. Aunt Cornelia said the Herberts were an old and respected family dating back to the arrival of William the Conqueror. Even if this was a cadet branch, she had an excellent background.

As to her aunt, she walked stiffly at the major's side, as though she wished she were anywhere else but was too polite to say a word of protest. He limped, his cane in his free hand, his other cupping her elbow.

The dining room was immediately next to the drawing room, a most congenial arrangement. The room was dim, and in spite of the lingering daylight, a great number of candles had been lit, casting a pretty glow to everyone and everything. The room needed more windows or something to help add light. Of course, windows allowed not only light but also chilly air to seep in, so perhaps they found the present arrangement a balance. Besides, candlelight was very flattering to a woman of any age.

The cherry-wood chairs had spoon feet and very pretty backs. Harriet had always admired Mr. Sheraton's designs, and these were extremely fine examples. The cushions were surprisingly comfortable. She couldn't begin to count the number of times she had been required to endure a meal while seated on a hard, uncushioned chair.

Once seated, she raised her gaze to meet that of Lord Stanhope directly across from her. Well, it was going to be a trifle disconcerting if she had to see that face, those dark, disturbing eyes, every time she looked up from her plate. She tried looking over his head only to discover one of those paintings of dead fowl and fish often found in dining rooms. Why anyone would wish such a depressing subject while dining, she didn't know. She had glimpsed a hunting scene behind where she sat, and would gladly have traded places with Miss Herbert on the other side of the table to improve her view. But that would have placed her beside Lord Stanhope. She was not certain if she wanted to hear what he might have to say.

She compelled herself to listen to Lord Nicholas embark on an enthusiastic account of designing a part of his course, or link, or whatever it was called. She couldn't be certain, for the terminology was totally unfamiliar to her. He was a trifle boring, his conversation consisting solely of golf. On the other hand, when she forced herself to listen to him, it kept her mind off Lord Stanhope.

The first course found an exquisite mushroom soup before her, and she ate it with pleasure. Her empty bowl was efficiently whisked away to be replaced by a fish that had been caught locally and prepared with a delicious sauce. Truly, the marquess and his wife were blessed with a fine cook.

"Nice to see a woman who enjoys her meals. I find it intolerable to watch food wasted on chits who continually refuse to eat more than a bite or two. Just looking at them will tell you that they must eat sometime," Lord Nicholas complained.

"I fancy they do, only they believe that by appearing to have a nonexistent appetite, they will give the impression they would be economical to have as a wife."

"You jest. Surely no one would buy such a fabrication." He stared at her with patent dismay.

"Someone must or why would so many do it?"

"Dashed silly, if you ask me."

"I notice that Miss Herbert does not toy with her food."

"Miss Nympha is a good sort. She'd never do anything so stupid." He didn't bother to examine the lady in question, but applied himself to his meal.

"I quite admire her. She is pretty, soft-spoken, and dresses with excellent taste."

He looked across the table to where Miss Herbert sat by his brother, talking in a vivacious way. "Never noticed."

"That is often the case when people live close by to one another. Tell me, do you know if your brother dislikes me? That is, has he made some remark? Oh, dear, I am making a hash of this. It is merely that earlier he stared at me in such an odd manner that I wondered if I had offended him when we met. I confess, it was rather unconventional." Harriet gave Lord Nicholas an uncertain look before returning to her fish.

"He's not said a word. Unconventional, eh? How unlike my dear brother. He is usually the soul of discretion."

"That explains it, then. I fear our meeting must have given him a very bad impression of me."

"Now, you must clarify that. I am intrigued."

She was saved a reply by the simple means of having her fish plate removed to be replaced by a clean plate upon which the footman served her excellent roast beef with a Yorkshire pudding beside it. The change of courses required she turn her attention to the gentleman at her other side. She wasn't certain what to expect from

Lord Lanstone. Did he talk about anything other than birds?

"You must view my latest acquisition, my dear girl." He twitched his fine mustache. "A yellow-breasted bunting! I was out in the south meadow when I chanced to see this very rare bird, one I'd never seen in these parts before. In fact, the Ornithology Society declared it extinct! Well, I happened to have my gun and shot it. Had I not, we might never have had it to study, you see."

Harriet choked on a bite of her beef. Had he not shot the bird, it might have bred and supplied more of the kind and not become extinct. "And now?" she gently queried, trying not to show her distaste for him and dead birds, extinct or otherwise.

"It just came back from the taxidermist, and I have had a fine glass case made for it. I will show you immediately after dinner. Can't tell you what pleasure it is to have an intelligent female take an interest. Good thinking!"

What his lordship might think if he knew her true feelings on the matter was best not considered. She ate very little of her beef and pudding, although it was delicious. The vision of a poor dead bird kept popping into her mind. What a loss to England if what he said was true.

The plate was removed, and a selection of sweets was set on the table. It was an unusual meal, in that fewer courses were served and the footmen saw to the serving of each person with the central dishes. Harriet was certain there would be far less waste, although that meant the servants would have to have something else. It was the custom for the help to consume whatever was left over. The serving platters and bowls looked quite empty.

With gratitude, she turned back to Lord Nicholas, hoping he had forgotten their previous topic.

He had not.

"Now, satisfy my curiosity that has been simmering all through the beef. Miss Cherry may be fine for Figg, but to my mind she lacks conversation. I demand to know what happened to overset my proper brother."

"It rained. I sought somewhere dry and found a storage barn in which to take refuge. Your brother had the same idea. That is how we met."

"Why do I have the idea that you have left out a considerable amount?"

"It is the bare bones of the event, and that is all you really need to know."

"Hm."

At that moment the footman offered a plate with a variety of delicacies on it. Harriet gladly requested several of the little sweets.

Lord Nicholas waved aside the plate. "You are not going to say another word, are you?"

"No, and that is final. Ask your brother if you must."

"I say, it just occurred to me that if you and dear Philip were alone for some *time,* you could claim to have been compromised." His face was solemn, but his eyes gleamed with mischief.

"Rest assured I would never pull such a trick on him or anyone else. When do you expect to complete work on your golfing course or whatever you call it?" She devoured one of the delicate sweets. Delicious.

"Very well, change the subject. I shall tax Philip later. I do enjoy a bit of mystery."

Harriet consumed the last of her wine and said nothing to his remark. Chancing to look down to the other end of the table, she saw Lady Lanstone signal for the women to rise and leave the gentlemen to their port. With more than a little relief, she slipped from her chair and walked from the dining room with as much speed as she dared. As to Lord Stanhope, she didn't so much as glance in his direction.

Once in the comfortable confines of the drawing room, Lady Lanstone begged her to play for them, and she gladly complied. Performing on the pianoforte made it impossible for anyone to quiz her on meeting Lord Stanhope or anything else. She had completed a delicate piece by Mozart when the gentlemen sauntered into the room.

"That was rather short," Lady Lanstone commented

loudly enough for Harriet to overhear when the men's voices blended with the women's more delicate tones. "I do hope Figg can arrange for the window," her voice faint. "He has little conversation, but is a worthy man for all that."

Harriet suppressed a smile. She would wager that the Mr. Figg and the quiet Miss Cherry found plenty to talk about when in company—their own, that is. She rose from the fine instrument, a Broadwood Grand, thinking they had heard sufficient of her music.

Mr. Figg claimed her attention with a query about window styles and what her opinion of Venetian windows might be in particular.

Harriet assured him that Venetian windows were quite the thing. When he explained that Lady Lanstone desired something of the sort, Harriet declared her pleasure at such an aspect. "For you must know that many London houses as well as country houses have had this sort of window installed. Where is it to go?"

"The dining room."

Well, he was short of conversation, but pleasant nonetheless. Then she observed Lord Stanhope glaring at them from not far away.

"I had best see to Miss Cherry. She is not accustomed to such elevated company." Mr. Figg took a hasty step back.

"That is most kind of you. It is horrid to feel awkward while at a dinner party."

She stood alone when he deserted her, but not for long.

"You found Figg interesting, Lady Harriet?"

"We discussed windows, my lord. You are arranging for a Venetian window to please your mother, I understand."

"Yes—for the south wall of the dining room. She claims the room too dark. What were you and Nick so engrossed in during dinner?"

"He spoke of his golfing plans," Harriet replied with care.

"Surely that wasn't all he discussed. Your eyes didn't

glaze over as usually happens." He leaned against the side of the grand piano, studying her with intent eyes.

"Miss Nympha Herbert listens, and her eyes don't glaze over, either," Harriet pertly responded.

"That may be, I have never paid the slightest attention to what Miss Herbert does. Come now, it cannot be scandalous. My brother may be a bit mischievous but he knows where to draw the line."

"Very well, he asked how we met. I told him I sought refuge in the storage barn from the rain. I then said that you had done the same. Period. Does he need to know more than that? After all, nothing happened."

He mulled her words over for a few moments, then sighed. "You realize that if others learn of this, it could mean you would be deemed compromised."

"How silly. Besides . . . the cat and kittens were there. We were not alone. Your horse as well." She compressed her lips to keep from laughing. He looked so angry for a moment. Would it have repulsed him so much to be compelled to marry her? "Rest assured that I have no desire to wed a man who has no love for me. You are safe from me, Lord Stanhope."

She was rewarded by a rather confused expression on his lordship's handsome face.

# Chapter Four

"How exceedingly, frightfully stupid!" Harriet paced the length of the drawing room, turned to face her aunt, then paced to the other end. "I refuse to even consider the matter."

"You may have to consider the matter, my dear. We have no assurances what Lord Nicholas may do or say. Should he be annoyed with his older brother, he might well refer to your chance-met time in the barn during a rain shower. 'Tis amazing what could be accomplished in a short time if two people put their minds to it." Aunt Cornelia sat serenely in the high-backed chair by the fireplace, looking for all the world as though she spoke of a commonplace circumstance, rather than something far more shocking.

"Well . . . nothing happened! I refuse to marry a man I do not particularly like, much less love, simply because some people have spiteful minds. Besides, he was behaving in a highly suspicious manner. I told you how he prowled about that barn as though searching for something."

"I cannot imagine what might be found in that barn." Her aunt picked up a dainty bit of needlework and resumed her embroidery. "No one ever goes there—usually."

Harriet paused before the fireplace to think back. She had picked up a little carved box when she first entered the barn. It fell when she put down her things. She'd tucked it down inside her bodice when she went to see the kittens. Could that possibly be what he hunted for and did not find?

"What is it? You have had an idea, I can see it." Cornelia held her needle poised in midair, intent on her niece.

"I am not sure. But I believe I will do a bit of sleuthing on my own." Harriet considered the idea at greater length, then started toward the door. "Could we reciprocate with a dinner invitation to the Hall? Lord and Lady Lanstone, and perhaps Lord Nicholas and Miss Herbert, and by all means Lord Stanhope." She paused to grin at her aunt before leaving the room. At the bottom of the stairs, she stopped again to call back, "I do not especially want the Plums. I shall leave that to you, since it *is* your dinner party. Oh, and I do believe you ought to invite that dashing Major Birch."

Her rush up the stairs prevented Harriet from hearing anything her aunt might have said in reply.

Inside the top drawer of her chest sat the little carved box, precisely where she had dropped it. She had completely forgotten it existed with all that had transpired since that fateful day. She removed it, eased the drawer closed, and took the box to the window so she could study it in good light. Could there be anything special about this beautifully carved little box?

The carving appeared fanciful, and she thought she could make out a sort of dragon on the top. Shaking her head in puzzlement, she turned the box over and over in her hand. Then she thought she saw a thin slit at the wide end. When she rotated the box, there was a duplicate slit at the opposite end. Since pushing on the center didn't open it, she tried pushing sideways. Little by little the top of the box moved!

Once she had the box completely open, the delicately carved dragon inside took her breath away. The ivory had mellowed over time and added depth to the exquisite detailing of the dragon. Surely this magnificent little thing must be what was sought by his lordship.

Well, whoever left this article would assuredly come back to look for it, but if Lord Stanhope had left it, he would have known precisely where it should have been. He hadn't. So, who had? She removed the little dragon from its concealment and, upon discovering a pin on the back, she promptly pinned it to the front of her gown.

When she returned to the drawing room, she marched up to her aunt, pointed to the pin, and asked, "Have you ever seen this before? Or this little box?" She handed the exquisitely carved box to her aunt and waited.

"Never. Where did you find it? No—let me guess. You found it that day in the barn. Am I correct?"

"I do not know how you can be so clever, but that is just what happened! How do you suppose it got there?" Harriet walked forward to gaze in the looking glass at the pin where it nestled in the little bow that adorned the bodice of her frock.

"It is a lovely thing, that little carving. What a mystery. Well, it will give you something to do before the milk thistles are in full bloom. I would so like a good painting of one." The wistful expression on Aunt Cornelia's face was quite enough to touch Harriet's heart.

She made a face. "Those leaves are dreadfully hard to paint. I would not do that for just anyone, you know."

"I know dear, which is why I am so grateful to you. Now, shall we plan a menu? Once we decide the main course, I will let Cook complete the rest."

"Oh, a good beef roast and perhaps a turkey? I fancy you know why I want the dinner? It is not simply to reciprocate our invitation to the hall. I mean to see if this pin has any significance to anyone from there. It might be Lord Stanhope, but it could be Lord Nicholas as well. From something Miss Herbert said, I gather that the older brother often has to help out the younger."

"That is often the way life is, my dear. Surely you helped your sister from time to time? You spend a good deal of time writing to her."

Harriet put aside the matter of her writing, thought back, and nodded. "True, I did." She decided her aunt was far better suited to planning the dinner than Harriet herself, and so excused herself to walk in the garden. Ostensibly, she intended to hunt for a milk thistle. That weed would poke up where least wanted, and she needed to find one before the gardener disposed of it. In reality, she wanted to mull over the matter of the ivory pin and who could have left it in the barn. It was a rather peculiar place to leave anything. But as her aunt said, no one ever goes there, so the person might have felt quite safe in doing so.

Slowly rounding the corner of the house, she collided with Lord Stanhope. "You! What are you doing here?" Then, realizing she did not sound gracious or welcoming, she amended her greeting. "What a pleasant surprise, my lord. We were not expecting you. Were we?" She wished she could have hidden the ivory pin. He was staring at it. She doubted very much if he would stare at her bosom in that odd manner!

"Ah, no. That is, I was out for a drive and thought I might stop to see how you fare. You suffered no ill effects from the dinner last evening?" He put his hands behind his back, watching her closely.

"No. Why? Was I supposed to? Suffer, that is." Harriet gestured to the stone bench at the edge of the garden, then walked at his side until they reached it. She sat first, motioning for him to join her. If they were going to talk, they might as well be reasonably comfortable. Not that a cold stone bench was all that cozy.

"Ah, yes, that is, no. You were not supposed to suffer, and I regret any thought of that." He fixed his gaze on the pin again. "What an unusual pin you are wearing. A gift from someone?"

"Why do you ask?" Harriet watched him shift a trifle uneasily.

"No particular reason. It is very lovely and beautifully carved. Could I look at it closer?"

Harriet considered his request. She could say no and insist if he wanted to see it, he would simply have to look at it where it was. On the other hand, that might be awkward, taking into account where it was pinned.

"I am sorry, but the pin is difficult to open. Perhaps another time, when I have had help to remove it." That was a prevarication of the first water, but how did she know he wouldn't take off with it? He had been snooping around that barn and would have taken it then had he found it.

He was obviously disappointed. "Actually, I came to see if you would consent to taking a drive with me. The countryside is pretty this time of the summer. There isn't a rain cloud in sight."

She gave him a derisive look at that remark. "Very well. How could I resist such a charming invitation? Especially the part about the lack of threatened rain."

"You will want to fetch a bonnet and shawl, I suppose?" He stared at the pin again, and Harriet fought the urge to giggle.

"How sweet of you to remind me." She beamed what she hoped was a ladylike smile at him, then rose from the bench. "Walk to the house with me, and you may greet Aunt Cornelia while I find a suitable bonnet and shawl."

He rose immediately and walked at her side to enter the house right behind her. Stalking, that was what he was doing.

Once in the entry she directed him to the drawing room, where he could wait while she went for her things. Fortunately, Aunt Cornelia had returned to her chair and was merely staring into the fire as though beset by a problem.

"Look who is here. Lord Stanhope has invited me to take a drive with him. If you have no need for me, I thought it might be lovely." She gave him a melting look, then after a nod from Cornelia, Harriet lightly ran up the stairs to her room.

Her maid found a shawl and bonnet in a trice while Harriet removed the pin to restore it to the box. When it was safely back in the drawer, she returned to the drawing room.

The first thing he did was to look at where the pin had been. Harriet wasn't stupid. She figured that he might find some way to remove that pin without her being aware of it. Quite how that would be accomplished, she hadn't the slightest notion. However, he was a clever—not to mention handsome—man and likely experienced at a goodly number of things. Whether removing a pin from a bodice was one of them was something she preferred not to find out.

"Shall we go?" she asked brightly.

He bowed over Aunt Cornelia's hand most correctly, then turned to join Harriet, where she lingered near the door.

"Are you aware that pretty pin is missing? I hope you didn't lose it while fetching your bonnet and shawl."

She withstood his searching study of her neatly garbed self with more composure than might be expected. "Actually, I removed the pin with my maid's help lest I do lose it. Such a pretty little thing, as you say."

"You never did say how you came by it." He guided her around to the side where a groom walked his horse and curricle.

Harriet thought rapidly while he assisted her into the carriage. She was invariably truthful, at least, as often as possible. A lie could be told only if a dire circumstance required such action. Could this be termed dire? Hardly. "If you must know, I found it."

"You don't say! Amazing." He became silent, and without another word being spoken, they drove out the gate and along the lane where not so very long ago they had first met.

Harriet had not done much traveling about since she moved in with her aunt. Cornelia was not in the least a recluse, but on the other hand she liked a simple life, one free from excessive socializing. To go for a drive in a smart curricle with a handsome gentleman was nice. Even if it was Lord Stanhope.

After a bit she examined him. "Is something troubling you, my lord?" She might as well plunge to the heart of whatever the matter might be, for she sensed something bothered him.

He paused a few moments before replying. "Actually, I am not certain what to say. First, I must tell you that I'd not wish to offend you or hurt your feelings in any way." Again, he paused before continuing. Harriet had the feeling his words were dragged from him against his will. "There is a problem, and I believe you may be able to help me with it. Can I trust you to say nothing to a soul about it? Or . . . must I muddle along by myself?"

"I can be as mute as a fish if circumstances demand." Harriet could well understand his dilemma. If you shared a secret, there was always a danger that it might accidentally be shared with another. Things like that happened to her too often not to be remembered—not that she had all that many secrets.

"That pin you found is identical to the one my brother is accused of stealing."

Harriet swallowed carefully, then turned on her seat to stare at his lordship. "Well, *I* did not take it from him or anyone else. I thought it was just a little box, not knowing there was anything inside. It was on the ledge where I had put my paints and pad in the barn where we first met. It fell when I set my things down. I picked it up to examine, then I heard the kittens. I dropped the little box inside my bodice, and not long after that you entered with your horse and curricle."

"That's it?" He took his eyes off the lane to study her face. Apparently satisfied with what he saw, he returned to watching the road. "Hm."

"May I inquire who has accused him of theft?"

"If I can trust you to help me, I suppose you have a right to know who it is. Baron Rothson claims Nick took it when we were over there for dinner some weeks ago. True, he admired it, we all did. It is very old, possibly Roman or even Chinese, and highly valuable, so the baron insists."

"Good heavens! And I dared to pin it on!" Harriet made a face. "What a good thing it is that I'm not given to swooning. I fancy *that* is enough to send a number of women into a faint."

"The thing is, we need to return it to the baron so he will not continue to threaten Nick. If our father learns of this, I hate to think of what he will say. He is not fond of the baron, but he would never countenance a theft. If we could sneak it back to the baron's collection room and him not be the wiser, all would be well."

"But Nick, that is Lord Nicholas, did not steal the pin. If he had, what would it be doing in the barn? And why would he take an old pin in the first place. I did not get the impression that Lord Nicholas is precisely at point non plus."

"True, he is not."

They turned off the lane onto the road leading to the village. That Baron Rothson lived in the same direction did not set easy in Harriet's mind. What did Lord Stanhope intend to do? Drive up to the baron's manor house and inform him that the woman in the carriage had his precious pin? That he could cease hounding Nicholas and begin harassing Harriet instead? Not if she had anything to do with it!

"I don't know. That does baffle me a bit."

"A bit! Well, please do tell me when you are flummoxed by something. I wish to see it!" Harriet sniffed and eased away from his aggravating lordship.

"I was afraid I'd offend you."

"Why ever would I be offended to have someone think that I am a thief? Where are we going? Or will that be another surprise?" She crossed her arms before her, then turned to glare at him. "What *do* you have in mind?"

"You would be surprised," he admitted, turning his head to give her a lopsided grin.

She must not like him, Harriet cautioned herself. If he desired silence, she would oblige. Not another word crossed her lips until they entered the village.

"Oh, my, would you look at that!" Harriet tugged at his sleeve, forgetting her intent to remain aloof. "They have begun work on the village fair. I can detect Miss Nympha Herbert's hand in this."

"I thought you did not know her well."

"You need not be so suspicious. It is just that no man would be so clever at decorating, and she did mention her theme for this year."

"I believe I see her sisters in front of the village shop over there. Claudia, Priscilla, Drucilla, and Tabitha, if my memory serves me right. The good rector chose the names from the New Testament."

"Goodness! Well, they appear to be lovely girls. I thought Claudia was married."

"The eldest did wed, but her husband lives close by so I suppose she came to lend a hand. They are a very close family, or so Mother said."

"Is the glebe land sufficient to help them?" Harriet knew that most clerics did not have much money, and she thought it might be difficult for some to go around collecting tithes from the landowners. They could not be shy! "With six children to support, the rector has his hands full. Does his son assist with the clerical duties? If the land that comes with the benefice is large enough, a good deal of produce and other sustenance can be had from it—chickens and cows, fruit and grain."

"He also rents some land so that he has ample to support his family, plus he has a private income. Tell me, why are we nattering on about the Herberts?"

"I tend to talk a lot when I am nervous." Harriet bit at her lower lip in vexation. She had not meant to say that.

He chuckled. "That is rather good to know." They continued through the village until they reached an imposing stone gate. He drew the curricle to the side of the road. In the distance rose an impressive Tudor manor house with every evidence of wealth and age possible. "That is the house belonging to Baron Rothson. *That* is where we must return the pin without him being the wiser."

"Good grief."

"I agree. There is a more recent addition in the back of the house. The collection of his prized artifacts is on the first floor, and there is no window access to that room other than narrow slits. He is conscious of the need to take precautions, you see."

"That does present a problem." She thought a minute, then added, "I must apologize. I had the silliest notion that you intended to drive up to his front door and hand me over to him as the one who has his precious pin."

"Good thought. Why did that not come to my mind?"

"Well." She sniffed again, folded her arms across her

chest, and sat back in the seat. "If you would be so kind
as to return me to my aunt's house, I am certain that I
will feel much better."

He obligingly set off at a clip, found a wide spot on
the road that made turning his vehicle a simple matter,
and headed in the direction she had requested. "Is there
nothing you wish in the village while we are here?"

"I think not. Aunt usually sends Mrs. Twig to the village for our needs, and on occasion she goes to the nearest market town for serious shopping."

"But not to London?"

"No. Aunt seems to prefer the country. Of course, she
inherited her house, and it suits her love of flowers and
gardens to be here."

"Tell me, did you sense a strain between your aunt
and Major Birch?"

"As a matter of fact, I did. She has said nothing in
that regard since. Although I did suggest she invite him
to the dinner she plans to give. We both enjoyed the
dinner at your home, and would wish to return the hospi-
tality," Harriet said with care.

"Will Major Birch be included?"

"I suggested that she invite him, but I received no
reply on that score. I ran upstairs to get the little carved
box I had just recalled, and upon examining it, discovered the pin inside. That quite put Major Birch completely out of my mind." Harriet relaxed a trifle as they
left the village behind. She was aware that every person
out and about had stared at the familiar vehicle. She
hadn't gone around much other than to church when the
weather was good. Her aunt's gig did not have a hood,
and the prospect of a drenching didn't appeal at all. They
remained home, read from the Bible, and had a quiet
day when it looked to rain on a Sunday.

"Well, we have a little mystery on our hands, in that
event. That makes two, does it not? Unless I should include the mystery of you being deep in the country when
the Season is not yet over."

"I can solve that for you fairly easily. My sister married, then mother wed as well, leaving me somewhat

stranded, not wishing to intrude on newly married couples. Fortunately, dearest Aunt Cornelia invited me to visit, and so here I am."

"Painting."

"Well, yes, that and other things." Harriet knew her face grew a bit pink. Those "other things" weren't scandalous, but one of her avocations did tend to get some annoying reactions from others, so she did not bandy it about.

She could see the puzzled expression on Lord Stanhope's face from around the edge of her neat little bonnet.

The groom ran forward to take the reins of the curricle so Lord Stanhope could assist Harriet from the carriage.

"I suppose you wish to come in? Goodness, that did not sound well at all, did it? I am merely surprised that you are free, since you want to restore that pin. I fancy you wish me to give it to you now?" Harriet looked at him, then walked along at his side, waiting for him to decide.

"I believe you should keep it for the time being. We have to think of a way to get it into that house. Have you met the baron?"

Harriet paused before the front door. "No, aunt says she scarcely knows the gentleman. He does not attend church, you see, and that is where she has met most of the people in the surrounding area. I am certain you know how it is—unless you have lived in an area forever, you are considered an outsider."

Lord Stanhope opened the door and stood aside for Harriet to enter the house, closely following behind her.

There was a box sitting in the entry hall. Puzzled, Harriet looked at the labeling to see her name on it.

"Whatever has come for you, dear?" Aunt Cornelia cried, joining them from the drawing room. She signaled to a footman to carry the box into the drawing room to place it on a low table.

Guessing what it might be, Harriet sought to put off opening the box. Her aunt would have none of that.

"I am certain there is a small knife you may use," Lord Stanhope said, gesturing to the footman again.

Harriet knew there was a knife on the writing desk and yielded graciously. There was nothing to do but open the box and perhaps lose the friendship of Lord Stanhope.

"Books?" Aunt Cornelia declared in surprise. "I know you like to read, but that is a rather large order, my dear."

Picking up one of the volumes, Harriet took a measure of delight in seeing her work in print. Naturally she had used a *nom de plume,* but still, it was hers.

"These are all the same book," Lord Stanhope said, as puzzled as Aunt Cornelia. "Some mistake has been made."

"There is no mistake. These are mine. That is, I wrote the book and the publisher has sent me these copies as part of my payment." Harriet clutched the first of the three-volume work to her chest. The slim little book was bound in a rich deep red and had red marbelized paper inside the cover. Stamped on the outside in fine gold was the title *The Rogue's Regret.*

"You wrote this?" Lord Stanhope sounded somewhat aghast.

"You truly wrote this?" Cornelia cried. "Why haven't you said anything? Had I written a book, and it had been accepted for publishing, I would be trumpeting it to the skies!" Aunt Cornelia enveloped Harriet in a warm, loving hug.

"Well, I did this as a lark, and now I find I am pleased with myself. I trust you will keep my secret, my lord?" Harriet studied Lord Stanhope, wondering if he was truly as appalled as he looked when first she confessed to her authorship.

"It is by all things wonderful. And you look so ordinary. Are you writing another book now?" He ceased to look appalled, seeming more curious than anything else.

"Yes, and you do not have to look as though I intend to bite." Harriet laughed to cover her dismay. "I assure you that I am as normal as you, possibly more so. And everything I compose is imaginary."

"We must celebrate. I cannot recall a celebrity in our

family before." Aunt Cornelia picked up the second volume, then the third so to inspect them. "They are bound very nicely. *The Rogue's Regret*. I must say it is an intriguing title. A gothic romance, dear?"

"A fanciful book, but not one of those whose silly heroine keeps swooning and there isn't one ghost!"

"I imagine your writing keeps you busy?" Lord Stanhope looked at her with a frown.

"Not so busy that I do not have time for friends and family. I write a bit each day. I fear if I write too long, I will get a cramp in my fingers. So I paint and . . . help others if I can." She gave what she hoped was a pleading look for his understanding. She would not desert him, but help him return the pin to Baron Rothson.

The frown disappeared. "Your painting is a talent that ought not be neglected."

"She plays the piano well, too, my lord. It would seem that Harriet is far more talented than ever I expected." Aunt Cornelia gave Harriet another hug, then rang for the maid. She requested a tray be brought with a nice wine and biscuits.

"A little celebration." Gesturing to a chair for him, she sat in her accustomed high-back chair by the fireplace, and studied Harriet.

"Goodness, you make me feel as though I'm notorious." Harriet laughed uneasily.

"I confess I am relieved that it is not my company that has sent you to your room, but your writing instead."

"And my painting sends me off to the meadows."

"You do not leave your aunt's property, do you?" Lord Stanhope inquired. He sounded as though he would issue a scold if he found her straying.

"Rest assured that I am quite the proper miss. I remain on Aunt Cornelia's estate at all times. There is a fascinating folly near the little ravine that is most inspiring."

"Take care a rock doesn't tumble on you. It has been neglected ever since I moved here," Cornelia cautioned.

"Yes, do take care," his lordship echoed.

Harriet welcomed the maid with the tray. The light

wine was poured, biscuits offered, and Harriet blushed when Lord Stanhope proposed a toast to the latest literary lioness.

"I shan't ask about your present book, but if ever you want a reader or whatever it is called, please ask me," Aunt Cornelia said, a twinkle lighting her blue eyes. "I can think of nothing more exciting than to read something before it is printed."

Harriet merely nodded, quite overcome with the attention and the expression in Lord Stanhope's eyes.

# Chapter Five

Philip gave his assurances that a dinner at Quince House would be warmly welcomed by his parents, his other relatives, and, he suspected, Major Birch.

"We are not precisely on what you would call the best of terms," Miss Quince said after a few moments of silence.

"I know you do not give a fig about even numbers, dear aunt." Harriet's voice held a wistful note. "However, I do believe there ought to be someone close to your own age. You are not so very old, you know."

Philip repressed a smile at Lady Harriet's earnest words. "That is true. You are too young to put on your caps and molder away."

The rose that bloomed on Miss Quince's delicate features was delightful. Usually it was the buds of Society who produced a blush when gently teased.

"I must leave." Philip rose, then turned to Miss Quince. "I hope Lady Harriet will do me the honor of painting with me tomorrow." He smiled at the expression on Lady Harriet's face. "I have mentioned that I also paint. The picturesque, of course. That folly sounded rather interesting as a subject."

Her expression was definitely wary. "You believe it will not rain?"

"If it does, we can go the next day. I doubt the folly will disappear overnight."

She looked to her aunt, for permission, no doubt, or perhaps an opinion.

"I see no reason why you cannot have a painting expedition with the maid to go along." The look she fixed on Philip was a promise of retribution should anything untoward occur.

"Would eleven in the morning be acceptable, directly following your breakfast, I daresay?" For some reason he truly wanted this painting trek. That he might enjoy company on his usually solitary painting excursion did not enter his mind. He did wish to see how she painted.

"Yes. Yes, indeed, it would be most agreeable. I shall warn you now that I have little to say when I am painting. I concentrate, you see. So, I fancy I am not very good company."

She looked as though she wanted him to beg off, or hoped he changed his mind. As though he would! Indeed, it had the effect of making him want it all the more. He was not accustomed to young women like her. As a rule girls sought him out, trying to capture his attention. Lady Harriet was just the opposite, and he had to confess it intrigued him. She intrigued him.

"I have little to say, either. We shall make a good pair." If she had more arguments, he could easily demolish them. He liked her company. She didn't flirt, or act silly as girls of nineteen were wont to do. In fact, she seemed remarkably mature for her years. But then, hadn't someone told him her mother had been a semi-invalid or something of the sort? She and her sister would have had to assume considerable responsibility, for certain.

Wariness turned to downright hostility in Lady Harriet's eyes. Good heavens, what could she possibly have heard to make *her* so distrustful of *him?* "Until tomorrow, then." Philip bowed over Miss Quince's hand, then turned to Lady Harriet. She had her hands behind her back, presenting him with a disconcerting smile while she avoided touching his hand. How curious. She might not like him, but the more she backed away, the more inclined he was to go after her. He had to confess it was refreshing after being hunted by those London belles of the matrimonial bazaar who gave new meaning to the word predatory.

"I shall be looking forward to seeing your painting,

my lord." Her words were polite, but suspicion tinged every word. Surely she did not doubt he could paint!

"I shall see you in the morning." Philip left the house, walking smartly to where his curricle and horse awaited him. Handing a coin to the young lad, Philip sprang into the vehicle and was off. He was not quite in a miff, but close enough. Even with looking for humor in it, he could not understand why Lady Harriet should be so mistrustful of him. Perhaps she did *not* believe he could paint. Well, he had never made much of it, but he did dabble from time to time, and had a number of paintings he deemed fit to frame. Of course, what he truly wanted was to discuss the ways and means of returning the pin to Baron Rothson.

He encountered Peel as soon as he entered Lanstone Hall. The butler offered him a silver salver upon which rested a letter. "The groom just brought this up from the village, milord."

Nodding his thanks, Philip broke open the seal, noting that Pericles Heron's father had franked the letter. A rapid perusal brought a smile. He glanced at Peel, who still stood at attention, obviously awaiting possible instructions.

"Mr. Heron has accepted my proposal to alter the dining room windows and design the addition to Father's library. It is becoming so full of birds, I feel as though I ought to chirp whenever I go in there."

"Indeed," Peel said with a regal nod. "Perhaps he will be able to give advice on the size of the room as well. The marquess seems to add glass cases for his stuffed birds at a steady rate. They do take room." He cleared his throat, then added, "One of the maids refused to go in there to clean. Said those beady eyes quite put her off. Normally we would have turned her off. Instead, she was assigned to the upstairs. It is becoming difficult to find proper help, my lord, what with being a bit remote in the country. So many of the young people wish to be closer to a village or town. Flighty things."

"Independent, too, if that is the case. Perhaps we may have to increase the wages?" Philip gave Peel an assessing look. Since Philip more or less ran the estate, the judgments usually fell on his shoulders. Wages was one area with which he dealt.

"It has not come to that as yet, sir."

"Inform Mrs. Cork that we will be having a guest for some duration. He likely will want a room in which he can draw, and will need whatever architects require in the line of a proper table. Mother will be pleased, no doubt, to acquire her window."

"Quite so." The butler stalked off in stately dignity to pass along the latest news to the housekeeper.

"Philip, there you are!" Nick strode along the hall with impatient steps, Rags trotting behind him with a wagging tail and doggy grin.

"What is it?" Philip waited outside the library door, knowing he was supposed to inspect his father's latest acquisition. It seemed as if one member of the family wasn't demanding his attention and help, another one was.

"Have a spot of trouble. There is a good-sized tree on that distant parcel of land adjacent to my course that I want to move to my greens. Can you think of a way we can accomplish it? My idea is to have a blacksmith make a huge shovel or pitchfork or something with a bend in it that would dig up the tree, and then we could use a sort of cart to move the tree where I want it."

"Can't be done. Resign yourself to planting one." Philip waved the letter in front of his brother. "I just had word that Pericles Heron accepted my offer. He will be here shortly to design the addition for the library and give instructions for altering the window in the dining room." Seeing Nick's blank expression, he added, "Mother wants a Venetian window in there."

"It would make the room lighter, for certain." Nicholas looked impatient, as he usually did when any topic other than his golf course was raised. Philip wondered what he would do when the course was completed.

"I have a short amount of time to help you," he said with more patience than he felt. "Tomorrow I have an excursion with Lady Harriet."

"Whatever for?" Nick stared at his older brother with frowning curiosity.

"That, my dear brother, is for me to know." Philip refrained from smiling at his brother's incredulous expression.

"And you would as soon keep it to yourself?" Nick frowned a few moments, then his brow cleared. "Well, no matter. I am too busy with my golf course. What do you think? Can we devise such a bit of equipment?"

"Let me look at father's latest bird, and I'll be with you." Philip placed a hand on the doorknob, ready to go in so that the new bird might be admired. Not that he usually admired them. He felt nothing except a bit of pity—for the bird as well as his father.

"I'd better join you. I've not seen the dratted bit of feathers and bone, either." Nick grimaced, sharing a look of resignation with his brother.

Philip rapped on the library and when bid to enter, went in with Nick at his side. The new bird was exquisite and likely the star of the collection. Philip had to admit he had never seen a bird like it—a soft yellow underbelly and pale greenish back with a dark head. The label on the case indicated it was a yellow-breasted bunting.

"Supposed to be extinct," the marquess declared with glee. "Yet *I* spotted it! Now all can admire it."

"Seems to me it could have had a mate somewhere. Had you not shot it, we might have had more." Philip gave his father a keen look, then backed away, standing with his hands behind his back. He tilted his head, trying to see what his father found so captivating.

"Rubbish, my boy. It likely would have flown off and I'd never have captured it." The marquess gave his son a reproving look before returning a rapturous gaze to his new acquisition, stroking his mustache as he contemplated the bird.

Philip and Nick exchanged a glance, said all that was proper, and left as soon as may be.

" 'Tis nice to know that to father we will always be boys," Nick said as they headed to the back entrance.

Without asking, Nick knew Philip would help him. He always did.

"Harriet, dear, I should like you to explain why you behaved as you did while Lord Stanhope was here. Surely you do not dislike him?"

"Do you really believe he paints? Dear aunt, I have heard a few interesting invitations to get me away from a chaperon before, but I must confess this is the most novel."

"Surely you do not think that he would . . . That he . . . No, I refuse to believe it." She shook her head and gave Harriet a distressed frown. "What is this world coming to? But you will take your maid." Aunt Cornelia took a turn before the fireplace, then sank down upon her favorite chair. She looked as frustrated as Harriet felt.

"You may be certain I will have not only a maid, and selection of paints and brushes, and my pad, but a dandy little knife. I always sharpen my pencils when needed, you know." Harriet's eyes gleamed with a hint of mischief.

"Heavens!" Her aunt gave Harriet a very shocked look.

"I wonder what his lordship finds to occupy his time?" Harriet mused aloud. "I fancy he is as idle as most of the peers I have met. All they seem to think about is gaming, their bits of muslin, and having pleasure, one way or another." Her tone made it clear how little she thought of these gentlemen.

"My dear, I suspect you may be underestimating the earl. I have heard he does a great deal about the Hall. He does not have the look of an idler. All those muscles, you know. And his family depend upon him to a great degree."

"Hmm. I sense you have a reservation regarding Major Birch? You are not inviting him to move in here, you know." Harriet assumed an innocent expression. "It is merely a dinner party. What is the great difficulty, dearest aunt?"

"That is the trouble. I do not know! He makes me uncomfortable. He looks at me, and I get all warm and restless and most peculiar inside. I cannot say I like that. He is not a comfortable sort of person, he never has been."

"How odd, for that is how I feel about Lord Stanhope—not that he is comfortable, but that he creates the most conflicting feelings within me." Harriet exchanged a confused look with her dearest aunt. While it might be comforting to know someone else had these strange feelings, it didn't help her solve the source of them—other than to know they were caused in some manner by Lord Stanhope.

The two women stared at one another, perplexed and a trifle bewildered.


"Are you certain you truly want to move this tree?" Philip pulled a pad of paper from his pocket, found a stub of a pencil, and began to draw.

"Well, I should think hazards other than gorse and an occasional pond would be desirable. And there are times when a spot of shade is nice, not to mention having it as a landmark." Nick strode about the area, studying the tree from all angles. "Think it can be done? You usually manage everything."

"I'll have to see about it. A cart most definitely, but the rest . . . I do not know. I'll discuss it with the blacksmith and see if there isn't something we might devise. Perhaps the gardener may be of help as well."

"I knew I could count on you to solve my dilemma."

"One of these days you will have to provide your own solutions—I might not be around. Think of that, will you?" Philip paused and gave Nick a searching look.

"Not planning to marry are you?" Nick grinned at his brother and swatted his shoulder with his gloves. "Can't think of a gal who would have you, old sober-sides that you are."

Philip didn't reply, just grinned back, then headed toward the outbuilding where the estate blacksmith could be found. Once there, the two men put their heads together to see what might be contrived with the assistance of the estate head gardener.

The following morning dawned clear with a bright sun shining in a cloudless sky. Clouds were bound to come up later in the day—they usually did. But this morning looked promising for the painting expedition. Not that Harriet actually welcomed the dratted gentleman along, mind you.

What to wear was her first problem. The old painting dress had been discarded: even her maid declared it beyond salvage. Finally, Harriet decided upon a pretty India muslin in a print of rose and pale green on an ivory background. Of course it was silly to wear such a dress for painting, but a spurt of vanity prompted her choice. Not that she would have admitted it to anyone.

Her maid was nowhere to be seen. An inquiry found that Abby was miserable with a cold. She dared not come near her mistress. Harriet managed to dress herself.

At last Harriet descended to breakfast. All was quiet on the main floor. She could hear Cook and Mrs. Twig beyond the green-baize door, voices raised as though they were across the room from one another.

The small dining room was vacant. She selected a roll and a bit of ham and cheese for her morning meal, poured a cup of tea, then sat at the table so she might see the view out of the window.

"You slept late, Harriet. I have been up for hours." Aunt Cornelia wafted into the room with an armload of summer flowers. She paused before collecting the vase on the sideboard in preparation to arranging her blooms. "Is everything to your liking?"

"All except this confounded painting thing," Harriet grumbled.

"I do like your gown—very flattering. I never feel comfortable when I am wearing something shabby. And, dearest, you must admit that old dress was definitely shabby."

"True," Harriet agreed. She hesitated a few moments,

then gave her aunt an inquiring look. "You do not think it is perhaps too nice, too good, that it will appear I am dressing up for him?"

Aunt Cornelia stuffed the flowers into the vase, then motioned Harriet to rise. "Now, turn around so that I might study you."

Harriet obediently twirled about.

"Not in the least, love. You look precisely as a young woman off on a painting spree should look. Just remember to select a wide-brimmed hat so your face will be shielded from this sun. It promises to be a warm day. Freckles are such a nuisance."

Harriet gave her aunt a stubborn look as Cornelia left the room, no doubt to arrange her flowers in the scullery. A large stone sink and the shelves above served her aunt for her flowers as well as the scullery maid for cleaning the pots and pans. All in all this was a tidy and well-organized house. Harriet did not welcome the thought of having to leave here. Perhaps her aunt would take in a permanent guest? For it seemed that Harriet, contrary to her sister's expectations, would not "take." There certainly was no sign of a suitor on the horizon—only that dratted painter-cum-investigator who plagued her. And likely all he truly wanted was to discuss the ivory dragon with her. She fled to her room.

Cornelia paused in the bedroom doorway. "Mrs. Twig says Abby has a miserable cold. I do not like sending you off without her, yet I cannot spare another maid today. We are in the midst of a major cleaning if we are to have guests for dinner. You will have to trust the earl."

"Oddly enough I do, but I will have that knife." She shot a conspiratorial glance at her aunt as she slid past her to head down the stairs.

Yet she was glad to see him in the entryway. One last glance in her looking glass had showed the gypsy bonnet with its wide brim and simple design just the thing for her outing. Now the look of approval in his eyes made her feel rather glowing inside, and that was silly.

Of course, he had not brought his painting equipment

into the house with him, it would be stowed in his carriage. But she would definitely check to see it was there. "Good morning, my lord. It appears you were right— this is going to be a lovely day."

"My groom insists it will rain before the day is over. Let's be on our way before the clouds come up." He held out his hands to take her collection of painting materials, then escorted her to his carriage. She didn't know why she had doubted him, for on the seat usually reserved for his groom was a case along with a large pad of watercolor paper.

She settled on the cushioned seat, glancing at him as he joined her. "You know how far we can go before we must leave the carriage behind?"

"Indeed—close to that storage barn where we first met. I thought we could leave the carriage in the barn in the event it does rain before we return. At least it would be dry. Where is your maid?" He glanced behind her as though expecting the girl to appear.

"In bed with a cold," Harriet added shortly. "I shall have to trust you." She noted that he seemed disconcerted at her words, but he said nothing.

They left the horse and carriage as planned, then ambled along the path that Harriet had taken so many times over this summer. She was beginning to know the estate very well and admired her aunt's management. A few cows occupied the next pasture, and sheep were beyond them. No pigs, but chickens were kept in abundance for their eggs and meat. There was little needed in town beyond sugar and salt, things like that. She inhaled deeply, relishing the country scents.

"You seem to enjoy being in the country." Lord Stanhope sounded rather surprised.

"Do you find that so unusual?" Harriet gave him a quizzing look before turning her attention back to the uneven path.

He did not reply, but stopped when the folly they sought came into view. "Where do you think would be the best place to view it?"

"Look, there is a creek that runs past it. Settle yourself

so you can draw in the creek as a diagonal with the folly rising on the hill beyond. There are some rather nice trees that show behind the folly from that point."

He left her side to stride to the spot she had pointed out and nodded. The view was charming and worthy of a sketch at the very least. "You must have considered painting the folly yourself to see the potential in the view." He gave her a somewhat quizzical look. "You have found something to paint?" he inquired as he returned for his case and pad.

"Yes." She didn't bother to tell him she had at last found a milk thistle to depict for her aunt. Harriet admitted the thistle flower was pretty enough, the deep purple tufts rising from the sharp green spikes of leaves at the base of the bloom. It was the mottled green and white leaves she found a bit tedious to paint with the preciseness she insisted upon. She watched as he strode across the grass to settle in the precise spot where he could capture the scene she had suggested. With amazement, she observed him pull a strange contraption from his case, unfold it, and proceed to sit on the odd little tripod stool.

With a sigh, she settled on the grass, naught but a cloth to cushion her from grass stains. Ignoring the tantalizing image of the earl totally engrossed in his sketch, she concentrated on the milk thistle, wondering why her aunt thought it so desirable. Dratted thing, with its spiky leaves and patchy colors.

The sun had moved a considerable distance by the time she completed the watercolor. She was so utterly absorbed in the detailed painting, she had not only lost track of the time but his lordship as well. Now she sat back to study her work, and then satisfied with it, she carefully put it aside to dry and turned to see her companion.

He wasn't aware of her scrutiny, for he was as engrossed in his painting as she had been in hers. Perhaps he had some talent after all? She had half expected him to pester her, tease her, or at the very least flirt with her. He had done none of these. Rather, he had done precisely what he had said he would do—paint. Carefully placing her things in a neat pile, she rose, stretched out her stiff limbs, and then gingerly approached the gentleman on the three-legged stool. One never knew how a painter would react to another creeping up behind him.

"I can hear you breathing," he muttered softly as he placed a dash of blue where he had sketched the creek.

"Heavens, you truly are very accomplished!" Harriet was astonished. The man was good, very good. The folly depicted in his painting had character, more than the real one did standing on the hill. And the creek seemed so real she could almost hear it burbling along over the stones and around the little bend. She shook her head. She might be able to depict flowers with precise detail and botanical correctness; she could never paint like this.

"Well, I am pleased you think so," he murmured as he wiped his brush on the grass before dipping it in the creek to clean it.

"I didn't believe you, you know." Harriet felt compelled to confess her doubts. "I half expected you to . . ." She halted her explanation, for she did not wish him to think she had wanted him to flirt with her. Not that she was so prim she didn't enjoy a bit of flirtation—she did. As long as it didn't get out of hand, that is.

Lord Stanhope picked up the now completed watercolor and held it away so he could study it. "I think it is fair. At least it looks a bit like the folly—don't you think?"

"Should you ever wish to part with it, I would very much like to have it. I have admired that folly since I first discovered it. To have a painting of it would be of all things pleasing."

"I'll make you a bargain. You help me figure out how to return that pin to the baron, and you can have the painting." His look could only be called calculating, she thought. Yet, could she blame him? His younger brother was accused of stealing the lovely object. Whoever had done so, it wasn't his brother. She believed that much.

"I wonder who actually took the pin and why they put it in the barn?" She gave his lordship a speculative look.

He turned away to gaze at the folly for a few moments, then turned back to face her. "I believe I know."

"Who, then?" Harriet took note of the distressed expression in his eyes. Whoever was the guilty person, it was someone he wanted to shield.

"I trust you to keep it a secret." There was a question in his voice that she immediately responded to at once.

"I shall not say a word to anyone, I promise."

"I believe my mother took it when we last had dinner with the baron. She said little, but she had the opportunity."

Harriet couldn't conceal her astonishment. "What!" Then, seeing the pain in his eyes, she sought to soften her reaction. "Is she given to doing things like that? I know some people are. It isn't that they need the items, they just seem to want them and take them on a whim." She hoped to atone her for original reaction of dismay.

"I confess I do not know as to whether she has done this before. I have my suspicions, but nothing I can voice other than the word of the groom who drove her to the barn. And he saw nothing."

"But why hide it in the barn?"

"I can only guess that she intended to retrieve it later. Her maid could have found it and possibly have mentioned it to my father."

"Which she would not have wanted? For him to know what she had done?" Harriet took a step back and regretted it instantly. She chanced to step on a wobbly stone at the edge of the creek, and before she could save herself she teetered, then fell back into the chilly water, splashing water everywhere. She came up sputtering. How fortunate it was a shallow creek!

# Chapter Six

"Let me give you a hand." She could see his lordship valiantly tried not to laugh. He compressed his lips, reached out to pull her from the creek, and set her on her feet. Then he laughed, a rich, delicious sound.

For some reason it made Harriet even angrier—mostly at herself for being such a ninny. She knew better than to back up without first looking, especially since she knew there was a creek close by, for pity's sake.

"I suppose you think this is exceedingly amusing," she demanded with a sniff, glaring at him with icy disdain. She stepped away from the creek, a difficult effort because her dress clung to her like a leech. "Ohhhh!" she exclaimed, utterly frustrated. She didn't dare to stamp a foot, for fear she would tumble back into the stream once more. Those stones turned out to be very unstable!

"If you could but see yourself." It was an effort, but he managed to subdue his laughter. Instead he assisted her from the stones to the long grass close to the creek.

Harriet looked down, plucking at her pretty India print muslin with dripping hands. The color was running, creating new patterns, not particularly pleasing ones. Goodness, the fabric was like a second skin. "If you had a decent thought in your head, you would look elsewhere, my lord," she said in an unconscious echo of her words when they had first met. She tried to squeeze out some of the water. It was difficult without lifting her skirt, and she thought she was disgraced quite enough without adding to it. What he might think of her then couldn't be imagined. Not that she truly cared, she reminded herself.

"It isn't easy," he murmured before he chanced to

meet her angry gaze. He sobered at once. Turning away, he collected his painting gear, neatly stowing all in the case. Then he gathered up her equipment and the two paintings as well. She was in no state to carry anything, and she had to admit it was nice of him to collect it all.

While his back was turned, she squeezed water from her skirt so that she might at least manage to walk.

She took a step, water squelching in her shoe. The other one squelched as well when she advanced. What a pity she was wet and cold, not to mention embarrassed— she *might* have laughed about this.

"Come, we may as well get started on our way back." He walked at Harriet's side, saying little, most likely wondering how they were to escape from this muddle. Should anyone chance to see the two of them *now*, well . . . It was truly a pity that Harriet had not insisted upon another servant to go with her. She devoutly hoped that this aspect of their predicament had escaped him for the nonce.

The clouds that had been creeping across the sky proved his groom had been right. No sooner than they had begun the trek back to the barn than the rain commenced. It was a gentle rain, but nonetheless a very wetting one after a time. Her wide-brimmed hat soon drooped on either side of her face. The worst of it was that he probably felt as though he had to stay with her. It would be ungentlemanly to walk off ahead, leaving her to fend for herself.

"It is just as well the maid remained at home. She would have an inflammation of the lungs had I insisted upon her joining us." Harriet tried to sound cheerful, but it wasn't easy. The rain might not be cold, but being wet and out in a gentle breeze made her feel downright freezing. She sneezed. "I cannot become any wetter. You had best go ahead to the barn. There is no point in ruining your coat or the paintings. Do protect those!"

He didn't argue, but dashed ahead, leaving Harriet to ponder the villainy of a gentleman's vanity. *He* hadn't been silly enough to fall into the water to be drenched to the skin. What hope had she of winning a gentleman's affection when she couldn't seem to stay out of trouble? Of course, she did not wish to gain his lordship's favor, but it was not an auspicious incident no matter how you looked at it.

Instead of remaining in the barn, within minutes the earl dashed back to her with a large white cloth in his hands. With one arm he held it over her, slipping his other arm about her to bring her close to his side. If she had shivered before, she trembled now with an awareness of his proximity.

"I had thought we might have a bit of cake and lemonade before returning. Instead of a cloth to sit on, I will hold it over you. I do not want *you* to catch an inflammation of the lungs!" He smiled down at her when she chanced to glance up at him.

"Th-thank you." Her teeth chattered, and she welcomed the shelter and warmth of his body. Shameless girl, she couldn't even refuse to share the cloth; it was far too agreeable. It did lessen the impact of the rain, however.

"And once inside, if you sit on a pile of hay you could retain more of your warmth."

They sped down the last of the slope to the barn, arriving breathless and dripping. They dashed inside the barn, then stamped feet, shook the cloth off, and in general attempted to improve their state.

Shivering with the wet clothes as well as the bit of wind that had risen, Harriet gratefully accepted the heavy white linen cloth, hugging it around her, thinking it a poor substitute for the warmth radiating from him. She sank down to huddle on the pile of hay and eyed the bottle of lemonade, wishing it were piping hot.

"This barn seems to be the site of one disaster after another," she murmured, looking about at the pile of hay still where it had been left days ago. Katy-cat with her kittens had returned to the kitchen following the previous debacle, so this time they were totally alone—except for the horse, and he scarcely counted.

It seemed that Lord Stanhope couldn't agree. "Well, I wouldn't say that."

He leaned down to adjust the cloth, coming so close she could feel the slight heat from his body. He hesitated, studying her face a time before stepping back with a faint sigh as though disappointed about something. Well, she must look a fright. She calculated she was correct when he reached out to remove her dripping bonnet from her head. The expression on his face disturbed her calm, and she dearly wished she knew what he was thinking. Not that it would do her much good. For a moment she thought he'd intended to kiss her. That had to be a silly fancy, what with her feeling like a bedraggled waif. Best think of something else.

"So," she began, sounding very purposeful, "you think your mother had something to do with the removal of the little box from the baron's collection? I suppose you cannot imagine why she did it? Or how? Or how it came to be left in this barn? It seems to me to be a very strange place to hide something so valuable." She wrapped the linen tighter with the hope of blotting up more water, and cast her gaze about the interior of the very ordinary and nondescript storage barn.

"I have no idea." He spoke with seeming reluctance, and Harriet could well understand that. It must be horridly embarrassing for him. "My first clue was from the groom who usually goes with mother when she is out in her little gig. I imagine she thought he wouldn't say a word about her stopping here. She told him she wanted to see what the inside looked like—quite as though she hadn't been in a barn before."

"You must confess her behavior does seem a trifle unusual." She wiped her face with a corner of the large white cloth, then made a tentative attempt to push her hair back from her face. Even though the bonnet had offered protection, she knew her hair must be untidy. What a blessing there was no looking glass to confirm her dilemma. It was quite bad enough to contemplate her ruination without seeing it.

He ignored her comment, giving her what she considered was a quelling look. "At any rate," he continued, "my guess is that she placed the box on that ledge—the same one you put your painting gear on. I suppose she thought she could return for it later whenever she had need of it.''

"But why would she need it? Surely if she desired a pretty little trinket, your father would be more than pleased to buy her whatever she wanted.'' Lady Harriet chewed at her lower lip, frowning in her bewilderment.

Lord Stanhope compressed his lips for a few moments. "As to that, my parents seldom see one another—except perhaps for dinner. I doubt if he would have the slightest inkling that she might wish for something. Unless it was an item like the dining room window that she mentioned during a meal, and that quite often.''

"How sad.'' She sniffled. "You ought to do something about that. Truly! I think it tragic for a couple to be so estranged. Your poor mother.''

Lord Stanhope looked surprised that she would have the slightest interest, much less care about his mother's difficulties. She found she did. There must be a reason behind that lady's bizarre dress other than to look different. She obviously needed help. Harriet had become rather good at giving help—even if the person in question didn't think they needed it.

"I think it is dreadful when a husband and wife drift apart.'' She gave her nose a tentative swipe. "My parents were not close while he lived. Looking back, I truly pity her, for she must have been quite lonely. I am so happy that Mama has found a husband to cherish her, as the general surely seems to do.''

"Cherish?'' Lord Stanhope seemed to think her choice of words odd.

"Well, and so I think. I would like to be cherished if I ever marry. Not that I have prospects at the moment. But in the event I did, I would like that. Cherish sounds much nicer than love.'' She surreptitiously wiped at her nose again, hoping he wouldn't notice. She'd taken care to let him believe she might have a beau, even if she didn't. For all he knew, it might be that lanky chap she'd sent off.

Philip looked away from her delightful being. She had

the appearance of a little girl wrapped in a towel, straight from her bath. Only . . . she was not a child. The sight of her in that wet, clinging gown had stirred him considerably, and he'd been glad when she suggested he go ahead to the barn. True, he had dashed back to offer a covering, but he had relished holding her so close. And now she sat in all innocence, staring up at him from wide blue eyes. At least she wasn't caterwauling all over the place about her gown, her chill, or worse. He found her curiously enticing.

He strode over to the open door, searching the sky to see if there was a chance the rain might let up soon. To risk being alone with her was courting more than disaster. It was a gamble with potentially dire consequences. And he had made it a point not to gamble with odds like these.

"I think I would like a bit of cake, if you please." She sniffled again. "What a pity we cannot heat that lemonade." Longing tinged her words.

Philip knew it would be folly to light any fire inside a barn, and it was hopeless to think of a fire out in the rain. Yet he wished he could, for her sake. "You could try a swallow of the brandy I have in the carriage. I always have a small flask tucked in a pocket, as one never knows when it might be needed."

She nodded with obvious hesitancy and rose to take a step in his direction. "I believe it is said to warm a person."

He considered her words a moment, then nodded. "It does that—among other things."

Once he found the little flask, he offered it to Harriet. She took a generous swallow, gulped, and sputtered, handing the flask back with a trembling hand. When she could breathe again, she admonished him. "You might have warned me!" She coughed and stumbled forward when he thumped her on her back.

Rounding on him, she cried, "I thank you not to do that."

"But you are warmed now, are you not?" He drew nearer to take back the flask. Now he was far too close for her comfort. He reached out to wipe a lingering drop of water from her cheek, touching her ever so gently.

"Perhaps we ought to leave," she whispered, not because her voice was failing her, but because of something else that had sprung up between them, something she didn't understand in the least.

"Yes, I imagine we should." His agreement was pronounced in a soft, polite voice totally at odds with the look in his eyes. His eyes said something else entirely, and whatever it was, it made Harriet feel as though she was aflame.

She swayed, and he reached out to steady her. That was a mistake, unless she missed her guess. For in an instant he was kissing her with an ardor that left her trembling. She clutched at his coat less she slither to that pile of hay behind her. Her bones had ceased to hold her properly, and she was certain her mind had stopped functioning. All she could absorb was that this had to be the most delightful sensation she had ever experienced in her entire life.

The damp linen tablecloth fell to the hay when she sought the warmth of his embrace more fully. Sliding her arms about him beneath his coat, she decided—with what thought she could summon—that kissing was an excellent way to ward off the cold. One scarcely was aware of it. The cold, that is. However, she was definitely aware of his firm, well-muscled body.

He at last withdrew and seemed to have as difficult a time breathing as she. He ran his knuckle lightly down her jawline, giving her a wary look as he did.

"That was not supposed to happen."

"No, I don't expect it was." She thought back to what she had said to her aunt about Lord Stanhope and his reputation. "But you are not given to this sort of thing, are you?" she concluded awkwardly.

"Well, I confess I do enjoy kissing a pretty girl—but I had not intended to commit such a misdeed while we were out on our painting expedition. I am aware you were very hesitant about trusting me. I'd not intended to betray that trust."

"I'd not call it a misdeed, precisely," she countered, the warmth of his kiss lingering on her lips. She stepped away from him, sorry at once when she lost his heat.

"What would you call it, then?" He tilted his head to study her face, a strange light in his dark eyes.

Feeling as though her cheeks must be rosy with chagrin, Harriet compressed her lips, then said, "Perhaps it was in aid of warming me? I must say that was accomplished rather well. I feel far better now."

His eyes lit with amusement, and his grin did strange little things to her heart. "I daresay you have the right of it, my dear girl."

"Oh, but I am not your dear anything. I am too tall for one thing, and for another . . ." She paused, groping for words that seemed to have fled from her brain.

"Now you are being foolish."

"I suppose I am. I frequently find myself in that position. It is the fate of our family, I suspect."

"I do not think I want to inquire into that too closely," he countered, a grin lighting his face.

Since Harriet did not particularly want to share a few of the escapades that she and her sister had fallen into while in London, she simply smiled and made no reply.

"The rain seems to be lessening. I can scarce hear it on the roof anymore. Perhaps we ought to leave here before someone stumbles on us—or discovers us, or something of that sort?" She reached down to pick up the white square of linen and her pathetic hat. Well, she hadn't been that fond of the thing, but hats were not easy to come by deep in the country. It certainly was ruined now. She held the limp straw with disdainful fingers, then dropped it to the floor. There was no point in taking it home. It would never look the same again even if her maid could block it.

"You promised that you would help me figure out how to return that pin to the baron if we went painting today. You did a splendid painting of a thistle—although why a thistle, I can't imagine."

"My aunt wanted it. As to returning the pin—just give it to him." Harriet glanced at Lord Stanhope before glid-

ing to the doorway to peer up to the sky. The clouds
were breaking up, and she was certain that was a sliver
of blue not far away. Few people traveled this road, but
she was positive that just because she did not want anyone to come, someone—like the rector—was certain to
do just that. And then the fat would hop into the fire
for sure.

"You have no imagination if you think that. He will
wonder how I acquired it and suspect my brother all the
more. I certainly do not want to explain that my mother
appropriated it—even if I could figure out precisely how
and when she did. Take it, that is."

"I understand. Perhaps if you take me home and I can
get into dry clothes, we could discuss the problem over
hot tea? I do think we ought to leave here as soon as
possible." She creased her brow in concern.

He responded with unflattering speed. Before she
could do no more than squeeze out more water from her
dress and wrap the linen square about her again, he had
the curricle ready to go.

She accepted his help up into the carriage. Once there,
she settled into her corner and stared before her, wondering what would result from this scandalous painting
expedition. She was quite certain he would never bother
to ask her again! When both were seated, he urged the
horse from the shelter and modest warmth of the barn
to the road that led to Quince House. They traveled in
silence, each absorbed in thought.

When they reached the house, a groom ran through
puddles to take the reins from Lord Stanhope, leaving
him free to assist Harriet. If he allowed his hand to linger
at her elbow a trifle longer than necessary, she paid it
no heed.

Mrs. Twig opened the door, evidently having been
watching for their return. She tut-tutted while taking
away the linen cloth, exposing the wet gown in the
process.

"Heavens!" Aunt Cornelia cried when she caught sight
of Harriet's ruined gown. "I daresay you were caught in
the rain after all. I had so hoped you would have noticed

the dark clouds and taken refuge. The storage barn can't have been too far from where you were painting?"

"Indeed, ma'am." The earl stepped forward to place Harriet's painting box on the hall table. "We were slow to see the rain approaching, but we did take shelter in the barn until the rain eased off."

"My lord, I hope you will wait here until I can change?" Harriet gave him a beseeching look. "We can have hot tea when I return." That they could discuss the matter that has been plaguing him was left unsaid. Mrs. Twig might be an estimable housekeeper; it wasn't likely she would keep her silence at hearing something of interest.

"Please do," Aunt Cornelia added in persuasion. "I should like to see the paintings."

"Forgot them!" He looked vexed at the oversight and swiveled to leave the house.

"I shall meet you in the drawing room shortly." Harriet nodded at him, then hurried up the stairs leaving a dripping trail behind her.

Abby was properly horrified at the sight of Harriet in the ruined gown. "Although, my lady, I think if I dip it in a salt bath, I might be able to save it." The maid gave her mistress a hopeful look while wiping her nose. "I can do it before it dries. You may find it just as pleasing."

"That would be of all things wonderful. I think I will put on a warm gown. Never mind that it is summer. I am chilly." With that, she sneezed.

Abby handed her a scrap of linen, then helped Harriet into a pretty long-sleeved gown of blue lutestring decorated with delicate white embroidery. She took a light shawl from a drawer to slip over her shoulders.

Once her hair was dressed, Harriet hurried down the stairs to the drawing room. A lady did not—in her estimation—keep a gentleman waiting. She was still adjusting the shawl when she entered the room. He faced her, his back to the fire in an effort to dry off. She could detect nothing from his expression.

"You are just in time for tea," her aunt declared with a hasty perusal of Harriet's attire. "I am glad you are a sensible girl. Too many would have put on a thin muslin and succumbed to a horrid cold as a result."

Harriet gave her dearest aunt a wobbly smile. Oh, indeed she was a very sensible girl. So sensible that she paid little heed to the weather when out with a dashing gentleman, and ended up stranded in a barn with him with naught but a horse as witness. No one else was the wiser—especially to that foolish kiss. But, sensible? Hardly.

The earl left the fireplace to join them, casting frequent glances at Harriet.

The three sat in silence for some moments, each apparently deep in thought. The clink of cups on saucers was all that could be heard for a time.

"The sun has come out," Aunt Cornelia murmured into the quiet of the room.

"Indeed," Harriet agreed. The hot tea was thawing out her chilled body quite nicely. That a neat fire burned in the grate not far from where Harriet had chosen to sit didn't hurt, either.

"I fetched the paintings we did today. Would you like to see them, Miss Quince?" Lord Stanhope rose from where he sat to pick up the two sheets of watercolor paper. He handed the first to Aunt Cornelia.

"Ah, you found a milk thistle for me. How nice." She gave an approving smile at her niece.

Diffident, he handed the second painting to her. Harriet rose from her cozy chair to peer over her aunt's shoulder. The painting was as she recalled, outstanding!

"That truly is very good!" she exclaimed. "There is atmosphere and charm about the folly not readily seen at first. Most picturesque," she concluded with a shy peek at the earl.

"Indeed, I must agree with Harriet." Miss Quince held up the paper at a distance, studying it at length.

"I fell in love with the folly the moment I saw it, and I couldn't hope to paint it half as well as you have done. Should I be so fortunate as to receive it, I will treasure it, you can be certain." Harriet tried to signal him that she would help with the matter of returning the ivory dragon, although she wasn't sure if he understood.

"In that case, I will be happy to give it to you. Perhaps you might allow me to frame it for you? Our carpenter is gifted at making frames and gilding them most expertly." What messages his eyes sent in return were quite beyond her ken. He had asked this in a modest manner, but Harriet sensed it was something he truly wished to do. Well, if he so wished, she would let him.

"I would be pleased. Thank you."

Mrs. Twig appeared at the door, requesting a moment of her mistress's time. Once her aunt was out of the door, although still not far away, Harriet motioned Lord Stanhope to join her.

"I fear I have not thought of how you might be able to return that pin to the baron. I promise I will consider it, and perhaps by tomorrow I can conceive of something. There has to be a way!" That she also intended to consider the matter of his dear, if eccentric, mother and her estrangement from his father she didn't mention.

"The village fair is coming up. I trust you plan to attend?" He set his cup and saucer on the table close to his chair, then studied Harriet with a slight frown creasing his brow. She wondered what prompted that.

"Of course. Nympha has talked about its delights so much that I would not miss it." Harriet gave him a questioning look.

"Yes." He smiled rather fondly, Harriet thought, and she experienced a strange pang in her heart.

"She is a clever girl. Oh, I have a guest coming soon— Mr. Pericles Heron, the architect. He has agreed to design an addition for my father's bird room—otherwise known as the library. It has more birds than books at the present. At the rate he goes, Father will run out of room before long." His voice was dry and his manner skeptical.

"Hmm," she replied absently. Did his remark about Nympha indicate an interest in that direction? His mother had placed them together at the dinner, and they appeared to be on close and companionable terms at that time. "Does he plan the window for your mother—the one she said she wants?"

The earl offered details of the sort of window his mother wanted installed. Harriet listened with one ear while she mulled over the matter of Nympha Herbert. The girl was charming and evidently in favor with the marchioness. There would be no obstacle in the way should his interest lean toward her.

"Does Miss Herbert have any solution to offer on replacing the pin?" Harriet inquired before she considered.

"No—why should she? Miss Herbert knows nothing of the disappearance of the pin from the baron's house." The earl wore a baffled expression.

"Ah . . . I was merely wondering." Harriet knew she fully deserved the odd look Lord Stanhope gave her. But she had to wonder if his handsome lordship had occasion to kiss Nympha Herbert, and if so, had it tingled through her as it had Harriet?

"Harriet . . ." Aunt Cornelia reentered the room holding the watercolor of the milk thistle in one hand. "I am so pleased with this. I shall have it framed to go with the others." To Lord Stanhope she added, "The upstairs hall is lined with Harriet's paintings of wildflowers. I bought quite a number of frames when I was last in Town. I wanted them all to match, you see. There is still room left, dear girl." She bestowed a kindly look on her niece.

"What do you wish next?" Harriet gave her aunt a wary look. If she thought there would be another painting expedition with Lord Stanhope, she was sadly off the mark. Even on a bright, sunny day there would be no repeat of today.

"I will think about it. Perhaps a wild gladiola or perhaps that stinking iris—which is truly lovely to see, even if it smells dreadful."

Grateful the topic was safely changed, Harriet smiled. "I can do both if I can locate them. I'd have to hunt for that iris in the woods, and if the gladiola can be found, it would be around the bushy heaths. They are not precisely common."

"I am impressed with your knowledge, Lady Harriet." The earl rose from the chair with his watercolor in hand once more. "Too often it seems young women know little about botany."

"My aunt has stimulated my interest, sir." She also rose, intending to walk with him to the door.

The groom was bringing the curricle around to the front as she opened the door. Nicely timed. Her aunt calculated the length of his visit to a tee.

"We must do this again," he said politely, nodding to Aunt Cornelia as he spoke.

Over her dead body, Harriet thought. "Perhaps." And that had to be as noncommittal an answer as she could find.

It wasn't that she had found going with him to paint objectionable, and even the rain hadn't been all that dreadful. It was the kiss that had upset her calm, pleasant life. She couldn't decide which would be worse—to have another kiss or to go with him and not experience that delight again!

## Chapter Seven

Philip had scarcely entered the house and handed his painting gear to Peel, when a traveling coach could be seen rumbling up the avenue. The butler set the gear on a side table to be dealt with later, then walked with a stately tread to open the front door.

Philip watched as the coach slowly drew to a halt before the front of the house. The device on the door panel was mud-splattered and impossible to decipher. He guessed the arrival to be Pericles Heron; he was due to arrive about this day from what his letter had said.

The groom hurried to let down the steps, and within minutes a tall, thin gentleman with a mop of pale blond hair exited the vehicle. His blue eyes roamed over the exterior of the house and seemed to approve of what he saw.

Philip stepped from the house, his damp apparel ignored. "Mr. Heron. Welcome. We have been expecting you. I trust the roads were tolerable?"

"Execrable, but one scarcely expects better, does one?" He gave Philip a most agreeable smile and walked over to join him. Together, they entered the house, Heron explaining that he had decided against any delay.

Peel had summoned Mrs. Cork, who stood waiting to escort the guest to his room.

Glancing at the servants, Philip suggested, "Why don't we both go to our rooms? I feel certain you will welcome a change from traveling clothes, and I need a dry coat. When you are ready, please join me in the drawing room." He vaguely waved in the direction of the rear of the house, but did not explain how he had come to be

so damp. It would be presumed that the recent rain had
something to do with his condition.

After asking Mrs. Cork which room had been assigned
to Mr. Heron, the two gentlemen sauntered up the wind-
ing staircase to the first floor, chatting as they went. The
more they talked, the more Philip found to like in the
architect. He decided that Pericles Heron would be precisely the man to enlarge the library and install just the
correct window for his mother. Lady Harriet's words regarding his mother returned. Was he to pity her?

Mrs. Cork had wisely placed Mr. Heron two doors
from Philip's room. The room caught the morning sun
and had an elegant blue-and-gray carpet, the colors of
which were picked up in the pale blue walls and blue-
and-gray-figured draperies, all of which went nicely with
the mahogany furniture. Philip smiled at the thought that
the colors were fitting for a man with the name of Heron.

Once changed from his damp coat and presentable to
meet with the stranger, Philip promptly made his way to
the drawing room. In a short time Mr. Heron joined
him to partake of a restorative drink. Philip directed the
conversation to the changes necessary in the dining room
and the addition needed in the library. They first strolled
to the dining room to survey the window wall.

"I can see what you mean about the lack of light in
the dining room, Lord Stanhope," Mr. Heron declared
as they walked purposefully from that room to the library. When he nosed about the library, particularly the
end wall, he nodded decisively from time to time. With
a polite glance at the various cases housing Lord Lanstone's birds, he ventured to smile. "I fancy your father
will soon run out of space if more room is not provided.
I shall at once begin measuring and drawing sketches for
your approval."

"You surely ought to rest the remainder of the day,"
Philip protested.

"I dozed in the coach. Quite comfortable, you know,
as traveling coaches go." He pulled a rather clever fold-
ing ruler from a coat pocket and began his work.

Philip had never seen anything like that folded ruler

before, and it reinforced his notion of what a fine fellow Mr. Heron was. Perhaps Mr. Heron was an inventor as well as an architect? He retired to the far end of the room to watch only to be interrupted by his Aunt Plum.

"Dear boy, I thought you agreed to have the carpenter make me some shelves? He made but one! I want several, if you please. See to it, will you?" She nodded her head, then sailed off to the staircase and up to her room.

Uncle Plum shuffled into the library a short time later, watched Mr. Heron for a time, then murmured, "I want to order a chest of sorts to hold my chess sets. Know of a likely source?"

"No, but perhaps Mr. Heron does. I will ask him when he is not occupied. Father's room comes first, you know."

Uncle Plum wandered off in the direction of the drawing room, and Philip went the opposite way. How he longed for a place all his own, without one relative to plague him. He knew he could afford it, but he also was aware of how dependent his family was upon him. If only he had the magic to make them all stand on their individual feet, independent and self-sufficient. He shook his head, thinking that he'd never see that day. He would be happy merely to see his aunt and uncle leave! Perhaps he made things too comfortable for them? It might be that if they did not get every whim satisfied, they would remove themselves, along with their dratted cupids and chess sets, and set up elsewhere!

He had picked up his painting gear before going upstairs, seeing Peel had somehow forgotten it, and once in his room opened his watercolor pad to look again at his painting of the folly. It wasn't bad at all. He'd order it framed for Lady Harriet at once, and a pox on Aunt Victoria's shelves. Upon removing his painting from the pad, he found something he hadn't expected. Beneath it reposed the incredibly detailed painting of the milk thistle done by Lady Harriet. He carried it to the window to better study it, marveling at the wealth of detail she had included. It was as good as many a botanical painting he had seen on exhibit.

Well, he would have to return it to her at once. He couldn't imagine how it had come to be in with his things. He was certain he had left the painting at Quince House. He found a hat, a pair of gloves, and dry coat, then left the house with his watercolor pad, the painting protected inside it, before anyone knew what he was about.

Harriet gazed thoughtfully out of the front window at the curricle coming up the avenue. "Lord Stanhope is returning, Aunt Cornelia. I wonder why? I should have thought he would have had quite enough of us—of my company in particular."

"Now, dear, he probably went home to change and thought of something he had to tell you—or something . . ."

Harriet stared at her aunt, a suspicion sneaking into her mind at her aunt's too innocent words, not to mention her expression. She said nothing, however, and retreated to the chair close to the fireplace where a gentle blaze warmed the damp chill from the room.

In short order Mrs. Twig opened the drawing room door to admit his lordship. "Lord Stanhope." Her introduction was most unnecessary as it was unlikely that either of the two women would have forgotten him in such a short time. However, Mrs. Twig was all that was correct.

"We are delighted to see you again, my lord. Is there something you forgot?" Aunt Cornelia crossed the room to meet his lordship, as he stood not far from the door looking rather uneasy.

"Actually, I have no idea how Lady Harriet's painting found its way into my watercolor pad. Here it is." He produced the painting of the milk thistle from within the pages of the pad to offer Aunt Cornelia, evidently thinking that she was the one who would want it. "I recall you seemed anxious to have it framed and hung. I must say it is very deserving. The painting is worthy of being used as a botanical illustration. It is very accurate."

"Thank you," Harriet said quietly from where she stood next to the chair that had been a refuge for a brief time.

"You ought to show Lord Stanhope a few of the others, dear." Aunt nodded her head toward the door.

"I doubt if he has the time at present. Did you not mention that you had a guest coming?" Harriet cocked her head, looking at him with the hope he would depart as quickly as he came. Although, why she felt this way, she was not certain. As she had told her aunt, he made her feel unsettled, stirred up, not like her usual calm self in the least. She had never in her life experienced this strange inner disquiet, and she was uncertain if she could adjust to it. Or perhaps it might go away? Maybe it would if she just nerved herself to be with him more— she would become accustomed to him, and the feeling would disappear.

"True," his lordship replied, a faint smile curving his lips. "He did arrive shortly after I returned to my house. However, Mr. Heron is already in the library, busy measuring and making notes. I believe the gentleman does not like to waste time."

"How nice. I'm sure he will do well—and please your mother also." Harriet cast him an inquiring look, wondering how his father would take the expected changes.

"I trust he will do well." Lord Stanhope also looked at the door, although he made no move to depart.

Harriet chanced to glance out of the front window again to observe the rectory gig approaching. "What a lovely surprise. I believe Miss Nympha Herbert is coming. I was told she is the only one of the rectory girls who is gifted with being able to drive their gig."

Aunt Cornelia looked vexed for a moment. Harriet decided that her aunt was not above a bit of matchmaking. What a pity Miss Herbert interrupted. Then another thought intruded. It would give Harriet an opportunity to discover just how Lord Stanhope felt about Miss Herbert . . . maybe.

Mrs. Twig ushered Nympha into the drawing room with a broad smile reserved for those people she liked.

"Miss Herbert, how lovely to see you," Cornelia Quince said. If she harbored any ill feelings at her plans being thwarted, they were extremely well concealed.

"I trust I am not coming at an inconvenient time?" Nympha sought Harriet's face, then Aunt Cornelia's, and lastly Lord Stanhope.

Harriet had her eyes on Lord Stanhope to see what manner of reaction he had to the lovely little blonde. In her pale blue gown and a bonnet tied beneath her chin with ribands of the same delicate blue, Nympha had the look of a Dresden shepherdess. Harriet noted that same fond expression cross his face, and decided that she had not been imagining things when she observed it before. Lord Stanhope harbored some feelings for Nympha. What they might be, or how strong they might be, she couldn't guess. She sniffed. So much for a kiss in the barn.

"I hope you are not coming down with a cold," Lord Stanhope said at once. To Nympha he added, "We were out on a painting expedition and were caught in that earlier rain."

"How dreadful. I am fortunate. I never catch a cold. Papa says I inherited his constitution." Miss Herbert smiled, and Harriet thought she might have posed for the angels that were arranged above the church altar.

"Well, if you must inherit something, that is a good thing to inherit," Harriet quipped, then chided herself for a rather inane remark.

"Yes," Nympha replied uncertainly. She gave Harriet an anxious look. "Actually, I wanted to consult you regarding the village fair. It is not far away now, and I need a few more ideas as to booths or something of that sort. Papa usually handles much of the arrangements, but this year he needs a bit of help."

"Well, I have attended quite a few of these fairs in the village, perhaps I can lend a hand—or head as the case may be?" Lord Stanhope stepped forward to stand by Nympha.

Harriet found the sight of the two so close together utterly dreadful. Then she chastised herself for being quite stupid. She had no interest in his lordship, so why should she care in the least who he found attractive! And Nympha was certainly all of that.

"Perhaps a cup of tea would be welcome? The day is not precisely chilly, but I find that after a rain a cup of tea is an agreeable drink. And I would imagine that tea is conducive to thinking as well." Aunt Cornelia gestured to the chairs and sofa drawn up close to the fireplace.

"By all means." Lord Stanhope touched Nympha Herbert's elbow lightly, guiding her to the sofa.

Harriet returned to the chair where she had been prior to their arrival. She mastered the inner feelings of annoyance and whatever else it was that bothered her, and became the gracious hostess.

Mrs. Twig apparently had anticipated the request for a tray, for no sooner had Cornelia tugged on the bellpull than she entered bearing a well-laden selection of biscuits and seed cake, along with an enormous pot of tea and the delicate blue and white china her aunt favored.

"Now," Aunt Cornelia began, "I should think the first thing to do is to make a list of what you have arranged to this point. Then we shall better know what might be added."

"Oh, good thinking, Aunt Cornelia," Harriet said lightly. "Perhaps I ought to fetch a little pad of paper to make notes."

"Now, that is excellent logic, Lady Harriet."

She glanced at Lord Stanhope to see if he was teasing, but found only what seemed to be admiration in his eyes. Did the man admire every woman he saw? Or was she being overly sensitive about everything?

"Papa said you have a guest. Is that true? And do you think he might enjoy the village fair?" Nympha Herbert asked Lord Stanhope.

Harriet considered that there could be a hint of calculation in those delft blue eyes, but then, Mr. Heron might be a horrible creature, not worth the batting of blue eyes in the least. It would be well to be prepared.

"Indeed. Seems most agreeable chap—tall, rather thin, but a kindly face for all that. I shouldn't be surprised if he is willing to join in for the day. Once he has things in train, he ought to have a bit of free time on his hands. Besides, if I suggest he join us, I should think he would."

"Oh, how lovely. Just think what a sensation such a distinguished gentleman would create at our little fair." Nympha beamed a smile of goodwill at Lord Stanhope, then turned her gaze to Harriet, still smiling.

She seemed such a dear creature, Harriet felt quite guilty for harboring the slightest ill will toward her.

"Now, what do you have planned so far?" Aunt Cornelia could be counted upon to be practical, and Harriet was very grateful for it at the moment.

"Well, we have the gypsy to tell fortunes, of course. There will be bobbing for apples and tables for the things the village women have made. Do you think we might invite some Morris dancers to liven things up?"

"I should think a footrace for the young girls and men as well would be acceptable. There would have to be prizes," Harriet added thoughtfully. "Did you not mention that a Punch-and-Judy show is usually set up?" She studied Nympha to see what reaction she had to this.

"Oh, indeed. The children are not the only ones who enjoy them. And I expect there will be a peddler or two to offer their wares."

"Plus the stalls for gingerbread and sausages. Last year I recall someone had a performing monkey, a funny little brown fellow," Lord Stanhope inserted, smiling down at Nympha Herbert in a far-from-avuncular manner.

"The blacksmith usually sets up a roundabout that is well patronized by all." Nympha looked up at Lord Stanhope with pleading eyes. "Can you think of anything else, sir?"

"Not in the least. I should think that everyone will be as pleased as a dog with two tails."

"You tease, my lord," Nympha said with a delightful chuckle.

Harriet clenched her teeth and wondered why in the world she should care one jot if the rector's daughter flirted with their neighbor. She would merely remain with her aunt for a time before . . . well . . . and that was her difficulty. She had not the slightest idea where she might go if she left here. There was little room with her mother and new stepfather. It did not seem right to insert herself into her sister's household, newly wed and all. The ideal situation was to marry. Otherwise she would have to beg her aunt for a home—not that dear Aunt Cornelia was anything but delightful. It was that somehow Lord Stanhope altered the situation. She didn't understand it in the least.

The door opened, and Mrs. Twig ushered Lord Stanhope's younger brother in to the room. "Lord Nicholas Stanhope." She gave an anxious look at the tea tray, then murmured something about bringing more cakes and tea before she disappeared.

"Well, brother, I find you at last." Lord Nicholas strode across the room to greet his brother, who had risen upon his entrance.

Harriet thought she observed a flicker of resignation cross his lordship's face before his expression altered to one of warm welcome. "Hello, Nick. What is it you are wanting now? I gather it is urgent for you to ride this far in search of me."

"The blacksmith finished that scoop thing for the tree. I thought perhaps the ladies from Quince House might like to join us in watching the tree being moved." He smiled at all of them, looking young and fresh from the out-of-doors. There was something particularly lively about Nicholas Stanhope; he had a vitality Harriet had not seen in the dandies in London. It wasn't that he failed to dress properly, for he was a proper gentleman in his garb. He simply looked so alive.

"You are moving a tree? I trust it is a little one." Aunt Cornelia held her teacup high before her, pausing before she took a sip, eyeing him over the rim.

"That is the beauty of it. It is a mature tree, but I am certain I can move it to my golf course."

Harriet gave him a dubious look. "Will it not die?"

"I'm taking a large ball of earth with it so as not to disturb the roots. I think it will survive." His enthusiasm was almost catching. Harriet began to think that perhaps he would do as he claimed. Certainly his brother did not deride his notions.

"We have been discussing the upcoming fair," Lord Stanhope inserted.

"What? You mean the Society for the Suppression of Vice hasn't shut it down? They have been trying to for years. Doesn't seem to have any effect, though. Most anyone can justify a fair on economic grounds," he added, accepting a cup of tea from Harriet with a sideglance at the plate of cakes and biscuits, now replenished. She hastily offered both plates to him and smiled inwardly as he helped himself rather generously. But then, being in the outdoors did give one an appetite.

"No, and they won't, either," Lord Stanhope declared. "They can hardly say it is vice if the rector has something to do with it!"

"When do you propose to move this tree?" Harriet decided she was quite tired of discussing the fair. In her view the thing would have a life of its own, with all the various peddlers and other participants doing what they usually did without prompting or organizing by Nympha or any others. Naturally, she didn't give voice to her thoughts.

"Well, as soon as we are finished with this tea, what say we all go to the site and watch. I have lined up a cart, and the blacksmith has moved his device to where the tree stands now."

Harriet sought her aunt's eyes for permission. Anything was better than sitting still by a fire on a summer's day. "Could I not watch, dear aunt?"

"If you feel sufficiently recovered, I do not see any reason why not. In fact, I believe I will join you."

That said, they all finished their tea. Nympha waited with the two Stanhope brothers while Harriet and her aunt went to their rooms to fetch bonnets and shawls.

Nicholas had ridden over on his horse, so Aunt Cornelia stepped up to the rectory gig, declaring, "I shall ride with Miss Herbert so we can talk a bit more regarding the fair."

Since that was Miss Herbert's aim in coming, there was little she could say to that.

Harriet was left to join Lord Stanhope in his curricle. In an amazingly short time, they set off down the avenue in the direction of the Lanstone estate, in particular the far end of it where Lord Nicholas was in the process of creating his beloved golf course.

When they neared the site, it was clear the vehicles would have to be left at some distance. It was with a cheerful smile and determination that the women left the gig and curricle to walk to where the massive digger was placed beside a grown tree.

"It will offer some shade, will it not?" Miss Herbert asked Lord Stanhope.

Harriet wondered why the girl didn't ask Lord Nicholas. After all, it was his plan, his course. However, the query served to confirm her suspicion that there most assuredly was "something" between those two. She watched as his lordship placed Miss Herbert's delicately gloved hand on his arm while he gallantly escorted her to a good position where she could see all.

"How fortunate that I am not in the least delicate," Aunt Cornelia murmured to Harriet as they walked behind the others, picking their way over clumps of grass and around the gorse bushes.

"Indeed." Harriet compressed her lips as she considered her feelings in the matter. Why should she care? Of what importance was it to her, anyway? She studied his lordship's fine profile for a few moments before it came to her. She had developed a decided fondness for him, and there was not a single thing she could do to alter circumstances. Could she barge up and demand he assist *her*? Hardly. That was not Harriet's way. For one thing it was rude, and another, she simply couldn't risk a snub from him.

"I trust we are sturdy souls," Harriet replied at length.

"I could wish otherwise at times." Aunt Cornelia clasped Harriet's hand, a most comforting touch, and urged her forward.

It truly was fascinating to see how the giant machine bit into the earth a distance from the tree. The machine was moved here and there, making a complete circle before it came to rest where it began. Then the blacksmith signaled his men, and the real work began. In less time than Harriet would have believed, the tree slowly rose in the air, a large mass of dirt with it, before burlap was wrapped about the ball of roots.

The cart stood ready to accept its burden, the horses waiting patiently before it.

"Four horses," Aunt Cornelia stated, sounding very impressed.

"You must admit that when the Stanhope brothers do something, they do it right," Harriet replied in an undertone. Off to her right and front, she could not help but notice Nympha clung to Lord Stanhope's strong arm. *He* didn't have to lift a finger. His brother was managing the whole with surprising efficiency. Somehow Harriet had thought him one to lean on others, wanting them to help him decide what was to be done. Evidently that was not the case when it came to his golf course. Good for him, it made him far more likable.

Once placed in the cart, it was Lord Nicholas who leaped up to drive the team. The group from Quince House, along with many of the estate workers, followed along at a safe distance to where the tree was to go.

The tree was carefully put down into the prepared hole, then the gardeners and a few extra men swiftly worked to tamp the earth about the tree. Lord Nicholas watched, directing when he thought necessary. When all was accomplished, he left the gardeners to finish the job and strode across to where Harriet and the others waited.

"Lord Nicholas," Harriet cried as he neared, "I think you have an excellent chance of that tree taking root. What a splendid thing you did!"

Nympha glanced at her, then to Lord Stanhope, but said little, other than to utter soft congratulations.

Ignoring Nympha and his bother, Lord Nicholas walked to stand at Harriet's side. He took her hand in his, clearly pleased with himself. "Well, if I do say so, it was a job well-done. Could not have managed without the blacksmith. Chips is an excellent fellow." Rather than drop Harriet's hand, he tucked it next to him and began to walk to the carriages.

"I suppose your head gardener will keep an eye on that tree now?" Harriet didn't tug her hand away, aware that Lord Stanhope was directly behind them. If he could lavish attention on Miss Herbert, she might as well enjoy the company of his younger brother. Not that it was what she wished, mind you. But wishes were not always realized.

"Right. And since I am in the area often, I shall as well." He beamed a broad smile at her.

Harriet could see the family resemblance in the two brothers. Philip was perhaps a bit more firm in his jawline, but they both had the same well-molded lips and eyes that had the power to mesmerize you. They wore their hair slightly different—Philip brushing his back from his forehead while Nicholas allowed his to tumble into a whirl of soft curls, a sort of Brutus cut.

Lord Nicholas assisted both ladies into their respective carriages, lingering by Harriet's side, continuing to hold her hand. "I do thank you for coming to see the tree get moved. I am pleased it proved to be successful."

She looked at their entwined hands and smiled at him. Such enthusiasm deserved a reward. Impulsively, she leaned forward to place a light kiss on his cheek. "To the victor."

"Belong the spoils?" Lord Stanhope had helped Nympha into the gig and now stood ready to enter the curricle. His strong nose looked as though it smelled something displeasing.

"If you see it that way, yes." Harriet gave him a defiant glare. If he elected to spend his time fawning over Miss Herbert, he could scarcely object to her smiling at his brother.

They returned to Quince House in silence.

# Chapter Eight

The silence was more than a bit strained by the time Harriet and Lord Stanhope reached Quince House. Harriet decided that if he wanted to say something, he could. *She* had nothing to say. At least, she amended, nothing that she *could* in all propriety say to him. As they turned up the avenue to the house, she observed the rectory gig drawn up before the front steps and her aunt, with Miss Herbert at her side, about to enter.

"Thank you for bringing me home," Harriet said with utmost politeness.

"What would we British do without our manners," he murmured. "You are entirely welcome, Lady Harriet. There is something I must ask before we join the others."

Harriet turned a wary gaze on him, wondering what on earth he might find to query her about.

"I would like to come over in the morning to look at that pin again. I feel sure you would not wish to bring it down while Miss Herbert is present." He sent her a look of great significance.

"Of course," she immediately replied, understanding at once that he would not want his mother to be the object of gossip, although to be honest, she probably already was considering the outrageous garments she favored. "Whenever you wish to call, I expect we will be here. Nothing is planned as far as I know."

"Perhaps eleven in the morning? Let us hope that Miss Herbert does not require more advice on how to organize the fair, which has doubtlessly been held here for a decade or two without the benefit of her care." He paused a few moments, then added as the horse slowed to a gentle walk, "That does not sound kind. But I deem it silly to make such a fuss over the fair."

"That I quite understand, sir." But, she wondered, how did that opinion sit with his hovering over Miss Herbert while they were at the site of the tree removal?

"Do you? I wonder."

"Well, I should hope that I am not prone to doing utterly silly, stupid things." At his expression she added, "Like falling into streams and that. I have observed that we all do foolish things from time to time. I suspect it is merely human nature not to be perfect. Or are you?"

"Am I what?" He looked absolutely baffled.

"Perfect, my lord." She offered a serious look.

"Not in the slightest. I tend to make at least one stupid blunder every day. Spices up my life, you see." He didn't smile, but his eyes seemed filled with mirth.

"Really? How quaint. I find it enlivening to try for, at the very least, two idiotic things per day. I suspect this conversation may qualify as one of them." She compressed her lips lest she burst into a laugh.

He grinned at her words. Her heart did a strange dance when his eyes met hers and held the bond for some seconds. She broke the connection by turning to look at the house.

"I imagine we are being wondered about, my lord. My aunt and Miss Herbert arrived here some minutes ago. If we proceed now, we should arrive just as the tea is being brought into the drawing room. My aunt is a great believer in tea for all occasions. Although she does have coffee in the house for those who prefer it, she usually serves tea. I'd not be surprised were she to believe that coffee is somehow un-English—even if coffee came here first."

He promptly set off toward the house, stopping just behind the gig. A groom came whisking around the corner from the tables to tend to the earl's carriage, ignoring the rig from the rectory. He listened to a few words from the earl, nodded, then led the earl's carriage toward the stable with the promise he would take the rectory gig there shortly.

Harriet ignored the matter, but resolved to speak to the stable hands later. It was understandable, even if rude, to take care of the earl first, but a lady, even from the rectory, was not to be ignored.

"Lord Stanhope," Aunt Cornelia said in her most lady-like manner—cool, distant, and only a trifle off-putting. "You must join us for tea."

Likely he thwarted her by agreeing at once. Harriet wanted to grin and didn't dare. Not understanding what was going on in his mind, she was not about to guess. She tossed her shawl on the back of a chair, and removed her bonnet, since she was at home rather than calling. Her gloves followed, and she caught the earl watching her. Surely he had seen other women do such things a hundred times or more. How curious that he watch her so.

Mrs. Twig entered with a generously loaded tray. Not only did she have seed cake, but a goodly variety of other eatables, including meat sandwiches.

"Ah, Mrs. Twig, you know just what a body wants after being out in the fresh air." His lordship smiled at her, and Harriet noted with delight the blush that tinged the housekeeper's cheeks.

"Certainly, sir. The gentlemen always seem to like a bit to eat."

More silence reigned until tea had been poured, cakes passed about, napkins draped over various knees, and the important task of the moment begun. The brisk warmth of Assam tea was sheer heaven.

Harriet nibbled a biscuit, quite unable to eat more than one. She noted without the slightest envy that the earl consumed several beef and watercress sandwiches, followed by a number of ginger biscuits, and at least three cups of tea which Harriet poured for him with proper care. The poor man must have been starved!

"I imagine you have solved most of your pressing questions, Miss Herbert?" Harriet gazed at her expectantly. The dear girl might take more upon herself than necessary, but perhaps it was all in aid of seeing a certain gentleman? Harriet gave the earl a considering look. Was he actually the one Nympha sought? It was hard to tell, given how shy Nympha was at times. As well, Harriet recalled the demure glances Nympha had shot in the direction of Lord Nicholas. Perhaps she had decided he was too engrossed in his golf course to pay attention to a girl and she needed someone else?

"Indeed, I have, Lady Harriet. You cannot know how much I appreciate being able to consult with you . . . all." The look she bestowed on the earl seemed to Harriet to be somewhat possessive. What a peculiar notion. Yet, as she carefully noted his reaction of a reassuring smile and nod, she wasn't so sure. It was none of her business, she knew that. But her strange response to the earl's touch, not to mention the memory of that all-too-wondrous kiss, assuredly prompted it.

"In such a small community, I imagine that everyone feels a certain responsibility for neighborhood activities." Lord Stanhope blotted his mouth with the dainty square of linen that had reposed on his knee while he sipped tea and consumed the quantity of delicacies. Harriet admired his unabashed enjoyment of the excellent food. If there was anything she disliked, it was someone who pretended not to be the slightest hungry, then ate plates loaded with edibles. Now, that was silly.

At last Miss Nympha Herbert decided she had better return home with the rectory gig. Mrs. Twig promised to relay the request at once. With a raise of an eyebrow at Harriet, his lordship indicated he would leave as well and she relayed this to Mrs. Twig. The look he gave Harriet doubtlessly wished to remind him of their morning meeting at eleven o'clock. As though she might forget.

Aunt Cornelia joined Harriet on the portico to watch the departure of the two carriages. She chatted briefly with Nympha while Harriet offered her hand to Lord Stanhope. He drew her hand to his mouth, placing a lingering kiss on it while gazing deeply into her eyes.

"Until tomorrow, my dear Lady Harriet."

"Tomorrow," she managed to reply in an unsteady voice. Really, the man had the most unnerving effect on her—and she wasn't his dear anything! She welcomed the return of her aunt to her side to observe Nympha leave first, followed closely by the earl.

"Miss Nympha is a dab hand with the reins, I should say." She gave Harriet a thoughtful look before turning to watch his lordship tool his curricle down the avenue. "And then, we have the earl, who is undoubtedly a nonpareil."

"Indeed, he must be." Harriet was careful not to put any inflection in her voice. It seemed to her there were not that many gentlemen who continued to kiss a woman's hand anymore, much less someone like the earl who managed to make it so sensual. Gracious, she could have lit a fire with the heat emanating from her hand.

"You dawdled coming up the drive." Her aunt studied Harriet with a far too shrewd gaze.

"Yes, he had a few things to say. He intends to come over in the morning to see that ivory dragon again. I wonder that he is content to take his time at returning it. He keeps asking *me* if I have any ideas as to how it might cleverly be restored. I can't say I have had any practice at returning stolen items."

"Harriet, never say stolen!" Aunt Cornelia took Harriet by the arm with the intent of returning to the drawing room.

"Well, it was taken, for what that is worth. I'll not discuss by whom, but of course it has to go back. Perhaps I shall simply hand it to him and let him worry about it. Or maybe Nympha Herbert can assist him? She seems intent upon running the fair single-handedly." Harriet paused in the doorway to glance back at the direction his lordship had gone.

"Harriet!" Aunt Cornelia looked taken aback.

"I am sorry, dear aunt. I think the sun must have touched me in the head. Oh, look. I do believe that is the carriage belonging to Major Birch approaching. What a pity I *must* go to my room." With that, Harriet dashed head into the drawing room, caught up her shawl and bonnet, plus her gloves, and hurried to the stairs, intent upon reaching that sanctuary before more company arrived. Her aunt scarcely needed protection from a gentleman who apparently was not an admirer. Or was he? Thank heavens it wasn't her problem. She had quite enough on her hands at the moment.

Philip wondered how he had managed to tumble into this muddle. Miss Herbert had flirted with him, and he would have been a cad to push her away . . . wouldn't he? Besides, Lady Harriet had been decidedly cool that past day or so. And then she had the audacity to kiss his brother. To be sure, it was on the cheek. But still. Philip seethed with righteous indignation. They would have to join together to solve the remaining problem of returning the ivory dragon to Baron Rothson, and it would be helpful if they were on agreeable terms when next they met. He thought Harriet had responded to his kiss on her hand. Positively, of course.

Tossing the reins to the groom who dashed up to meet him outside the stables, Philip left the curricle in his capable hands to head for the house. He wondered what might have gone wrong now. Something usually had if he absented himself for long.

He was partway across the stable yard when the carpenter left his workroom to meet him.

"Milord, a word, if you please?"

"What is it, Parrot? Problems?"

"Not at all, sir. The frame you wished for is ready. Do you want it now?" The carpenter wore a pleased smile, for he had managed to surprise his master.

"Amazing. I'd not have expected it so quickly."

The carpenter nodded. "Well, as to that, I keep some picture molding of that sort on hand, just in case. Never know when you might want a bit of it."

Philip followed him into the workshop, inhaling the aroma of freshly cut wood and gilding. Within minutes he was off again, his thanks hanging in the air. The frame was precisely as he wished, and he had to admit the painting looked even better when matted and framed with gold.

Peel met him in the hallway, bowing politely and indicating he would like a word.

Philip hoped it would be agreeable. He found the day had tired him, and he'd like nothing more than a bit of quiet.

"The architect is settled in his room with his tools. He requested I invite you to join him when you returned to the house. If you please, that is." Peel kept his stiffly erect posture, but Philip suspected that he was inwardly pleased about something.

"Really? Well, and so I shall. I must say this is a pleasant homecoming for a change."

"Lord and Lady Plum have gone calling. Your mother is in her suite. Your father has gone out bird watching."

"Thank you, Peel. That explains a great deal." Indeed, if they were not around, they were unlikely to think of some demand on his time. One of these days he intended to make some changes around here.

The butler bowed again and marched off toward the pantry. Humming.

A knock on his guest's door brought forth a distant "Enter."

Philip hesitantly opened it and went in to find Heron near the window. He had pulled a table close to it, and found a sturdy wooden chair to use while drawing.

"Come in, come in. I have made a sketch to show you—just an idea, mind you, but something to give me a notion of what you like."

"It is for my father," Philip reminded.

"You will inherit this house before too many years are gone by. I think it is even more important that you approve. You will have to live with it as well." He gave Philip an astute look of understanding.

Since this was indisputable, Philip merely nodded, then went to the table to study the sketch. "I like it," he pronounced at last. "I think it will fit in well and . . ." A sudden vision of youngsters romping through the room, a fire burning in the grate, and a lovely lady with auburn hair curled up beside him on the sofa crept into his mind.

"It ought to be very versatile." At Heron's questioning look, he added, "For a family, that is."

"Indeed so. You plan upon marrying before long?" The architect wore a considering expression. Philip wondered if he intended to make other changes to the room on that speculation.

"Perhaps. One must always think ahead." Philip grinned at the chap, who sat so tidily on the wooden chair. He suddenly felt as though what he wanted might eventually come to pass. As to the lady who would be at his side? That little matter had yet to be finalized.

The following day did not begin well. His mother demanded to see the plans for her window. Fortunately for all concerned, she liked them. She thought.

Then his father, totally ignoring his wife, insisted upon reviewing the plans for the expansion of the library. As far as Philip knew, he had not paid the slightest bit of attention when it was discussed previously. He did not like the plans in the least. When asked what his objections were, he was vague to the point of irritating absurdity. It took all of Philip's powers of persuasion to convince the marquess that he would have adequate room for his blasted birds and books.

"The library needs more shelves, and provisions have been included for them in Mr. Heron's plans."

"Hmpf," Lord Lanstone replied, looking highly displeased, his mustache bristling with annoyance.

He stalked off to consult with the architect while Philip took note of the time. It was half past the hour of ten, and he intended to leave come what may!

The groom had received the message to have the curricle ready and waiting, so all Philip had to do was to climb in and head out of the stable yard, using the alternate road. The road was little more than a path to the main road that led to the village. However, it had the advantage of being a considerable distance from the avenue leading to the house, not to mention closer in the direction of Quince House.

A groom met him to take the curricle and his chestnut to the stable. Miss Quince was blessed with good service.

Lady Harriet opened the door to invite him inside. She glanced at the drawing room door, then guided him along the hall to the library.

"Come, I believe we can be private here. My aunt is occupied in the drawing room at the moment." Harriet cast a concerned look in the direction where her aunt and her guest had been closeted for the past twenty minutes.

"I trust there is no problem?"

"No, at least none that I know of at present. Now," she said with a sigh, "come to the window so you may see the dragon properly. It is a lovely day, is it not?" she murmured absently as she walked to stand by the window that had been opened to let in the lovely summer breeze.

The earl followed her closely, observing that while she had left the door ajar, the window where she led him was out of direct sight of anyone in the hall. He wondered if she was aware of her omission.

"The sun will help us to more clearly see the little slit that shows where to open the box. How delicately it is carved." She held it in her hand, admiring the exquisite carving, wishing she owned such a pretty little thing.

After removing his gloves, he picked up the box to turn it over in his capable hands. Harriet thought them strong-looking, yet she knew full well how gentle he could be if holding a woman in his arms. There was an ache within to know those arms again, and wasn't that a foolish desire? He did not seem the least happy to see her this morning, and had been all business when she met him at the doorway. What if she had never worn the pin where he could see it? Why, he would still be wandering in search of the blessed thing.

"Ah, I see the slit now. You are right—the sun does help see it much better. Would you do the honors? I'd like to see the dragon again, and then we can discuss how we shall slip this dratted thing back into the baron's house. At this point, I would be satisfied merely to place it anywhere within his four walls!"

Harriet took the little box and with gentle fingers slid the top back to reveal the delicately carved ivory dragon. Using care, she put it in the palm of her hand so it would show to better advantage. She moved her hand so the sunshine might highlight the design. It was a decided mistake. The earl edged closer to study the design, and in so doing nudged her arm. The pin simply flew from her palm to land outside on the grass!

"Oh, good grief! Come, quickly, we had best hurry. I'd not wish anything to happen to the baron's precious ivory dragon." Harriet tossed him a pointed look, then rushed from the room.

He followed at once down the hall, out the front door, and along the side of the house until they reached the library window.

The grass had not been scythed for at least a week, and was rather tall. Harriet knelt just outside and below the window, noting the kitchen dog trotting off around the house as she did. She hunted through what seemed like every blade of grass, but found nothing.

"Allow me," Lord Stanhope said, dropping to her side to begin his own search. He had no better luck than she did.

"I do not see how the pin could simply disappear," Harriet said, her vexation ringing clear in her voice.

"Had I not seen it flip out of the window, I would think it was in the house. Or is it? Could we have imagined it went out there? Let us look near the window, on the inside this time."

"Oh, do." Harriet was beginning to feel panic rising within her. It would be her fault. She had meant to help him, show him how lovely that little pin was before restoring it to the box and the owner, and this is what happened! Perhaps she was jinxed? She grabbed his hand and led the way back to the library. All was as it had been before . . . wasn't it?

She frowned as they both knelt before the window. Spotlessly polished oak flooring with a fine Turkey carpet close by was all they saw. There was no little carved ivory dragon to be seen anywhere.

She slumped against the wall, allowing the breeze to ruffle the top of her head. She closed her eyes in anguish. "Nothing. I cannot tell you how sorry I am. This is like a nightmare—or do I say daymare instead? I meant to help, and instead I am the worst sort of assistant." She couldn't prevent the tears that filled her eyes, one or two to spill over. Studying her hand didn't help at all. No clue could be found there.

"You could not help what happened. Had I not bumped your hand in my clumsy way, the dragon would never have leaped over the sill."

"You are never clumsy." She sniffed, wishing for a handkerchief.

"Harriet, do not blame yourself." The whispered command brought her gaze to meet his.

Afterward, she remembered that it was as though she had no power to do else but accept his kiss. If it was meant to be comforting, perhaps it was—at first. Then something seemed to take flame between them, and she melted against him. She was enfolded in his strong arms and kissed nearly senseless. The kiss was infinitely better than her first—the one in the barn.

At last she withdrew, giving him a tentative and misty smile.

"Harriet . . . I suppose I ought to apologize for that. I'd not intended to kiss you again, but, dear girl, you are the most tempting of creatures. And as to an apology, I'll be hanged if I will beg pardon for something I enjoyed so much. And unless I miss my guess, you did as well." He searched her face as though wanting a reply in the affirmative.

She gave him a straight look in his eyes and nodded. "I confess I did. Enjoy it, that is. I do not know what you must think of me. Label me a wanton, I suppose. But I think it would be quite silly of me to lie." Then the memory of what had happened before popped into her mind, and she gasped.

"What is it? You look as though someone just stabbed you!"

"And well they might. That ivory dragon has gone missing. We still have the little carved box, but that scarcely compensates for the ivory dragon that ought to be inside. How do we explain that to the baron, pray tell?" She rose to her feet to take several steps away from the tantalizing gentleman she had come to care about far too much. She spun around to face the earl. "What do we do now?"

"Hm. Let us go outside once again and look around. Perhaps we missed something." He grabbed her hand and tugged her behind him until they arrived back outside the library window.

In vain did they search for the tiny little bit of ivory. Nothing could be found tucked in the blades of grass. The dog returned and sat watching them, as though they were daft.

"I wish I had never seen the dratted thing," Harriet declared fervently.

"I wish Mother had thought of something else to snabble from the baron's collection."

"True." Harriet sat back on her heels, staring off into the distance and seeing nothing.

"Was there anyone about?" He also stared, but rather than off into the distance, he stared intently at Harriet.

"Not a soul. I could see a gardener off in the distance, but he didn't come near the house. I doubt you observed anyone, either." She rose to her feet, reluctant to end the search.

He rose to his feet as well, then took her hand in his. "Look at me." When Harriet obeyed he continued. "I want you to understand that this could have happened to anyone. Do not blame yourself for what was a freakish accident."

"Nevertheless, it did happen to me, and I feel dreadful. What will we do now?" She was grateful that he didn't dump all the blame on her. It was a series of misadventures. Had she left that little wood box in the barn, had she told him immediately about what she had found, had she insisted he take the pin with its box with him sooner, had she not gone to the window for the sunshine, for that matter, had his mother not taken the thing in the first place, all would be well. She wouldn't blame him were he to have nothing to do with her in the least, or until the ivory dragon had been found.

"Your mother needs something else to take her interest," Harriet said upon reflection. "You cannot permit her to continue in this line. She could find herself in serious trouble, and then where would you be?"

"It is a responsibility, you may be certain." He tucked her arm against him and began to walk toward the rear of the house. "Not only does my mother need watching, but my father wants nothing to do with the running of the estate. He is of the opinion that I can handle it now, as I must once he is gone aloft."

"Never say so! You scarce have a moment to yourself, it would seem. And here I thought you one of those carefree *Men About Town* I observed when in London." She gave him a concerned frown, thinking his family certainly did impose upon him. What he needed was a wife to help him, to persuade those pesky relatives to stand on their own two feet as it were.

"Hardly."

"You are a very gallant gentleman, I perceive, a rare gentleman who truly cares for his family, sees them more than a duty."

"I am no saint, madam. There are times when I would like to send the lot of them packing. Or take off and let them muddle along on their own. The difficulty with that is that I would hate to see the estate fall into rack and ruin." He ran a hand through his hair, quite obviously frustrated by it all.

"But would it? Surely if you were indisposed, your father would step up to take the helm, manage as he knows he must? Or perhaps Lord Nicholas would take command?"

"Nick? Perhaps one day he might. He is the best of chaps when he doesn't have a bee in his bonnet over something he wants to do."

"Like the golf course." Harriet nodded in agreement. 'I see how it is."

"As to Father, well, I'd not wish to put the theory to the test." His mouth tilted up to one side in derision.

"So you are their dependable bastion of support, a man they all—including your aunt and uncle—figure they can turn their problems over to and have them all solved. Who solves *your* problems, pray tell?"

"No one. I must depend on myself." This was said without a note of pity in his voice, but rather a simple statement of fact.

"You need help." And Harriet was certain she knew just the person to fill those shoes.

# Chapter Nine

Harriet watched Lord Stanhope enter his curricle to return home. Each had promised to consider where the pin might have gone, although how that might help, she wasn't sure. She left the rear of the house to go to the drawing room to seek her aunt. What she found was her usually calm aunt in a dither. It seemed her guest had proposed a startling scheme.

"He wants to what?" Harriet cried, certain she had not heard right.

"Major Birch wants to court me. It is as simple and as difficult as that." Aunt Cornelia shredded a cambric handkerchief as she slowly paced the floor from the window to the fireplace and back again. "We argued years ago. I confess I was astounded when he moved near here. He had this silly thing about his limp, as though I would care about that, and I told him he was an utter fool."

Harriet sank down on her favorite chair to absorb this shock. Of course she ought to have realized that something was in the wind. He was here yesterday, and Aunt had said nothing about the visit, other than he had wanted to discuss something with her. Now this morning, and *such* momentous news. "I can see that it is simple—I mean," she continued awkwardly, "courting is courting, is it not? But why is it difficult?"

"Because, dear girl, I shall have to make a decision sooner or later. I do not know what to do." Cornelia hesitated by the window, staring out at nothing in particular from what Harriet could tell. Then she resumed her pacing, which was more of a meandering walk than a purposeful stride. "My head says I have my independence, that I have a lovely home, dear friends, my lovely gardens."

"What does your heart tell you to do?" Harriet leaned back in the chair, steepling her fingers before her chin with her elbows propped on the arms of the chair. The thought crossed her mind that everyone around her was either married or in the process of doing so. Soon she might find herself on the hunt for another home. "I should think a woman might welcome the attentions of so handsome a gentleman as Major Birch. He has a rugged face, true, but it is a face of integrity. I rather like the way his hair curls at the nape of his neck, even though he brushes it back from his forehead rather severely. I think it an interesting contradiction in him. I saw him when he arrived, you know. His biscuit coat fit him to perfection, and his neck cloth was very well-done. I should think a single lady living alone in the country would welcome a strong gentleman to protect her. Surely his limp would be no deterrent to protecting you?"

"Protect me? And why should I need protection, pray tell? There has never been any difficulty around here." Cornelia paused in her pacing to stare at Harriet, eyebrows raised.

"You never know what might occur. You will not believe what happened a while ago. Lord Stanhope came over precisely at eleven of the clock as he had promised. He intended to take that carved box and the ivory dragon home with him. I wish he had taken it before. We were looking at the little dragon—and it flipped out of the window! Just like that! He nudged my elbow and off it went. I could not believe it. *And* when we went out to hunt for it, the pin had vanished, quite as though it was magical. Dear aunt, that pin did not walk off by itself! Someone crept up and took it—I just know that is what must have happened! How else could it disappear?"

"Oh, dear. It is quite valuable, and now it is gone again? Well, you know what I mean," she amended when Harriet gave her a look.

"I wonder why his mother takes these things, for that is what occurred. She is the one who placed it in the barn, likely storing it until later for some obscure reason. Do you think things like that can run in the family? His Aunt Plum is a bit strange as well."

"I am not certain, but I suppose it is possible. They both *seem* like very acceptable ladies. What will you do now?"

"She needs help," Harriet mused aloud, echoing her earlier thoughts.

"No, dear, about the pin?" Cornelia walked closer to where Harriet sat to gaze down at her with welcome sympathy.

"It was and it wasn't my fault, if you see what I mean. I didn't take the dratted pin in the first place. If his lordship hadn't nudged my elbow, he'd have the thing in his pocket right now, instead of who knows where. Fortunately, the baron has not made any formal complaint. He could not, because he is merely guessing. It seems to me that any number of people could have had access to the thing. How Lady Lanstone was able to sneak it from the display case is beyond me. From what Philip—that is Lord Stanhope—said, the cases are extremely well protected."

"It would seem that the baron's security is not as good as he thinks if a mere woman can purloin an object from under his nose." Cornelia's tone was more than a little ironic, her mouth compressed.

"True," Harriet murmured. "I think I shall go back outside to see if by chance we somehow missed that silly pin. I will be seeing dragons in my dreams. Will you excuse me?"

"I believe I see Miss Herbert coming up the avenue in the rectory gig. Dear girl, how tedious she becomes when she is involved in some project."

"She is sweet and tenacious; both are good qualities when properly directed. I think what Lady Lanstone needs is a project to involve her in something of great interest." Harriet rose from her chair to glance out of the window, then back at her aunt. "Why do you suppose her ladyship dresses as she does? Her husband quite ignores her, so she fails to attract his notice if that is what she wants. Lord Stanhope said his father is not apt to pay her any attention."

"That might have some bearing on her difficulty."

"What an interesting notion. I suppose you want me to remain in here to chat with Nympha?"

"Please."

Harriet remained standing to greet their guest with well-disguised impatience. The ivory dragon couldn't have gone off on its own. It had to be there yet. Somehow they had missed it. What she needed was a better tool to rake the blades of grass. If it was on end, it might seem to disappear. Perhaps not, but what else could she think?

Philip was not in a good mood when he returned to the estate. He had hoped to have the ivory dragon and box in his pocket so he could return them to the baron. It was impossible the ivory dragon could vanish, even though his eyes told him it was not to be seen.

When he rode into the stable yard, he could hear his aunt's querulous voice raised to Parrot. The patient carpenter would likely be ready to decamp after enduring one of her tirades. Philip left the curricle and horse to the groom, then walked toward the carpenter's shop.

"May I be of some assistance, Aunt Victoria?" He paused in the doorway to assess the problem. Most likely she was fussing about her dratted shelves.

"I have not yet received those shelves you said you would order for me, and this man said you never did. I accused him of lying." Her gray eyes were stormy.

"Actually, something came up and I forgot. Don't blame him, Aunt Victoria." He stepped back as his aunt rounded on him in her indignation.

"Well, if he had made me several shelves in the first place, I would not have this problem now. I found a dear little cupid while we stopped in the village. I need another shelf." She crossed her arms over her ample bosom and stared at Philip.

It was then he decided he had at last had enough of his mother's sister and her husband. One way or another, they were going to leave. He didn't know how, but he would think of something.

"You will have it as soon as Parrot can manage it." Philip soothed her even as he guided her to the doorway. The last thing he needed was more histrionics.

Appeased, she left the shop to return to the house. Philip wondered if she actually had bought a cupid, or if she was like his mother and helped herself to something she spotted where she was out calling with Uncle Melrose. He supposed he best check to see where they had been.

Once in the house he found his mother dithering in the hall. It was quite obvious she was in a state, looking anxious and fretting.

"What seems to be the trouble, Mother?"

"I, er, lost something. I have looked and looked and cannot find it."

"What did you lose?" He had some idea as to what it might be, but then for all he knew she could have taken something else from who knows where.

"Ah, er, I could not say." She wrung her hands while edging away from him, looking to the stairs as though she intended to flee.

"Was it something you admired, perhaps?"

"Oh, yes. Indeed, it was. Very admired. I did, to be sure." She made her way to the first step and placed one hand on the banister, frowning as though in deep thought.

"And it is something you cannot tell me about?"

"Oh, no," she cried, airily waving her other hand in the air. "I feel certain it will pop up . . . somewhere. If I could just think where," she muttered while making good her escape up the stairs to her suite, her purple-and-green draperies floating madly about her as she went.

Philip had to smile even with the severity of the situation. She was a dear lady in spite of all her faults. He moved forward to the library to see if anything had changed there. When he entered, he found a great deal had altered. The end of the room where the addition was to be made had been cleared of everything that had originally been there. On the wall Heron had meticu-

lously drawn the outline of the proposed archway to the
new addition. Philip paused to admire the design.

"Well, what do you think? It is sufficiently wide to
take the boxes your father uses for his stuffed birds? We
could make the opening wider and then insert a couple
of Ionic columns for support if you like. That is a bearing
wall, after all." He looked to Philip for a decision.

"I think that might be a fine idea. It would offer more
light, for one thing. Yes. Proceed on that premise."

"I have designed the Venetian window for the dining
room." Heron pulled forth a sheaf of papers on which
the window was carefully drawn.

Philip approved that as well. At least there was progress on the home front, and if his mother worried a bit
about her missing object, that might be all to the good.
Perhaps she would turn her skills to something other
than appropriating items that didn't belong to her.

"Your carpenter is cooperating well. I will request a
few specialists to join me, if that meets with your approval. I found they can be housed at the inn in the
village, a very good sort of place I understand. And I
was told there is an excellent glazier not far from here.
That will help a great deal."

It was with a much lighter heart that Philip left the
house, intent upon returning to Quince House and the
mystery of the disappearing dragon.

The groom looked understandably confused when
Philip requested his horse this time. It wasn't like him
to be in and out as often as he had been today.

Ignoring the fine summer day, other than note the rip-
ening fields to either side of the road, he concentrated
on the missing ivory dragon.

No solution had offered itself by the time he stopped
before Quince House. The front door stood open, and
within moments Miss Quince appeared, smiling as
though relieved about something. Perhaps the ivory
dragon had been found!

"She is around the side of the house, just outside the
library window. She refuses to give up her search."

"Then, the dragon hasn't been found?"

"I am so sorry, but no, not as yet." She withdrew into the house, leaving the door open for the gentle breeze. The weather was warmer than it had been, and likely she welcomed the fresh air.

After handing his steed to the groom, he went around the corner. He spotted Harriet at once. She was on all fours, combing the grass—with a comb!

"I daresay that is the first time a comb has been used for the grass." Philip hunched down beside her.

"I keep hoping I'll find it." She glanced up at him, then blew a wayward auburn curl away from her face. What a delectable girl she was, scented with primrose today and looking as fresh as one. Philip could think of other ways he would enjoy passing the time with this charming creature besides looking for that ivory dragon.

"Think back. Are you certain that no one was around at the time." As he spoke, the kitchen dog came nosing around where Harriet now sat.

"Only this dog." She looked at the dog, then turned her gaze to Philip, her eyes widening at her thoughts. "You do not suppose . . . ? No. Or could it have?"

"You think the dog made off with it?"

"Do you have a better idea?" She jumped to her feet and motioned to the dog, begging it to come. It thought some sort of game was in the offing and trotted off to the front of the house. Harriet dashed after it, with Philip close behind.

"It's going into the house. We *must* catch that dog." Harriet raced up the steps to chase the dog down the long hall. Only she didn't. Rather, she slipped on the entry rug and fell to the floor, one leg beneath her. Philip was not quick enough to catch her.

Forgetting the blasted dog, he knelt beside Harriet's still form. "Harriet, can you hear me?"

"Oh, yes, I can hear you," she said in a stifled voice. "I believe this is one of my idiotic things for the day." She shifted a little in an attempt to rise, and subsided. "I suspect I have done something to my right ankle. At least it hurts like the very devil."

"Harriet! What has happened?" Aunt Cornelia, followed by Major Birch, hurried to Harriet's crumpled form.

Philip helped Harriet to sit up, then looked to her aunt. "I will carry her up to her room. Her ankle should be checked to see if there is a break."

"I can make my own way, thank you," Harriet said primly. Of course, when she made the attempt the pain was impossible.

Philip scooped Harriet into his arms to make his way up the stairs. "Which room is yours?"

Cornelia called, "I shall fetch something for the swelling, dear." Leaving the major behind, she hurried off to the kitchen.

"This is so stupid. I never fall! The one over there, third door from the end." She leaned her head against his shoulder, something that felt very good and right. He was sorry that he would soon put her down. Holding her so intimately brought her enticingly close, surrounding him with the scent of primroses.

He shifted her in his arms to open the door, and Harriet clung to his neck. "Oh, please do not drop me!" She clutched him even closer, and he couldn't help the grin that escaped. Oh, to be tightly held by a charming and very well-endowed young woman.

"I promise I won't." He kicked the door open, then carried her to her bed, where he set her down as gently as possible. She scooted back, eyeing him as though she wasn't quite certain what he intended to do next. "Let me have a look. I'm rather good with sprains and what, with Nick tumbling into trouble now and again."

Once her foot was hesitantly extended, he sat on the edge of the bed to examine a very nicely shaped slim ankle that showed some bruising. "Beginning to swell a little, but I doubt any permanent damage has been done." He probed the ankle, ignoring her winces and gasps. While he explored for injuries, he chanced to look about her room a little and liked what he saw. Then he returned his gaze to Harriet's pleasing curves. The sight was by far the most engaging.

"Your aunt should be here shortly with a soothing poultice," Philip said to offer comfort of a sort.

"I wonder how long it will be before she leaves."

"She is thinking of moving?" Philip reluctantly removed his hands from the ankle, deciding that while it might be painful, there was no serious damage done.

"You observed Major Birch downstairs? I will have you know that he is courting my aunt. This is all a secret for the moment, mind you, but I imagine not for long. He seems a very determined man."

"Here I thought he did not care for the ladies!"

"Evidently he altered his opinion. She has said little to me so far, but I'd not be surprised if she accepts his hand. Evidently they have known each other a long time."

"Will she sell this house? Where will you go if she does?" Philip was amazed at the turn of events. He decided to speak to Miss Quince regarding her house in case she chose to wed the major. The major's income wouldn't extend to maintaining two homes unless he rented one, and Philip had designs on Quince House.

Harriet gave him a wide-eyed stare and whispered, "I really do not know."

"Well, in all the romantic stories, something happens at the last moment so the heroine is saved." Philip took her hand in his. He admired her courage and resilience. No vapors for her. Her hand was dainty, delicate, and he liked the satiny feel of it. "As to her selling, if she is so inclined, I would buy the house. It has been well maintained, and her land marches with ours."

"I see."

Philip tilted his head to watch her. She looked rather forlorn. Did living here mean so much to her? "Surely you could live with your mother?"

"Perhaps." She wiggled her foot, wincing only slightly at the pain. "I do not think this is so very bad. But that dratted dog got clean away. What shall we do now?" She struggled to ease herself up on the bed.

"Here, let me help you. The skirt of your gown is

tangled about your, ah, limbs." A gentleman was not supposed to mention legs—or limbs, for that matter. Somehow he did not think he had shocked her.

"Legs. I have two just like everyone else." She gave him a direct look, a small smile creeping across her face. What a lovely creature she was, her gorgeous auburn hair tumbling about her face, a face that was now admittedly a trifle pale. He bent over to place a pillow behind her head and discovered he was far too close for propriety. He wanted to kiss her again, to know the taste of her lips, hold her in his arms, absorb the very essence of her.

"What did you decide, Lord Stanhope?" Miss Quince said as she swept into the room.

Philip stood at once.

"Do you think there is a break?" Miss Quince continued. If she observed his closeness to her niece, she made no comment.

"A slight sprain is all she suffered in my estimation, ma'am. Of course, you could call the apothecary if you wish a more learned opinion than mine."

"Please do not," Harriet implored. "He is such a fussy old man. I am sure he would keep me in bed for a week. I cannot spend a week in bed when there are things to be done."

Philip smiled at her passionate plea. He couldn't say he blamed her. Mr. Berry was a nice enough fellow, but inclined to stew over every little thing.

"I promised to help Miss Herbert with a few things—the fair, you know," Lady Harriet added.

"Ah, the estimable Miss Herbert. She has even impressed Nick with her organizational abilities," Philip added.

At those words Lady Harriet turned her face away from him. "I think I should like to rest for a time. You can hunt for that dog if you wish. Normally he is found near the kitchen, but I doubt he is allowed to bring anything in there. Look about if you please." Her words were clearly dismissive. Philip had little choice but to leave the room and the house as well.

He chatted briefly with the major before heading to

the stables, where he intended to look around for the missing dog. No one appeared to have seen the dratted animal, and he certainly did not spot it. A cat, presumably the one that had her kittens in the barn on that fateful day, sauntered across the stable yard. No dog.

"Well, what a dilemma this is, dear aunt. Just when I need to be able to hunt for that miserable ivory dragon, I injure my ankle. What more can happen?"

"You will ignore the dragon for the moment, you hear? And I wish you to recover from that dreadful fall before you even think of assisting Miss Herbert."

"Nympha reminded me that the fair is in a few days. Lord Stanhope is offering the prizes for the various races and will be there to present them. I must attend."

"You are attracted to Lord Stanhope, I believe. And I suspect he may be attracted to you, as well. Whether it is the sort of attraction you would like is something else. Well, I shall leave you to rest for the moment. Try to stay out of trouble until I return!" Aunt Cornelia bestowed an admonitory smile before departing.

Harriet could hear her talking to someone in the hallway and surmised it would be the major. He had arrived while Harriet was combing the grass. It certainly seemed that once the major made up his mind regarding Aunt Cornelia, he intended to wage a vigorous campaign to win her. He practically lived here now.

Thinking back to the tree moving, Harriet attempted to recapture the reactions she had while watching Lord Stanhope with Nympha. Had there been a lover-like attitude? And what about Lord Nicholas? Had he ignored Nympha with his brother? Harriet was of the opinion that Nympha and Lord Nicholas would make a wonderful pair. Yet, it seemed that it would not be. Rather, she didn't know how anyone would end, especially herself.

Lord Stanhope mentioned he would like to buy Aunt Cornelia's house in the event her aunt married. Why? Did he intend to move in here with a bride? When he mentioned buying the house, he had given her a significant look, and for one tantalizing moment, Harriet had the delirious notion that his decision involved her. But in the next instant she realized it was probably because he wanted a place where he could escape his family, or perhaps bring a bride. It would be good for his parents and other relatives if they were left on their own, but who would be the bride? The mere thought of Nympha Herbert marrying his lordship to reside in this charming house was more than Harriet could bear.

She buried her head in the pillow and willed herself to sleep, so when her aunt returned to check on her, she was dreaming, albeit restlessly.

"Drat it all, Nick, you are going to have to solve your own problems." Philip looked up from the sheaf of drawings in his hands to stare at his younger brother. "In fact, I am tired of not only you, but Father and Mother, and the Plums, and anyone else who expects me to be a magician and resolve every impediment to their happiness." Philip paced the floor of the library, where he had gone to inspect the final sketches of the library addition. He dropped the papers on the desk, then defiantly faced Nick, waiting to see what his reaction might be.

"I don't see why you never said anything to me about it." Nick was clearly provoked. "I've been busy, you know that. Besides, you never seemed to mind. I thought you liked solving our problems! If you had complained, I'd have done something about it." He gave Philip an engaging, boyish grin. He had breezed into the library, smelling of earth and the out-of-doors, his cheeks rosy and his eyes sparkling.

"I know. And instead of making you think on your own, I found it simpler to just do things for you. That was a mistake I intend to rectify at once. I have some plans for the future that I hope to realize . . ."

"Regarding a wife? Someone I know?" Nick inquired, his curiosity piqued.

"You know her," Philip admitted.

"Who, then? Lady Harriet? She'd be a welcome armful. Or Nympha Herbert? You'd catch cold at that one, dear brother. I scarce think she is the one for you."

When Philip remained silent, Nick stuck his hands in his pockets and stared. "That does affect things around here, doesn't it? I imagine we will all have to learn how to fend for ourselves. Moving far away from here?" he inquired idly.

"No. I will always be close by. After all, someday I will have to take over here. Would you believe that I would like a life of my own now, rather than later?"

"What about Mother?" Nick's forehead creased in thought. "She has a problem, you know."

"Ah, yes, Mother and her problems. Lady Harriet is of the opinion that she needs help. What do you think we could do for her?" Philip picked up a paperweight and tossed it in his hand.

"Lady Harriet or Mother?" Nick grinned at his brother.

"Mother, of course. Maybe we could persuade Lady Harriet to interest Mother in some pastime? Perhaps assist Miss Herbert with the fair? The locals would be in alt to have the marchioness assisting in any capacity." Philip tried to keep the irony from his voice, and quite failed to do so.

"She'd never do it," Nick opined. "Besides, Nympha Herbert is too impertinent." He looked more than a bit disgruntled. "I can't abide pushy females."

"Well, I hope that Lady Harriet can think of some manner to deal with Mother. She simply cannot continue as she has been. You *do* recall that Baron Rothson accused *you* of stealing his ivory carving? Are you aware Mother is the one who made off with it? She hid it in that old barn for some daft reason, Lady Harriet found the thing, and now it has disappeared—just when I thought I could return it." Philip rubbed his chin, sighing in exasperation.

"What?" Nick's head snapped up, his dismay almost comical. "Why in the world would she do a thing like that!"

"Lady Harriet is convinced it is because she wants attention. From Father, no less." When Nick scoffed, Philip continued, "Sneer if you will, but I believe Lady

Harriet may have something. Think about it, Nick. Why do *you* suppose Mother wears those outlandish gowns?"

Nick looked nonplussed. "I begin to see what you mean. She wasn't like that when we were young, was she? Didn't she start dressing like that after Father took an interest in his bloody birds?"

"Right. That's not the only problem on our hands." Philip enlightened Nick with the detailed account of his trials in his attempt to recover the ivory dragon.

"Egad! I had no idea all that has been going on!"

"And that is my fault. I should have brought you into the matter before now."

"Well . . . I daresay if you and I and Lady Harriet put our heads together, we ought to find a resolution to this."

Philip shook his head. "If she remains in the area. She may be out of a home. Miss Quince is being courted by none other than Major Birch. No one is supposed to know about it, but I saw him there with my own eyes. That would mean she must hope to find a room with her mother or sister, both of whom are newly wed."

Nick studied his older brother. "She could get married, I suppose."

"True. She might well wish to, since I decided to offer Miss Quince for her house." Philip clasped his hands behind him, trying to sound very offhand, wanting to see how his brother reacted to his bit of news. "I should think she would sell if she weds the major. Her property marches with ours, and her land will be a welcome addition."

"What would you do with the house? It's a nice bit of property." Nick's manner was casual, but his eyes were fixed intently on his brother.

"I have a few ideas. First, I must complete the purchase, and then I can think of how to use it. Perhaps I will move in there." He grinned at Nick, wondering if he had any inkling as to what intentions he nurtured.

"Well, as to that, I'd not blame you. I'd give a monkey to see how you intend to get rid of the Plums, though."

"I may just murder them with those blasted cupids!"

# Chapter Ten

"If Lord Stanhope has come, I do want to see him. Since it isn't proper for him to come to my room, I will go down to the drawing room. And if he has something for me—as you say he does—I wish to see it immediately, while he is here."

Harriet gave her aunt a stubborn look and swung her feet over the edge of the bed. Her attempt to hobble across the room was not much of a success. She couldn't even leave her bed without stabs of pain shooting through her ankle. She debated on what she might use as a cane when her aunt spoke.

"I guessed you would feel that way. You are dressed, so I see no reason why his lordship cannot carry you down." Aunt Cornelia opened the door, and Lord Stanhope entered the room.

"How is your ankle?" he queried. He strode to her bed, bending over to study the affected foot when he reached her side.

"Tolerable." Harriet shifted uneasily on the edge of her bed. She didn't know if she was ready for this. She admitted the close contact was something she would relish. On the other hand, she really ought to keep her distance from the man who had the power to throw her nerves into such turmoil. As much as she was attracted to him, there was little indication as to his intentions toward her.

At least her aunt was present to lend respectability. For some peculiar reason Aunt Cornelia had not been there yesterday when he carried Harriet to her bed. It was so unlike her that Harriet had wondered what had happened while she was with Major Birch. However, flushed cheeks and vague conversation put paid to any inquiries. It was obvious that whatever had kept them apart in the past had been resolved—to some degree.

"If you would try to stand on your one good foot, I can scoop you into my arms with no trouble." His smile was warm—at least she thought she detected a tenderness in his eyes. Perhaps she was indulging in wishful thinking? She suspected that girls did that when they wished for a gentleman's regard.

Harriet stood as he requested, wrapping her arm loosely about his neck. He smelled of shaving soap and a faint scent of eau de cologne. His neck cloth was again a miracle of perfection. She had to admire the understated elegance of his stickpin, a simple engraved design on a gold oval. Obviously he felt no need to dazzle with a spectacular emerald.

It was amazing how nicely she fit in his arms and against the solid comfort of his chest. Oh, how lovely it would be to rest her head on his shoulder and simply nestle there. With that scandalous thought, she pulled away from him and attempted to be very proper, as young ladies were supposed to be. It would never do to let him know how attracted she was to him. No doubt a man as handsome as he became accustomed to female admiration. But when at the Young Lady's Academy, she'd been drilled in proper behavior toward a gentleman. It did not include casting oneself onto his chest and wrapping one's arms about his neck.

However, she could use her reaction in the new book she was writing. Her heroine would not swoon, but fall deeply under the hero's spell.

"I shall be totally spoiled," she said in a joking manner. "I will not wish to walk down the stairs ever again. Aunt Cornelia, perhaps I might have a footman designated to carry me up and down."

"I do not think there is one of them who could cope with toting a lovely woman around in his arms," Lord Stanhope inserted. He glanced down at Harriet, while making light work of the stairs and bringing her to the drawing room sofa with a flourish, where he placed her ever so gently.

Once she was comfortably settled, she pinned him with an inquiring gaze. "Aunt Cornelia said you had something for me." There was little point in being coy. He should know her better than that by now.

"I do. Recall I promised to give you a picture of the folly once I had it framed?" He picked up a frame from beside the sofa. "Here it is." In a rather diffident manner, he held it up for her to see, then gave it to her so she might examine it more closely.

"Do be seated, my lord." Aunt Cornelia gestured to the chair close to where Harriet reclined on the sofa. Then she joined her niece to look at the gift.

Harriet studied the painting, a feeling of pleasure washing over her. "Ah, I thought it a handsome piece before. I declare it quite excellent now. I will never part with it." She smiled at the earl. His gaze was warm, and its expression sent a tremor right to her toes. She hastily turned her eyes to the painting. "Truly, I am honored that you would present it to me. Thank you very much."

She turned to her aunt, "Where shall we hang it, Aunt? It merits a place of honor."

Cornelia studied the walls. "Why not here?" She pointed to a spot above a side table. "Since it has been painted on my property, I may as well enjoy it, too."

Harriet nodded her agreement. "I can see it from where I usually sit, then. That will look charming. Thank you as well, Aunt Cornelia. I would not blame you if you preferred not to have a hole punched in the wall just to hang the painting when I suspect I will be gone before too long." Harriet watched her aunt's face with care, taking note of any change in expression. There was a slight softening of her face, but no words.

Lord Stanhope reminded, "Fortunately, a painting is quite portable."

"Yes, wherever I go I can take a bit of Quince House with me." Harriet smiled, hoping they didn't know what it cost her to do so. She had become amazingly fond of this house, not to mention her aunt. It would not be easy to leave here. "I should like to know where you inherited your painting skills, Lord Stanhope? Are either of your parents artistic?"

"My father's artistic ability extends as far as having a yellow-breasted bunting stuffed and mounted for display. He does rather well on displaying his birds. No, it is my mother who was the artist in the family. I have seen watercolors she painted as a young woman. Her family provided the finest of teachers for her, and she rewarded them with her efforts. I believe there are several of her paintings in her sitting room. I will show them to you the next time you come. I think you might like them very much."

"I look forward to seeing them." Harriet considered his revelation. This would bear some reflection. "She does not paint anymore?"

"Not as far as I know. It's the sort of thing young women do before they marry and have a family, is it not?" His eyes held warmth and something more.

Harriet nodded, mulling over his reply. She supposed he was quite correct. It was a pity, though, that a woman ceased to enjoy painting when she was so very good at it, as she suspected Lady Lanstone probably was. She doubted Lord Lanstone would praise his mother without good reason.

"Now, I must check your ankle." He gave her a roguish look and knelt by the sofa. Her heel cradled in his hand; he probed the ankle with gentle fingers. "I see it is much better today. The swelling is nearly gone. I should think you will be able to attend the fair by tomorrow if the ankle is well wrapped and you have a strong arm upon which to lean."

"I'd not stay at home, of that you may be certain!" Harriet chuckled at his expression. "If I had to hobble with a cane, I would come—even in a Bath chair! Do you imagine that after all the advice I have given Nympha Herbert, I'd miss the chance to see if it was taken?"

His shoulders shook with silent laughter. "I see."

"Not that she isn't all that is capable and delightful.

You probably know she has had to learn how to manage a significant number of things for her father. Her mother is occupied, so Aunt tells me, with preserving and coping with the glebe farm produce. I believe she even raises elegant fowl—ones that have speckled feathers as well as eggs! Nympha handles the sales for her."

Harriet watched his lordship carefully. What would be his reaction to her reference to Nympha? As far as she could see, he had no reaction at all. Either he was very good at concealing his thoughts or he really did not care much one way or the other regarding Miss Nympha Herbert. Harriet hoped it was the latter.

"Did you chance to look around outside again? Or do you feel as I do—that the dog made off with the pin and there is no use looking anymore?" She leaned back on the sofa to listen to his reply. He had returned to the chair and now watched her.

"The dog, of course. I searched the stable as well as the yard, and if he dropped the dragon pin, it has disappeared." The earl sat with a grace unusual for a large man, at least one so tall. He rested his elbow on the arm of the chair, putting his hand against his chin while studying her with a disconcerting thoroughness.

"Well, I do not see how the baron can charge your brother with taking the pin when he has no proof."

"True. I feel uncomfortable about the removal, however. If I cannot locate the pin I feel obligated to replace it, if that is possible. A rare object is not always an easy matter to duplicate."

He looked so bleak that Harriet longed to comfort him, pat him on his back or something. But to call the theft of the dragon pin as a removal was indulgent in the extreme! Something was going to have to be done with that mother of his. Something quite drastic, she feared.

"I trust your brother is managing his recently moved tree with no difficulty?" Aunt Cornelia inquired with gentle tact.

Lord Stanhope brightened considerably. "Absolutely.

He is so pleased with the results, he contemplates moving another tree to where he thinks some shade might be welcome."

"Do you golf?" Harriet asked hesitantly. She thought it a silly game, but she would not wish to offend him by an unkind comment.

"I have no time to be knocking a little ball over some grass and sand traps." His lordship shook his head. "I believe he intends to have Nympha make up a neatly printed copy of the rules he obtained from the St. Andrews course. He wants it to be printed so he can hand it out to prospective golfers." He exchanged an amused look with Harriet, and she felt a warmth uncoil within her.

"I suppose everyone is rather new to this game," Harriet reflected. "But the desire to chase a little ball around a length of green grass, avoiding puddles of water and traps of sand, is quite beyond my understanding."

She shared a smile with the earl, feeling a certain amount of delight that he didn't poker up at her.

"That dog is running about in the far lawn," Aunt Cornelia said from the window where she had been studying the scenery while Harriet and the earl chatted. "You know, the one that you chased yesterday?"

"Oh, the kitchen dog. But no one confessed to having seen the dragon pin." Harriet supposed she sounded disgusted, as well she was. "It was so frustrating, to be so close to returning it, and than have it simply jump out of my hand and disappear." She grimaced and shook her head.

Aunt Cornelia nodded. "One would think it possessed magic."

The earl rose to his feet in a fluid motion. "I had best return to the house now that I have ascertained Lady Harriet is better and the painting has been delivered into her hands." The earl evidently decided it better not to dwell on anything magical.

"The architect is to begin work on the dining room window today. He has summoned help from London and the surrounding area, and they ought to arrive shortly. Heron is an amazing chap, extremely clever."

"I think you are rather remarkable yourself, sir," Harriet said with an impish look.

"How so?" He stood by the sofa and towered over her, staring at her with an odd expression in his eyes.

"Well," she fiddled with the sash of her gown, refusing to meet his gaze, "you are a superb manager of your estate, or I should say, your father's estate. Few sons are so devoted or clever."

"It is a case of managing because I must, not because I wish. I am no hero, Lady Harriet."

"I believe you are, in spite of what you say." She tilted her head, a stubborn note in her voice. Mama said she was too resolute for her own good and perhaps she was. "Too often fine men do not receive the praise they are due."

He bowed, and turned to leave.

"I see Miss Herbert coming up the avenue in the rectory gig." Aunt Cornelia left the window to join Lord Stanhope. "She will be agog with news of the fair, I am certain. Perhaps you wish to remain?"

"I truly must return. One must keep an eye on matters, you know." He darted a glance to the avenue where Miss Herbert approached. "I will slip out the back way, if I might. It will be closer to the stables, and I could look for the pin while on my way there. I may have missed it."

Aunt Cornelia smiled. "Please do. Let us know if you succeed in finding it." She quitted the room to greet their arriving guest, relegating Lord Stanhope to the status of a family friend with the freedom to go through the house as he pleased.

He took a few steps, then paused. "You will go with me to the fair on the morrow?"

"That does not sound like a question. I think you have made up your mind, and I shall go willy-nilly." Harriet smiled to take away any sting from her words.

"True. I would deem it a kindness if you go with me. Think how well we agree on things of importance."

"Like golf clubs and other such?"

"See, I believe we shall be admirable company." At her answering nod, he swiftly left the room by the door that led to the dining room, then out to the back hall.

It was surprising how he knew his way around this house, or was he merely anxious to avoid an encounter with the chatty Miss Herbert? If that was the case, Harriet could only be pleased. Harriet settled back on the sofa, the injured foot elevated on a cushion. She contemplated the conversation with his lordship and knew a slight elevation of spirits. When their guest entered the room, Harriet was able to greet her with a much lighter heart.

"Miss Herbert—Nympha." She altered her greeting in light of the chastising look from their caller. "You have come to cheer the invalid."

"Oh, dear, I do hope you will be able to attend the fair. Lady Lanstone is to declare it open, you know."

"Umm," Harriet replied, her thoughts at once going to that lady and her history of painting. It was so sad she had ceased to paint. Perhaps she might like to join on a painting expedition? On a day that promised no rain.

"Oh, you will like it excessively, I am persuaded."

Harriet considered her escort and allowed as how she might.

Fortunately, the opening day of the fair proved to be as hoped. There were a few clouds, but the temperature was pleasant and only a little breeze fluttered the flags that attracted the fair-goers.

Harriet perched carefully in the curricle, aware that a number of people took note of her escort. While she was pleased to be in his company, she didn't want those attending the fair to make any assumptions. That could prove to be irksome if the gossips made too much of it.

"Where shall we begin our tour?" Lord Stanhope inquired once he'd lifted Harriet from the curricle.

"I would like to see everything, but perhaps first the stalls where the villagers have products for sale. Aunt Cornelia always buys as many things as she can. I will as well. They make such lovely items."

She missed the approving look from her escort, being far too occupied with all that could be seen. To appease the fair critics there were mounds of cheese, a gaggle of geese, with a few of Mrs. Herbert's feathered hens also on display. Harriet suspected she would sell the fertile eggs for a goodly sum. The gypsies had brought several horses to sell or trade. A number of farmers were eyeing them with shrewd study.

At every little stall she spotted multitudes of household articles, not to mention trinkets over which the maidens were sighing. Harriet was glad her aunt had the smart notion to bind her ankle securely. It made walking almost easy. They avoided the produce stalls, their tables heaped with onions and other vegetables and summer fruit.

"I am not hungry in the least, and the sight of food does not tempt me."

"What does, pray tell?"

He teased, certainly, but she thought she detected a curious note in his voice, almost sensual. She cast a look up at him, but did not reply.

Beggars hovered at the side of the lane, and a magician performed clever tricks to amuse and amaze the farmers and villagers alike. The Punch and Judy show was doing a splendid business. Nearby, a juggler tossed balls while a youngster tried to imitate him, to the amusement of the crowd.

"My lord, do you see what I see? That woman! Over there! Please note what sort of pin she has on her shawl. If that is not our ivory dragon, I will eat the entire mound of onions! And the cheese as well." Harriet clutched his arm, while attempting to sidle cautiously near the woman.

"Do you have any notion as to who she is?" Philip guided Harriet closer at her urging. There was no doubt in his mind that the pin was the same.

"To my knowledge, she is mother to our pot boy. It is possible that he found the pin, and thinking it a pretty thing, brought it home to his mother."

The crowd made it difficult to edge as close as he would like. "How do we retrieve the pin?"

"I suppose it would never do to simply walk up and request that it be returned. That would likely be too simple. Do you realize that should the baron attend the fair and spot that pin, he might have her arrested for theft? The poor woman would be hung before she knew what was happening."

"Then, by all means it is our duty to recover it." Philip studied the woman as unobtrusively as he could. Years ago at Oxford, he and his best friend had attempted to remove a pin from another student who had stolen it from his friend. They had practiced and practiced, and now he wondered if he could do it again. He had been successful, but would his ploy work on an old woman?

"How?"

"Could you admire her shawl?"

"It is a hideous thing, is it not? Would she believe me if I admired it?" Lady Harriet looked amusingly doubtful.

"Look, she has paused before the stall selling tea caddies." Philip nudged Harriet lightly. "Perhaps you could pretend an interest in them as well. Jostle her just a trifle, and I will come to her rescue."

"Would it not be easier to hire a pickpocket to obtain it for us?"

"Ah, but not nearly as challenging. If I fail, I will do just as you suggest. Does that please you?"

Philip couldn't guess what was in her thoughts when she glanced at him, but whatever it was brought a pretty rose to her cheeks. So, she thought about being pleased? He smiled.

She did as he suggested. Edging up to the stall where a really nice selection of tea caddies was displayed, she examined one after another, finally purchasing one. Then as she turned, she paused.

"Did you see a tea caddy you admire, ma'am?" she inquired politely, treating the poor woman far above her station. She was met with a blank stare before the pot boy's mother nodded, pointing to one close to where she stood.

"That is a nice shawl you are wearing. Did you buy it

at the fair?" Harriet held her purchase in her arms, turning to face the woman.

"No, ma'am." The woman mumbled her reply, looking as though she might collapse with the shock of a gentry lady complimenting her.

Harriet stepped forward as though she intended to finger the shawl. She faked a stumble and fell against the woman. "Oh, forgive me," Harriet cried. "My ankle is still not as it ought to be."

Philip rushed to the rescue. He caught the woman, his arm going securely around her to keep her from falling. Her cry of alarm abated when she realized she wasn't going to go down.

"Are you hurt, ma'am?" Philip inquired solicitously, his hands on her shoulders to steady her. He adjusted her shawl with a courtly air and righted the hat on her head.

"Thankee, milord. Nothin' more than a bit of a fright." The woman still looked overcome at this attention from the gentry.

"Madam, I insist upon buying you that tea caddy you were admiring. It is only just, after all." He plucked the item from the board upon which it sat, paid for it, and thrust it into the woman's hands before she could form a reply.

Lady Harriet grabbed his arm, leaning against him in a theatrical way. "Oh, please, I need to sit down. My ankle . . ."

"Allow me, my dear." Philip repressed a grin at her dramatics while he helped her to a wooden bench not too far away.

"You have the pin. I saw it simply disappear from sight. How did you do that?" She spoke so softly he could barely hear her.

"A schoolboy's prank recalled. We shall trust she does not remember where she was when the pin disappeared."

"It was a clever move to give her the tea caddy. She is so intent upon clutching it tightly that I doubt she will miss the pin until much later."

"By which time we will be far away." Philip helped Lady Harriet to her feet.

"I cannot believe we have the pin back. Who would have dreamed we would find it at the fair?"

"Indeed. Now all we have to do is return it to its rightful owner without being detected." Philip gave her a rueful look. It would not be as easy as they might think.

"Shall we leave right now?"

Philip studied her wistful face. "I think we might stay a little longer—but at the other end of the fair as far from that woman as possible."

"I have a hunch that she will avoid us as well." Lady Harriet glanced back through the throng of people. Apparently she didn't see her. "She probably thinks we are daft, and likely imagines we might demand the caddy be returned. A woman like her tends to be suspicious. Life is generally not very kind to her sort, and when it is, she does not quite trust it."

Philip couldn't see the woman either when he searched the clusters of merrymakers. "I did not like doing that, but at last we have the ivory dragon back."

"And as I said, should the baron see her . . . I'd not like to see the pot boy orphaned."

Philip tucked Lady Harriet's arm in his, and together they slowly made their way to the curricle, which was being watched by a village lad. Harriet paused at several booths along the way to buy some little thing, particularly if it had been made locally. The women in the stalls took pride in their handicrafts, and all beamed smiles whenever Lady Harriet made a purchase, taking her words of praise to heart.

"Look, there is a gingerbread stand. I think it would do your ankle good to rest while you nibble a piece." Philip urged her to sit on another little bench while he made the purchase. The gingerbread was still warm and fragrant.

"Do you think we are safe?" Lady Harriet murmured around her gingerbread.

"I have tried to avoid anyone who looked remotely like a pickpocket." He patted his pocket, then relaxed. "It is still where I put it."

"I will feel better when we return to the house. The

box is still in my room. I see Aunt Cornelia with Major Birch on the far side across from the Punch and Judy show. I hope they are not arguing. It certainly looks like it."

"Perhaps they merely experienced a polite difference of opinion."

"She has never said what caused the problem in the first place. I learned they argued, but over what, I am not certain. Surely it could not have been his limp?"

"I believe him to be a good man."

"Even if he looks rather fierce? I suppose one's looks do not determine what is inside." Lady Harriet rose to brush off the crumbs from her dress, then took a step toward the curricle not too far from where they had sat. "I suppose we had best leave."

"With regrets, I feel certain."

As they spoke, some lads came dashing along, pushing people out of their way. Philip caught Harriet, as she was about to tumble to one side. He set her on her feet, then looked up to see his mother bearing down upon them.

"Philip, dear boy. Did you see me open the fair this morning?" Lady Lanstone, wearing a relatively subdued dress, bustled up to confront her son.

"I fear I was delayed. I stopped to pick up Lady Harriet and had to check on her injury."

Harriet obliged by holding forth her neatly bound ankle. "My dear aunt took care of it for me. I am most fortunate to have so loving a relative."

"And I am as well." The marchioness smiled and gave her son a squeeze on his arm. "Philip is the only one who looks after me." She turned to Harriet. "I see you bought one of those tea caddies. They make such nice presents, I believe I will purchase one as well. Philip, do you have a few shillings I might have?"

"Of course." He dug into his pocket, found some change, then watched as she headed in the direction of the stall where the tea caddies were.

Time to depart—it was important they get away before anything happened to the ivory dragon.

Once on the road, they both breathed a sigh of relief.

"Well, at last I can be easy again. This was a most rewarding excursion." Harriet lightly touched Philip's arm. "Might I look at the ivory dragon again, just to reassure myself that we truly have it safe?"

Philip chuckled. "Naturally," he replied, slipping his hand into his pocket. He frowned and checked his other pocket, then halted the horse and began frantically patting the front of his coat.

"What's wrong?"

"It's gone! I know I put it in my pocket!"

Harriet groaned. "Do you suppose those lads who came dashing through the throng of people took it? One of them bumped against you."

"I do not know. I don't see how a lad could get into my pocket without my being aware of it."

"Be that as it may, someone did. Now what shall we do?"

For once, Philip had no answer.

# Chapter Eleven

"I simply cannot believe we were so close to success and now have nothing. You have not the slightest idea as to who took the pin from your pocket?" Harriet placed her hands on Lord Stanhope's shoulders as he lifted her down from the curricle. "That is most difficult to accept." She quite ignored the tingle that swept through her at his touch. That *had* to be disregarded were she to retain some semblance of dignity.

"Had I the slightest notion some thief was dipping into my pocket, I would have stopped him! You cannot think I want the pin to remain missing!" He frowned at her, then began pacing back and forth on the neatly graveled sweep.

"At this moment I scarce know what to think—about you or the pin. Had I not seen it with my own eyes, I would believe you fabricated the entire incident." She shook her head in dismay. "Might I point out that had you not nudged my elbow, the pin would never have popped out of the window in the first place?"

"That was an accident, and well you know it." He paused in his pacing. "May I point out that had you not taken the pin from the barn, I would not be traipsing over the countryside hunting for it. I could have returned it to the baron long ago." He was all hauteur and offended dignity worthy of an earl.

"If your mother had not taken it in the first place, we would have never had the slightest problem. And that, my lord, is where the most severe difficulty is. If your mother took something once, what is to prevent her from taking something again? Or has she done this before?"

Harriet crossed her arms before her, tapping her foot on the crushed rock of the drive. This nodcock must realize that his mother could fall into serious trouble if someone did not take her in hand and persuade her to cease her pilfering before it was too late.

"You needn't look at me as though *I* am the criminal. To my knowledge she has taken nothing else. As worried as she is at the moment, I very much doubt she will take anything else again." Harriet noted the irony in his voice. He rubbed his chin and shook his head as he stared out over the lawn before turning to Harriet once again, his expression bleak.

"Has she confided in you? Has she admitted something is missing?" Harriet couldn't imagine that the marchioness would do anything of the sort.

"No. I can tell from the way she behaves and what little she has said. She knows." He nudged a pebble with his shoe, and when he raised his head to look at Harriet, his gaze was steely.

"She didn't seem very upset when we saw her at the fair earlier, my lord. In fact, when we parted she was downright jolly." Harriet felt compelled to point out his mother's excellent spirits. It was inconsistent with a guilty conscience, if she had one.

"True. Perhaps she looked forward to buying the tea caddy. Most women enjoy shopping." He crossed his arms again, taking a stance not far from where she watched him. He was too close, but she'd not retreat. That would be a sign of weakness!

"Well, as to that, I admit I do as well. But jolly? She was positively vivacious."

"I cannot say. But may I suggest that if you have a notion how to deal with her, it is more than I have."

"I daresay I could come up with something better than you have done so far, which is merely to follow your mother trying to undo what she has done.

His eyes narrowed to slits. "Very well, I challenge you to produce a better solution." He shot Harriet a provocative look, one that defied her to accept.

"I accept your challenge."

For a moment they stared at each other, the air charged with tension. Harriet was the first to look away from the potent depths of the earl's eyes.

"When do I begin?" Harriet observed that her voice sounded amazingly normal, although her insides were churning.

"You seem the expert. Tell me!" He unfolded his arms and looked at Harriet as though she were an enemy. Perhaps she was, in a way. Perhaps he was justified in his annoyance, but her pride was involved as well. She refused to be daunted by the earl's fierce scowl.

"You said your mother once painted," Harriet coolly reminded him. She unfolded her arms, giving him an equally chilly look.

"I mentioned it. I intended to show her paintings to you at some time or other." His eyes narrowed again, in speculation, most likely.

"Why do I not invite her on a painting expedition with me? If we can direct her interests to something that will captivate her, keep her occupied, it might well succeed to keep her from her other pursuits."

"That sounds sensible. Pick a time and a day, and I will smooth the way for you." He wore the satisfied expression of a man who has achieved precisely what he wanted.

Harriet knew a twinge of doubt. "And you are so certain she will go with me?" Harriet gave him a dubious look. "Would your mother actually go painting with someone she scarce knows?"

He smiled, and it was of the sort she didn't trust in the least. "It is up to you to convince her—unless you prefer me to do it for you? If you feel inadequate to the task . . ."

"I will be at Lanstone Hall tomorrow at eleven of the clock, if that pleases you."

He bowed, "Indeed, it does."

Harriet nodded with what she hoped was regal grace. "Morning is best for the sun, as you well know. I will assume the sun will be shining, at least in part. If it rains, the day is canceled." Had she just hoisted herself on her own petard?

"But naturally." He almost smiled.

Harriet did not return that look. It had a devious quality to it that she was certain she couldn't match if she tried. Besides, he was standing far too close, and she felt intimidated, even if he possibly did not intend that effect. Another step or two and they would be touching.

"I would go along with you, but I wish to be at the house in the event the architect desires to consult with me." He affected the manner of one whose time is scarcely his own, and that might be the case, but she doubted it. She suspected he could leave if he truly wished to do so.

"What is he working on at present?" Harriet found her curiosity piqued. Surely the architect would rather his patron be off and about instead of lingering over his shoulder as it were.

"The Venetian window. Today the old windows are to come out, and they will commence framing in the new."

"Let us hope that the rain holds off, in that event." Harriet instinctively looked at the sky, assessing the chance of rain in the near future.

"They have tarpolins."

Suddenly recalling the manners that had been drilled into her at an early age, Harriet said with chilly politeness, "Would you care for tea, my lord?"

"Thank you, but I think not."

He bowed, not attempting to take one of her hands. Of course they were tucked close to her body, but he might have tried, her thoughts being quite perverse.

Once seated in the curricle, he held the reins lightly in his hand and looked down to where she waited. His farewell was civil in the extreme. As was hers.

She watched him flick the reins, then head off along the avenue without looking back at her. Annoyed beyond reason, Harriet stomped into the house, shutting the door behind her with unnecessary firmness. Her ankle protested at the strain, and she limped toward the stairs.

Mrs. Twig peered around the green-baize door, her

brows knit in bewilderment. "Was the fair a disappointment, my lady?"

"Yes and no. All I expected to see was there, and a few surprises as well."

Mrs. Twig's confusion increased at Harriet's cryptic reply. "I see," she answered in a vague little voice.

"Ask my aunt. She doubtless had a far better time." With that, Harriet tottered up to her room. She tugged her bonnet from her head to toss it on the bed, wishing she might toss it at his lordship's head, instead.

Not one to cavil at what had to be done, she gathered her painting equipment, made sure the blocks of watercolors were neatly stowed in the wooden box, together with her brushes, and found her pad of watercolor paper. She located an empty jar on the bottom of her wardrobe and added that to her collection. She could fill it with water from any stream.

Oh, she would be at that house precisely at the dot of eleven. And this time she would *not* wear her worst frock. Lady Lanstone deserved a neatly dressed companion, she argued with herself. Of course she would not dream of dressing to please his nasty lordship. He probably wouldn't even show up! He'd probably have Peel show her the paintings in the sitting room. The butler was certain to know where they were to be seen.

As to how she was to persuade Lady Lanstone to go with her, well, she would hope to view those paintings Lord Stanhope had mentioned, then go from there.

His audacity still stung. He had tricked her into doing precisely as he wished. At least it had seemed that way. Oh, he was a clever man, he was. He disturbed her. What else he stirred within her was best left unexamined—she had a notion it would be too disquieting by far.

The following morning on the dot of eleven, it being a sunny day with but a very few clouds in the distance, she presented herself at Lanstone Hall. She wore a pretty gown of sky-blue lutestring trimmed with a frill at the hem and petal sleeves. That it was her most becoming gown, one that showed her figure to best advantage, she quite ignored.

Her paints and paper she left in her gig. They could just as well ride to whatever scene they chose to paint.

Peel ushered her inside, looking behind her to see if a maid had accompanied her.

"I will not need a maid today, Peel. Is Lord Stanhope around by any chance?" Harriet just knew he would be nowhere to be found. She was willing to bet on it.

"One moment, ma'am. I believe he is in the library. He wished to view the framing for the new window her ladyship wants installed."

Leaving Harriet to her disbelieving self, he made a stately progress to the library door, something Harriet had to admire. Only frightfully superior butlers could manage a walk like that.

Within moments, he returned. Alone. Harriet smiled. It was just as she calculated. His handsome lordship couldn't be bothered. She prepared to be escorted by Peel to see the paintings.

"His lordship wished to know if you would like to view what has been done."

Surprised, Harriet nodded, then followed the butler to the library, where she discovered a hive of activity. The far end of the room had been nearly removed—at least to a generous height. Two rectangular frames were in place and the workmen were in process of creating a lovely curve for the top of the center section. "The Venetian window," she said at last.

Rather than reply, the earl pulled up a piece of paper from under the Holland cloth that protected the desk. "Here is Heron's suggestion for drapery. What do you think of it?" He offered it to Harriet.

Gingerly accepting the paper, she studied it with care. Faint tones of green striped the panels that hung to either side, then the fabric was draped in swags above the window. Two layers, she noted, swag upon swag. Deep green was designated for the long fringe, a most impressive effect.

"Your mother ought to be in alt with this when it is completed. The result will be imposing. Do you intend to have the chair seats covered with a matching fabric?"

"For the time being. I hope my wife will create some tapestry covers at a future date."

She felt as though a strong, cold draft had hit her. For a moment she felt unable to speak. "I was unaware you had plans to marry soon. Is it anyone I know?" she stammered at last, struggling to regain her composure.

"Yes, it is."

"I see." Harriet swallowed with great care. "Well, I am happy for you." There had been a slight catch in her voice, and she prayed he failed to notice.

"Thank you. However, I have had little time for courting what with all that is going on here, not to mention that dratted pin."

"I will do my best to aid you." Her mind whirled with speculation. Quite unable to think whom the earl intended as his bride, she managed to offer a bright, utterly false smile. "Am I to view the watercolors now, sir?"

He nodded, smiling at something that had amused him as he escorted her from the library and up the stairs to a large room full of sunshine. The walls were painted a creamy yellow, and Harriet received the impression of a light summer day. There were comfortable-looking chairs here and there with a table by the window. She paid little attention to furniture, however. Seated by the window was Lady Lanstone. On a table not far away sat the promised accoutrements for a painting expedition evidently placed there by the earl, for his mother ignored them.

"Lady Harriet, how nice to see you on this lovely day. My son tells me you like to paint. It has been a long time since I painted."

"He mentioned I might see your watercolors." Harriet caught sight of several exquisite paintings beautifully framed and hung in small groups. She couldn't resist stepping closer to view them. The technique was amazing, with a quality that would not have shamed a Society of Watercolorists exposition.

Harriet spun around to offer a genuine smile. "I think it a shame you ceased your painting. What a marvelous sense of perspective you have, my lady. And your use of color cannot be faulted. These are beautiful. Oh, how I wish you could come painting with me."

There was no mistaking the look of longing in her ladyship's eyes. "I fear I would be extremely rusty." Lady Lanstone rose to join them. She wore a gown of yellow and cerise printed with chartreuse.

Harriet couldn't help but wonder where on earth she found such fabric. For certain, Harriet had not seen anything like it in London while she was in Town. "Indeed, Mother possessed an unerring instinct for color."

Harriet darted a look at the earl, wondering if she imagined the irony in his voice.

"Well, I would be pleased for your company today. It is much nicer if one is not alone."

"Well, I suppose I might try," the marchioness said vaguely, but with a slight hint of excitement in her voice.

Harriet turned to look at him. "These are truly wonderful. I am so glad you had these framed, for they deserve it. You must be pleased, ma'am." When Harriet looked about, the lady had vanished.

"I suspect she went to don a bonnet and pick up her large sunshade."

"Does she do this sort of thing often—disappear without saying a word?" Then at his silence, she added, "I only inquire because I would have to frequently check on her while we are out if that is the case."

"I daresay she will let you know if she wants to wander about. You know how it is with finding a suitable site for painting."

"I will make sure we are not too close to a stream."

He smiled at that, then went to the table to pick up the painting supplies before ushering Harriet to the hall. Here they encountered her ladyship.

Harriet tried not to stare at the creation worn on her head. It consisted of yellow and cerise roses on chartreuse straw with wide ivory bows tucked in between the roses. Obviously, it was intended as an ensemble, and as such Harriet had to admit it was a success, of a sort. That is, provided one did not mind the color combination.

"Shall we go?"

"I have my aunt's gig with me if that is agreeable with you."

"When Philip told me you were coming over with your painting gear and wished to go painting on the estate, I felt the first stirring of a desire to paint that I've had in years. You are certain I will be no trouble?"

"There is nothing I would like better, ma'am. Shall we go now?"

"I would like that," Lady Lanstone crowed.

Her delight seemed genuine, and Harriet was thankful she did not have a recalcitrant painter on her hands. She recalled girls she had gone to school with who hated painting and did all manner of tricks to be excused. But then, considering the quality of the work her ladyship had done in the past, it was unlikely she would be too reluctant.

Lord Stanhope stowed the painting equipment in the little compartment Harriet had persuaded the carpenter to create for the gig. It sat where a groom might have, had there been one. Underneath it was a neat basket with a light lunch in the event they became hungry. Harriet had tried to think of everything to keep Lady Lanstone at her watercolors.

"Have a good day of painting, ladies. A pity I am required here. I should like to have gone with you."

Harriet shot him a disbelieving look, then flicked the reins and they were off. She didn't look behind.

Philip chatted with Heron, wondering all the while how the painters were doing. The weather held, the breeze was most acceptable, and unless they ended at daggers drawn, they should do well.

He watched the carpenters put the last of the framework in place while the glazier carefully moved the first section of eight-paned glass into place in one of the rectangular window openings. Ah, it was going to look splendid. And, as his mother insisted, it would bring far more light into the room.

Eventually he left the library to go outside. He'd check on those shelves for Aunt Victoria. He also needed to come up with a means of ridding the house of their presence.

Even his long-suffering mother had indicated she was becoming tired of her sister. They had quarreled over a rather tawdry cupid Aunt bought. To make matters worse, Aunt thought the hideous thing ought to be displayed in the entry. Philip had barely refrained from applause when Mother had told Aunt Victoria that either the cupid retired to her room, or she could take her leave.

Philip had hoped Aunt would be angry enough to say she would depart—taking her miserable husband with her. She had not. And now it was up to Philip to nudge them from the house. Unpleasant though it might be, he rather relished his duty.

Leaving the house behind him, he crossed the stable yard to where the carpenter spent his days.

"Parrot, there you are." He looked about the carpenter's workshop, spotting the shelves leaning against a wall. They were finished in a manner worthy of Sheraton, at the very least.

"Fine, fine," Philip murmured as he studied the work. "I thank you, Parrot. My aunt is unworthy of such skill. I know she will not appreciate them as they ought to be. Please know that I do. And with God's blessing, perhaps we will be rid of her before long. Who knows?"

Parrot said nothing, but nodded as though in full agreement.

After giving direction as to the disposition of the shelves, Philip went back to the stable yard, his boots clicking as he made his way across the cobbles to the stable itself. Once inside he requested his horse be saddled.

He waited out in the sun. From here he could see the new addition taking shape at the end of the library. All the walls and the roof would be in place and somewhat finished before the wall between the new and old would have the arch cut through. It would be quite fine, he decided. And when his father had gone aloft, Philip would enjoy that room very much. His earlier vision of a cozy family ensconced before a fireplace returned, and he smiled.

"Here you are, milord," his groom said as he brought out Vulcan.

Offering thanks, Philip easily swung himself into the saddle, then took off in the direction where he thought he might find Harriet and his mother. He did not need to go, he knew. Harriet has shown herself to be quite capable. But it didn't hurt to see how they did.

He cantered along until he spotted the gig under a spreading oak. The horse looked contented with the abundance of lush grass for his cropping. It looked up to survey Philip's approach.

In the near distance Philip could see two feminine figures seated so as to view a stream with a slight waterfall, just enough to make a pretty splash. At the memory of Harriet utterly drenched and furious, a grin spread across his face. He would have to tease her about the stream. There was no way he would avoid it. It was far too delightful a memory.

After he tied Vulcan to another tree not far away, Philip leisurely approached the painters, hoping to steal a sight of their work. "Good afternoon, ladies. I thought I would see how you fare. No one fell in the stream, I see."

Harriet looked daggers at him, but said nothing, no doubt because his mother looked at him, then her, with such an innocently puzzled face.

"Why should anyone fall into the stream, Philip? 'Tis a good thing it is shallow. But there are a small number of trout to be seen, nevertheless. Do you plan on a bit of fishing? Cook would like a few trout, I am sure."

"Another day, perhaps." He strolled to where Harriet sat with her watercolor block propped on her lap, her paints handy, and a brush poised in midair.

She did not disappoint him. The scene on her paper brought to life a slightly romanticized version of the stream, the waterfall, and a totally imaginary willow and a craggy mountain she had added for character. "Nice."

His mother on the other hand, had painted the scene as it was, precise and delicately beautiful.

"It is amazing how two artists can come up with such totally different results."

Harriet gave him a suspicious look. "Is that so? I trust you are not disappointed. Your mother has enjoyed herself enormously."

"Then, how could I be otherwise than pleased?"

"Somehow I think you could manage it if you tried," Harriet muttered.

"You are most amusing, even when you do not try," he murmured back.

"Well!" She finished the last of her strokes, then rinsed the brush in the jar of water.

"I'd not thought to find you by water. Have you learned anything of interest?" He crouched by her side as though to study her painting.

Her expression was guarded. "Your mother said she had always wanted to paint this view. Since the sun is shining and you were not present, I thought it safe enough. If we go again, I will suggest she try something else."

"Ouch. I don't think I deserved that cut."

"Perhaps not," she acceded, "but nonetheless, there you are. Things tend to happen when you are around."

"What a nice thing to say. I am gratified you do not think me dull."

"As if anyone could!" Apparently she'd not intended to utter those words, for she bit her lip in obvious vexation and glanced at him as though to see how he reacted to her words. He merely looked back at her, not even tempting to smile. Not that she didn't tempt him otherwise, sitting on the grassy slope with her sky-blue gown clinging nicely to her figure. Her arms had acquired a faint tan below the petal-shaped sleeves, and on her nose a few freckles were lightly sprinkled. He was far too kind to mention them.

"Have you given any thought to the problem?"

"The missing ivory dragon, I assume. Or do you have another problem on your mind?" She turned away to check her watercolor to see if it had completely dried.

"You would be surprised at what is on my mind."

"Perhaps, perhaps not."

There was a tense silence for a time, then he ventured to say, "I wish to see the last of the Plums."

"Well, if they have overstayed their welcome, why do you not simply tell them you need their rooms?"

"Too simple, and besides, they would never accept that, since the house is so large and there are other rooms."

She shook her head. "I am convinced that with people like that you must be blunt and direct. Civility can go just so far, you know."

"Philip, it is extremely rude to leave me out of the conversation." His mother glared at him as only she could.

"We were discussing your sister and her husband. I believe they have been with us for quite some time?"

"Indeed so. I wish they would find a place in which to live. Mr. Plum lost everything on a bad investment, and they are without a roof over their heads."

"Hmm." Philip stared at his mother. How could he have forgotten that precious bit of information? "No home at all?"

"Do something, Philip. If I see another cupid, I declare I shall be ill."

"I had no idea you felt like this about them." He thought for a bit, then continued, "It is possible I could have them remove to one of our lesser estates. Isn't there one in Derbyshire that came down through Father's family?"

"Quite so! Now, why did I not think of it?"

"Perhaps that is our solution, then. I will check with Father. Unless he knows of a reason why they couldn't be sent there, off they will go."

"It is so lovely to have such a masterful son. Do you not agree, Lady Harriet?"

Harriet looked as though she did anything but agree. As matter of fact, she appeared as though she had bitten a sour pickle. "Of course, ma'am. A dutiful son is of all things to be desired."

"Ah, but I said masterful, and that is even better!"

Her ladyship rose, gestured to Philip to collect her painting things, then wandered off to look at some
wildflowers.

"If she thinks you are masterful, do not expect me to
agree. I call you demanding and pushing. Not to mention
the most aggravating man alive." Harriet also rose to
confront him. She held her watercolor pad in her hands,
the wooden box containing her blocks of paint and the
brushes still sitting at her feet.

"True, I am probably all of those." He glanced to
where his mother inspected a flower, then turned his attention to Harriet. He hastily stole a kiss to prove his
words.

"You see what I mean?" Harriet demanded. "Whatever would your mother think if she saw you?"

"That I am a clever chap." He suspected she was more
affected than she revealed. Upon close inspection, her
cheeks had turned faintly rosy, and he'd sworn she trembled ever so little.

"If you think that I am going to rise to that bait, think
again." She sniffed, bent over to gather up the rest of
her belongings, then marched away to where the gig
awaited her.

Philip followed, allowing a smile to emerge from where
it had been hiding.

"And do not forget to inform the Plums they are to
remove themselves to Devonshire. It is what your mother
desires above all things, I think."

"I doubt that she desires it above *all* things. But I will
do as you suggest." He knew she wondered about the *all*.

"I will not ask."

"I shall tell you anyway. She wants me married."

The silence following his remark was broken only by
his mother when she came up to show them a pretty
flower and to ask Harriet if she knew its identity.

She identified it, then left for Lanstone Hall within
minutes once his mother was settled.

Oh, things indeed looked promising, Philip mused. If
only they could find that dratted pin, life would be perfect. He would be free to seek the woman he loved.

# *Chapter Twelve*

Again, Harriet stormed into the house, indignant at her confrontation with Lord Stanhope. That dratted man had kissed her, sending that tingling sensation from her top to her toes. Then when they reached his house, he had the audacity to propose she go painting with his mother again the next nice day. Not that she disliked his mother. *He* was the outside of enough!

However, she liked her painting. It was one of the better landscapes she had done, perhaps influenced by the exquisite work that flowed from Lady Lanstone's brush.

Then she wondered if Nympha Herbert painted and couldn't recall any mention of such talent by that young lady. Upon that cheering thought, she entered the drawing room to see how her aunt had fared this morning. Major Birch was supposed to come this morning, and Harriet wondered what had occurred.

Her aunt smiled with the brilliance of a lamp on a cloudy day. Harriet guessed that whatever occurred, it definitely had been good.

"I cannot believe all that has happened, simply because of a stupid misunderstanding." Aunt Cornelia sat at her ease near the drawing room fireplace. She worked a highly masculine monogram on a square of cambric.

"A misunderstanding all this time? I mean," Harriet said, feeling exceedingly curious, "did neither of you ever attempt to set matters straight?"

"It was Major Birch's stupid pride and my firm belief that he had rejected me. When I saw him again at the dinner held at the Lanstone house, I wanted to pierce that armor he wears about him. He looked so aloof, so smug, so utterly impossible!"

"How did you resolve matters?" Harriet placed her watercolor pad on a table, then took off her bonnet, examining the ribands with an absent gaze. It truly didn't matter *how* her aunt and the major had resolved things. The resolution meant that before too long Harriet would be on the move again. Well, perhaps that was for the better. She could leave Lord Stanhope behind, along with Nympha Herbert, Lord Nicholas, and Lady Lanstone. Perhaps she might persuade Aunt Cornelia to keep her informed of the news of the area. However, if Lord Stanhope married before long, Harriet wanted to be gone.

"Well, I accused him of being too proud. Then he accused me of being stubborn. We argued, and it was amazing how that cleared the air. He believed I could not accept him because of his limp—as though that made the slightest bit of difference to me. And I admitted that it was very stubborn of me not to inquire regarding his refusal to visit. And now he has proposed, and I have accepted."

"I am so very pleased, dear aunt." Inwardly Harriet thought it a great shame that the misunderstanding had stood in the way of their marriage all this time.

"That is why he bought the house in this area, you know. He sought to reestablish a friendship at the very least. Dear man, he did not think he could win my hand after so long a time. He claims he was astonished that I had never wed. As though I could after loving him for so very long."

"You are not so old now. You should have many years of happiness together." Harriet's pleasure for her aunt was genuine, only slightly dimmed by the knowledge that she must part from her.

"You will help me with my wedding clothes? You must have helped your sister, possibly your mother as well. I feel certain you will know just the things for me to order."

"But of course, dearest of aunts." Harriet played with

the ribands on her bonnet while she considered her own future. Was she to be a consultant to brides and never one herself? As to that, she could scarcely ask a gentleman to marry her! And while she might have hopes, there was not a great deal she might do to promote them.

"Now, you must tell me the results of your painting excursion. Did Lady Lanstone agree to paint? And if so, what?"

"Yes! She went with me to a pretty site on the estate where we both painted a scene. She truly is most gifted. And I enjoyed talking with her. Whatever else she might be, she is not stupid."

"I had hoped you would find one of those wild gladiolas for me. Perhaps you could persuade her ladyship to go with you again? It is far more agreeable to have someone along with whom you can converse pleasantly."

"Well, if I paint a flower in detail, she may wonder what she can paint, unless we find another acceptable landscape view. I did agree to go with her again after Lord Stanhope more or less put me in the position of having to consent. Not that I mind." Harriet set her bonnet—the ribands now mangled beyond redemption—on the table with her watercolor pad.

"Let me see what you did?"

Harriet brought the pad to her aunt, who set aside the handkerchief that had a very nice letter *B* begun on it. "How nice! It is very lovely, and not so far from where my new home will be once I marry the major. I should very much like to have it. Please?"

"By all means. Perhaps we could persuade the carpenter at Lanstone to frame it for you?" Harriet wandered to the window, supposedly to look at the scenery.

"It is possible you will be there tomorrow. Why do you not take it with you? As attentive as he has been, I make no doubt that his lordship will be happy to oblige you." Her aunt's smile could only be called devious.

"He has been attentive only because of that pin. We are no closer to finding that miserable ivory dragon. How I wish I had never seen it!"

"Pity. It is a lovely little thing. I wonder what the pickpocket did with it? Would he take it to a pawnshop? And where would the nearest one of those be?"

Harriet whirled about, the scene outside forgotten in her sudden excitement. "A pawnshop? I'd not thought of that. I wonder if the earl has? I'll grant you he has a lot on his mind. The men are working on the dining room Venetian window and the extension of the library. His brother Nicholas demands his attention far too often. Oh—he did decide what to do about the Plums. There is a small estate in Derbyshire that wants caretaking." She gave her aunt a significant look that sent Cornelia into chuckles.

"His mother agreed that the small place in Derbyshire would be perfect. It seems her ladyship was utterly wearied with cupids."

Cornelia burst into laughter, wiped her eyes, then patted the sofa. "I must hear every detail."

"Oh, yes, you will love the part about the hideous cupid. Shall I ring for tea? The nuncheon I brought along was rather small and long ago."

"You poor dear. Inform Mrs. Twig that we shall wish a generous tea."

"Well, do you have any other news that I have missed?"

"Major Birch suggested we host a small party at his home for the neighbors. We could wait until after we are wed, but this will announce the engagement and coming marriage. Besides, we plan a honeymoon to a warmer climate so his leg might not be bothered by the winter weather."

"That would be nice." Harriet wondered if she might remain here while they were gone, to act as a caretaker, much as the Plums would in Devonshire.

"I thought about having the party here, but it would be agreeable to have it in my future home. Did I tell you that the earl wishes to buy this house? I do not know what he plans to do with it, but I shall sell it, for it will be a substantial dowry to take with me."

Harriet absorbed this news with a sinking heart. There

was no reason at all for the earl to buy this property unless he intended to live here with his bride until such time that his father died. She voiced her speculation to her aunt, who seemed to agree.

"That would make sense in a way. He must become tired of dealing with all the family problems. While he would be close enough to handle estate affairs, they wouldn't be his twenty-four hours a day. On the other hand, love, he may just want to add to the family holdings. I believe that long ago this property belonged to the Lanstone family. Just how it went out of their hands, I have no idea."

Harriet rose and went to the hall to tell Mrs. Twig just how lavish the tea tray ought to be. Within a short time the tray was brought with not just tea, but dainty sandwiches, scones, ginger biscuits, and a scrumptious chocolate cake.

"Heavens, I know you are hungry, but this is a great deal of food!" Cornelia looked at Harriet with amusement as she began to arrange tiny sandwiches on two plates.

The door knocker sounded loudly in the front hall, penetrating even the drawing room. Harriet exchanged a questioning look with her aunt.

Mrs. Twig soon satisfied their curiosity. "Lord Stanhope and Major Birch, ma'am."

"Ah, I see we have arrived at the proper moment. Nothing better than a good tea, I always say," the major declared as he limped across the room to the side of his betrothed.

Harriet rose to greet the men, wondering what in the world had brought the earl here now. She had seen him not an hour ago.

Nothing was said to that point for the moment, tea consuming their attention. The sandwiches all disappeared in a trice, the scones and ginger biscuits were sampled, and the chocolate cake was praised with each person having a generous slice.

Once the tea was done, the major begged his betrothed to walk in the garden with him. She didn't even appear to give a thought to Harriet's being alone with the earl. She simply rose, offered him her hand, and off they went, heads together in conversation.

"I am surprised to see you again, that is, so soon. It is not long that I was at Lanstone Hall. Not that I object to your call. I am merely surprised," Harriet explained, feeling more than a little gauche. She rose to lead him from the house.

"I wanted you to learn what I have done. I informed dear Aunt and Uncle Plum that they are the happy couple to occupy the estate in Derbyshire in the foreseeable future. They were not pleased—to say the least. I fancy that if they are sufficiently unhappy—after all, there are no gaming houses for uncle there—my uncle and aunt can find some other spot to occupy. The only difficulty I can see with that idea is that he has spent all my aunt's dowry, and there is not much of his own inheritance remaining."

"He has no income at all?" Their steps were contrapuntal—hers soft, his hard.

"Well, as to that, his notion of investing money is to play the lottery. He likes to gamble far too much. Somehow Derbyshire does not seem like a hotbed of gaming."

"I would hazard that he could find a game of cards just about anywhere in England if he is determined," Harriet pointed out in a reasonable way as they paused on the terrace.

"But he will not have me to pull him out anymore, and he now knows it. I refuse to support him for the rest of his life." Lord Stanhope maneuvered Harriet from the terrace out to the grassy slope that led to a small pond.

"That is good. Who knows, they may actually enjoy life there?"

"It is possible, but I doubt it." They strolled on, each absorbed in their thoughts for a few minutes.

"My aunt was wondering if you have thought about looking into the pawnshops, perhaps with the chance of finding the ivory dragon." Harriet paused, staring off at the pond, where a pretty little bird perched on a rock.

He stopped, also looking off at the pond. "I hate to admit it, but I had not given that possibility a thought. I will explore that direction just as soon as I can."

"My aunt and Major Birch are planning a party for a few neighbors to celebrate their engagement and coming marriage." She began to head to the pond again, not knowing what else to do.

"Will they marry soon?" the earl inquired. "Of course, I imagine they find little reason to wait."

"True." Harriet smiled, even though she had mixed feelings about the marriage. Happy on one part, sad on the other.

"What will you do?"

He was certainly casual in his query, she thought. It seemed to her that he was merely being polite. "I thought to remain here until they return. From what Aunt said, they will be away for at least six months. Surely they would not wish the house to be empty all that time?"

"But she promised to sell it to me. I should like to take possession of it as soon as she is wed."

"Oh. I had forgotten you plan to marry. Perhaps you wish to take your bride here?" Harriet swallowed the lump in her throat with difficulty. But she smiled gallantly at her escort, as though he wasn't smashing all her dreams.

"I had thought it a pleasant notion. I feel that it is difficult for a young bride to settle in with her husband's parents. In my observation, a newly married couple is better off alone. What do you think?"

"It is a lovely house, and I should think any bride would be happy to live here. Not that your parents aren't dear. On the other hand, as vast as your house is, I should think you might occupy one wing while your parents are in the other and meet only when you wish."

She knew she sounded diffident, but then, she was. What was it to her what he did with the house once he bought it? She guessed that Nympha Herbert would be thrilled to live in either house. And it had to be Nympha, for what other woman had he paid the slightest attention to these past weeks? The time she had spent with him was to search for the ivory dragon. Somehow he did not seem like the sort of man who had a betrothed off in some distant part of the country to be whisked forward in time for a wedding!

"I wonder if your mother would like to paint birds?" Harriet suddenly exclaimed. "That is a dear little feathered creature on that rock. I would wager she could paint it quite beautifully—she is excellent at details. And I wonder that your father might not like it very well."

He halted, staring at her in amazement.

"Well, it was just a thought," Harriet said dryly.

"A very brilliant one, nonetheless."

"You do not know if she can even draw a bird, let alone paint one. And remember, we do not know if she wants to go painting again!"

"She does, she said so after we entered the house. She couldn't recall when she had enjoyed herself so much."

"Well, I am glad if our excursion gave her pleasure."

He reached out to take her hand, which caused her to chance a look at him.

"I need to apologize. Earlier I ought not to have kissed you as I did. It was badly done of me, for it must have made you think I toyed with your affections, and that is the last thing I would wish you to believe."

Before Harriet could think of a reply, a horrible squawking issued from the pond. A swan, apparently feeling they had come far too close to her cygnets, came flying at them in full wing.

"Oh, good grief!" Harriet cried.

The earl didn't waste any time commenting on the swan. He scooped Harriet into his arms and made a strategic dash for the upper lawn. Here he set her down just as Cornelia and the major came around the corner.

"I see you have made acquaintance with the swan. The pen has a nasty temper for all her beauty." Cornelia had her arm tucked comfortably close to the major's side, and she had the pleased look of a woman who has been well kissed. Perhaps she had convinced the major that having a limp did not interfere with important things like kisses.

"Thank goodness not all beauties have a temper. We poor men would all be unmarried." The major gave his beloved a nudge.

"Women are not the only ones who have tempers, my dear," Cornelia said with a gentle laugh.

Recalling what her aunt had said about the past, Harriet could only marvel that all could be forgiven so easily.

"Lord Stanhope came to tell me that the Plums will shortly be removing to Derbyshire."

"What a pity, they will miss our party. Unless, my dear, we could put it forward?" Cornelia gave her betrothed an earnest smile.

"If you think we can manage it, by all means." To the earl, he added, "I have sent for a special license, so we need not wait the customary three weeks for banns. I have waited quite long enough for Miss Quince to be my bride."

"Then, let the party be soon."

They fell to discussing the time and date, allowing Harriet to fall into a speculation as to where she might go when it came time. She would have to disturb her mother's contentment, that was all there was to it.

"You look as though you have reached a conclusion of some sort."

The earl studied her with too astute a gaze. Harriet shifted uneasily. But then, it mattered little what he thought of her plans. They did not concern him. "I will leave for my mother's new home shortly after Aunt Cornelia's wedding. I have no other choice."

"Don't be in a hurry to make plans. I hope you will not go until we have found the ivory dragon. I need a partner in my hunt." His gaze was downright bewitching.

"Well, if you do locate it at some pawnshop, you will not need me at all." She smiled brightly, hoping she looked pleased. Her reply did not seem to perturb him in the least. He merely nodded.

"I shall count on your help."

The four strolled toward the garden, Cornelia pointing out the various plants and flowers, of which she was very proud. "I warn you, now, I shall take my gardener with me. He would be impossible to replace."

"Why not?" Lord Stanhope replied. "May I suggest you also have him dig up any plants you particularly favor?"

The three of them discussed what was to be done. Harriet walked in silence, having no interest in the matter at all. The sooner the men left, the sooner she might go to her room and organize her things for packing. It was amazing how much one could accumulate in a short time.

The earl departed first, shortly followed by the major, who promised to return for dinner that evening.

After they had gone, Harriet teased, "The major is living in your pocket, dear aunt."

"Yes, I know. Is it not delightful?" Her expression could only be described as self-satisfied.

Harriet thought back to her sister and Marcus. They had behaved the same way. Oh, deliver her from engaged couples!

At Lanstone Hall a storm was brewing. Mrs. Plum was furious at the thought of removing to Derbyshire.

"How could you do such a thing? Derbyshire! We might as well be going to the ends of the world. Say something to your son, Beatrice." Victoria Plum paced back and forth in the yellow sitting room.

"I will not, sister, dear. We have housed you for at least two years. That is rather long for a visit, which is what you indicated when you first wrote. I think that both my husband and sons have been incredibly patient. I did not care so much until you began bringing those dreadful cupids into the house. That was the final straw." She sniffed her disdain.

"Oh, to think that I should have such an ungrateful sister."

"Rubbish. Why do you not go up and begin packing those appalling cupids of yours. I, for one, intend to see the carpenter about framing the watercolor I did today. I am quite taken with it. I am rather taken with Lady Harriet as well. Lovely gel."

Victoria Plum stalked from the room, muttering nasty remarks under her breath.

"I must congratulate you, Mother. I had begun to think they would reside here forever." Philip shifted his position before the fireplace. He had watched the confrontation with great interest.

"I once liked my sister very well. However, she became a silly twit when she married Melrose, and she hasn't improved with time. What do *you* think of Lady Harriet?"

"I like her better than Aunt Victoria, not to mention Uncle Melrose." Philip leaned against the fireplace mantel again, bestowing a fond look on his mother.

"If the weather is decent tomorrow, I should like to paint again. I had quite forgotten what an agreeable pastime it is."

"She has agreed to go with you, if that is what you are hinting."

"I never hint. I ask."

"Miss Quince and the major are to be married soon. I trust you will receive an invitation to their coming party before long. He is that eager to claim his bride."

"Any man of sense feels the same. What about you? When are you going to settle down with the bride of your choice?"

"When she will have me. I have a minor problem to finish first. I dare not hint. Like you, I prefer to ask."

"Think she'll have you? For all that you are a good catch, not every girl is smitten by your looks or title."

"This one isn't, for certain." Philip gave his mother—who was proving far too astute for comfort—a grin. "No. I'd wager she would as soon trounce me with a bucket as agree to be my bride as things stand now."

"Your father didn't have a silver tongue, either."

"Yet, you married him." Philip could not recall when he had talked with his mother like this—very illuminating.

"That was before he became nutty for birds. Those feathered creatures are difficult competition. There isn't much can be done to be rid of them, especially once they are stuffed."

"I once heard a man say if you cannot beat them, it is time to join them."

"You don't say?" Lady Lanstone tilted her head in a considering manner, then rose to leave the room, murmuring that she had some thinking to do.

Philip ran down the stairs only to find Nick waiting for him.

"I know you are busy, but I'd like to talk."

"That ought not take long. Come with me, and you can inspect the window progress at the same time that we talk."

Nick walked with Philip into the dining room, impatiently looked at the Venetian window, and then turned to face his brother.

"I heard you ordered Aunt and Uncle to leave."

"True, for once the gossip is correct."

"What about me?" Nick gave Philip a belligerent glare.

"What about you? You are my brother, and I assume that someday you will want your own home. Until then, you are welcome to reside here. In fact, *I* may move out," Philip said, quite aware he was dropping a rock in Nick's quiet pond.

"You? Why?" Nick queried. He looked concerned and not a little puzzled.

"I am buying the Quince House. Miss Quince wants the money for a dowry, she said. No house should sit empty, so I may settle there for a time."

Instead of arguing as Philip expected, Nick frowned. "Are you also planning to marry?"

"What if I might? Surely you do not expect me to remain single? Or do you relish the thought you are next in line?" Philip had not thought Nick to be so inclined, but he had learned that feelings were not always obvious.

"Oh, go ahead and marry for all I care. Do I know

the lucky girl?" He cocked his head at Philip, looking for all the world like a bantam rooster.

"You do. Actually, I intend to marry Lady Harriet. As soon as I can get this business of the pin settled. I refuse to ask for her hand with that cloud hanging over my head."

"I can't say I am terribly surprised. You do seem to linger around her." Nick grinned, nodding his approval. "I won't say a word to spoil matters for you."

Uncle Melrose came lumbering into the room, looking as though he had lost his last pence. "Victoria informs me that we are moving to Derbyshire as soon as may be. That quick? She is throwing a tizzy because Beatrice doesn't like the cupids. Tell the truth, I don't, either."

"It would be a shame if they were lost or broken on the way," Nick said with a perfectly straight face.

"I always said you were a bright lad. I know we have been a sad trial to you, Philip, but I've learned my lesson. No more gaming for me. I'll try to look after matters for you up there."

Philip and Nick murmured suitable words before Melrose Plum ambled from the room.

"I don't believe what I just heard," Nick said in an undertone, not wanting his uncle to overhear him.

"Time will tell if he really means what he said. It would be nice, though, would it not?" he murmured, seconded by Nick.

"Perhaps Aunt Victoria would toss out the cupids—the ones that survive the trip—if he improves?"

"Don't expect miracles!"

# Chapter Thirteen

"It promises to be a beautiful day." Harriet gazed at the rain pouring from the sky and smiled. It was so agreeable when the weather cooperated with what one wished. True, it did remind her of when she first met Lord Stanhope during the deluge. In time she ought to be able to forget that man. Until then, she would hold up her head and pretend she felt nothing for him.

"I do not see how you can say that. It is raining, love." Aunt Cornelia glanced up from her embroidery to give Harriet a puzzled look.

"I do not make much sense, do I? I suppose it is a perverse notion. I dislike it when people tell me I *must* do such and such. Lord Stanhope was so certain that it would be a lovely day today, and I *must* go to paint. 'Tis a pity that even he cannot order the weather." Harriet made a droll face at her aunt.

"I thought you were in charity with him?" Cornelia tucked the needle into the fabric and placed her hands in her lap, the embroidery momentarily forgotten.

"Well, I confess I am not angry, or anything of that sort. He sets my nerves on edge if you must know."

A soft smile lingered about Cornelia's mouth. "I am aware of that feeling, yes. Perhaps matters will improve?"

"I rather doubt it." Directing her thoughts and words on a different course, Harriet said, "Lord Stanhope remarked that he intends to marry. I'd not be the slightest surprised if he plans to move in here once he does. He thinks that it might be difficult for a bride to contend with the husband's parents."

"He likely has a good point. It is fortunate for me that he wishes to buy this house. It means that I will have money for refurbishing the major's place. The draperies are a trifle shabby, and that drawing room sofa requires new covering. I should have you help me with that—you are so good with color. I am leaning to a gold damask for both."

"I will likely be with Mother by the time you return," Harriet replied in a bleak tone. It wasn't that she did not love her mother. Things had changed so much, circumstances were so different now.

Cornelia gave Harriet an arrested look, quite as though she had an inspiring idea. "It occurs to me that you might reside in the major's house while we are away. It is not good to have a house sitting empty, as you know. Perhaps the earl would permit you to reside here until we have left for Italy?"

A spark of hope lit within Harriet. "It would do no harm to ask, would it?" Her eyes gleamed with the very notion. After all, the earl had not announced whom he intended to wed. *There is many a slip betwixt the cup and the lip,* as the old saying went.

"None at all. He seems such a generous man, kind and caring for the people on his estate. Never mind that his father is the marquess. It is Lord Stanhope that runs the place—all the workers look to him for leadership. As to his mother, well, perhaps you may think of a means to help her?" Cornelia studied her niece with a kind expression.

"I want to paint your wild gladiola, and I was thinking that it might be possible to persuade Lady Lanstone to try painting a bird. She and Lord Lanstone seem to be at daggers drawn from what the earl has said. I wondered if she showed an interest in birds, or did something to do with his diversion that he might look more kindly on her."

"That seems a positively brilliant notion to me." Aunt Cornelia pushed the embroidery aside and rose to give the bellpull a tug. When Mrs. Twig popped around the corner, tea was requested along with a few biscuits.

"Rainy days are better with a cup of tea," Harriet observed.

"Not to mention ginger biscuits." Cornelia walked over to join Harriet by the window, watching the rain pound the gravel on the sweep before the house.

"Any chocolate cake left, do you think?" Harriet said after a time.

"If I know Mrs. Twig, there might be two small pieces on the tray when it comes."

"Oh, good. All of a sudden I am famished." Harriet exchanged a smile with her aunt. Oh, she was going to miss her very much.

"Perhaps we had best increase the request for biscuits and cake. Is that not a carriage making its way through the puddles? Who on earth would be out in this deluge?" Cornelia clutched her hands before her, as though apprehensive.

Harriet grinned. "I cannot imagine, unless it might be the major. He seems to spend a great deal of time here."

"Oh, good. We can ask him about your taking care of the house while we are away." Cornelia left the room in a dash, rushing to open the door for her future husband. In a very short time, he could be heard in the entryway, stomping his feet and speaking to Cornelia. His weatherproof cape crackled when he took it off. The silence that followed amused Harriet, for she had a very good idea what was occurring.

When they entered the room together, Cornelia had a rather self-conscious expression and the major looked quite pleased with himself.

"Mrs. Twig will be here shortly with hot tea to warm you, William. Harriet thought a rainy day a very good time to have tea." Cornelia linked her arm with his, walking to the fireplace so he might warm himself. It might be summer, but a rainy day was usually a bit chilly.

"I suspect any day is a good time for tea as far as Lady Harriet is concerned." His smile was at odds with his gravelly voice. It was rich and rough, but suited him, however.

"True. I am fond of a good cup of China tea." Harriet met his gaze with composure.

There was no time for more conversation at the moment, for Mrs. Twig entered with the promised ginger biscuits and the remains of the chocolate cake, just as Cornelia had prophesied.

Harriet did the honors, pouring tea and dispensing the cake and biscuits.

Mrs. Twig entered to light a few candles against the gloom, as stormy clouds made the day darker.

Those around the tea table hardly noticed, for Harriet was entranced by the itinerary for the Italian trip. Since the major had been there before, he had strong notions as to what must be seen. Cornelia seemed happy just to listen to his plans.

Well, thought Harriet, she would be as well if she contemplated such exotic places as Venice, Rome, and Florence.

"We might go to the south if the weather is not as warm as usual. We will write you if plans change." The major studied Harriet for a moment. "Where will you be?"

"That is the thing, dear." Cornelia placed a slim hand on his arm. "I was wondering about our house. I do not like having it sit empty. Were Harriet to reside there while we are away, I would feel far more at ease. And she can see to the hanging of the new draperies I wish, not to mention having the sofa recovered. I had thought a rich gold damask if you agree?"

"Gold? Hmm. As to Harriet staying there, I do not see why she can't. I have an excellent housekeeper and butler, but nothing can replace the eye of a gentlewoman when it comes to what is needing to be done about a place."

"Then I may?" Harriet inquired breathlessly.

"Didn't I just say that?"

"Indeed, you did." Harriet nodded with vigor. It seemed as though her wish was to be granted. She'd have a haven for the coming months, allowing her time to think of something else. Not that she wished to observe the new occupants of Quince House, but she would rather remain here then foist herself on Mama.

"You do not desire to go home?" He raised an eyebrow at the thought of her not wanting to be with her family.

"I have no home at present. I've not heard from Mama since I came here. I trust she is quite busy with the house and all," Harriet concluded vaguely. "Although, I most likely could visit her."

Suddenly steps were heard in the hall, loud steps and not at all like those of Mrs. Twig. Whoever it was approached from the rear of the house, as though from the kitchen or stables. All faces turned to the doorway as one, curious to see who else braved the inclement weather.

"Lord Stanhope," Cornelia cried with pleasure when he appeared.

"Ah, in time for tea, am I? I can always depend on that. I thought I might find the major here. I need to ask you about your plans for next year's crops before you take off. Good time to talk when it is raining cats and dogs outside. We might order seed together and save a bit." He walked across the room to where they had gathered. "And your house—you have adequate provision for protection? I could have my man check on it from time to time for you."

"Actually," Cornelia inserted, "Harriet is going to stay there. You will allow her to remain here until we leave for Italy, will you not? Then she can take over the reins of our house—deal with the draperies I shall order and the sofa, you know."

"No, I did not know, but she is welcome to stay here." He glanced at Harriet, and what he might be thinking was beyond her. His expression was enigmatic at best.

"You will not require it immediately, then?" Harriet hesitated to ask, but she needed to know. For one thing, she would have to go somewhere else if he required this house, and the rector's house bulged with family as it was. She could think of no one else who would have room. Of course Lanstone Hall had rooms galore, but she'd not ask for shelter there!

Lord Stanhope gave her a slow, almost intimate smile. "Rest assured that you will be as fine here as at the major's house." He turned his attention back to the major. "You must decide on what to call your place. Birch Court, perhaps? Birch Hall?" He took the chair next to Harriet's and accepted the tea she poured into the fragile Wedgwood cup. When she offered him cake or biscuits, he nodded to the ginger biscuits.

"I rather like Birch House." Cornelia placed her hand back on the major's arm. "What do you think?"

"It was called Rush Hall, but I'm not fond of that name. I rather like Birch House instead." The major glanced at Harriet, then back to the earl. "You are buying this house. I suppose you will call it something else?"

"Well, Father would call it Bird House, I imagine."

They all chuckled at that sally.

"Harriet was saying earlier that she hopes to persuade your mother to paint a few birds." Cornelia's eyes gleamed with mischief.

"Quite so. It is worth a try."

Harriet thought she detected a hint of concern in his eyes, but it disappeared so quickly she was not certain.

"If the weather is much improved tomorrow, I will venture forth. I promised Aunt that I would paint her a wild gladiola. I believe I saw a small patch of them not far off the road and near that swampy area on your land. Would you mind?" She could compromise if necessary. Just because she didn't paint today, didn't mean she refused tomorrow.

"Not if you take Mother with you."

"She will agree?" Harriet gave him a dubious look. He seemed far too sure of what other people would do.

"Of course. After a day spent inside, she will welcome the chance to get out to paint." He met her gaze with that enigmatic expression in his eyes once again.

"You may recall I intend to persuade her to paint a bird. You think she will be amenable?" Harriet persisted.

"Let us hope so." He seemed so assured that Harriet decided perhaps he was right.

The two men fell to discussing what crops they intended to have the following year and what was most profitable. The major liked the idea of rotating the crops when the earl pointed out that he had found it beneficial.

"He did not object to gold, did he," Cornelia asked in an undertone.

"Not in the least. He did not approve, either," she felt obliged to point out.

"Well, I will have to persuade him, in that event."

Harriet wasn't sure what means her aunt intended to use, but it seemed it was not an unpleasant one. She smiled in a most delighted manner.

There was no backing out of it the next morning. The sun shone, making every drop of moisture seem a diamond. The birds warbled brightly, and Harriet felt her happiness stirring. It would be a good day—she knew it.

She presented herself at Lanstone Hall promptly, wearing a gown of sea-green jaconet muslin. She liked the pointed lace treble ruff at the neck, and thought the broad flounce around the lower edge of the dress quite dashing. She only hoped that the lace on the lower edge of the sleeve that fell almost to her fingers wouldn't get into her paint. It wasn't a practical gown to wear while painting, but after previous excursions, she wasn't going to be caught in an old rag this time.

Peel opened the door at once, inviting her into the house. "I shall notify her ladyship at once that you are here, my lady. Her painting things were sent down some time ago."

Harriet thanked him, then wandered over to the door of the dining room that stood wide open. She didn't think it would matter if she inspected what was being done.

She thought the Venetian window proved to be a wonderful success. There was a certain grace in that upper curve of the central portion, and in all, the three sections were precisely right for the room.

"Admiring my new window? I believe they are to paint it today sometime." The marchioness glanced about the room in a vague way. "I believe the color must match the rest of the room. What think you, Lady Harriet?"

"Oh, I agree, definitely." Harriet took note of her purple-and-blue ensemble with a dazzling jonquil bonnet.

They both turned from the dining room to head for the front door. Lady Lanstone gave Harriet a serene smile. "I am looking forward to painting again. My goodness, if I'd had someone to paint with in the past, I might have been painting for years. It is so nice to have company."

"True. Although I confess once I am absorbed in doing a flower, I tend to forget all else around me."

"Philip says you write as well. Is it the same with writing? Both are creative."

"Yes, ma'am. I have been a trifle remiss of late. But the writing is pleasant to occupy my hours at times." She proffered the painting she had done before. "Lord Stanhope suggested I have his carpenter make a frame for this. Aunt Cornelia wishes it for her new home."

"Of course. Peel will see to it." She gestured to the butler, who accepted the painting with forbearance.

Harriet searched the entryway for a sign of Lord Stanhope; then once they were outside, she again glanced about to see if he was anywhere to be seen. She thought she had been cautious in her scan of the area, but knew that to be false when her ladyship spoke.

"Philip went to town to seek out some shop or other. Perhaps you know what it is he is hunting for? He was very reticent about it, I must say." Her ladyship seemed most put out.

The pawnbrokers! Harriet strongly suspected that when he awoke to see sunshine and few clouds, he had taken it as a sign that he ought to check every pawnbroker within a reasonable range. He'd not be home until late, if today, perhaps even tomorrow. She tried to think of some other reason he might go to town.

"Perhaps it has to do with the purchase of Quince House? His lawyer would have to handle the paperwork,

I daresay?" Harriet hoped that would divert her ladyship from more speculation.

"Of course! Why did I not think of that? What a sensible girl you are, to be sure." She entered the gig with a groom's help, and in a short time they were headed down the avenue to locate the wild gladiolas.

"Have you considered trying to paint a bird?" Harriet inquired with caution after a time. Circumspection was needed at a moment like this.

"Why?"

The stubborn expression on her ladyship's face was not a good omen. "I thought it might be interesting to try a detailed subject for a change from a landscape. I dearly enjoy painting the wildflowers for my aunt. Perhaps Lord Lanstone would be pleased if you painted a bird?"

"A yellow-breasted bunting, no doubt." Her voice was dry, and Harriet noted she clasped her fingers tightly together.

"Are those the rare birds?" Wasn't that the name of the bird he shot and had stuffed?

"Not in northern Russia, I understand. He said they rarely fly this far to the east. We shall see what presents itself."

With that, Harriet had to be content. At least for the moment.

Philip entered the third pawnbroker's shop with little hope of any success. Nothing had turned up so far.

He explained what he sought. Although there was a pretty little ivory pin, it was not the dragon he hoped to find.

"Never seen the like of what you describe," the old fellow said, his voice sounding as dry and papery as his face appeared. "Lots o' other pins iffen you care to have a look."

Philip politely studied the tray of little pins, wondering if he might find something similar that would please his mother.

Nothing looked the sort to appeal to her.

After the last of the pawnshops in the town, he returned to where he had stabled his horse, and set off for Tunbridge Wells. This could take longer than he planned. When he reached his destination after a hard ride, he met with the same results. Nothing to be found, although one little shop tucked back into a side street had an ivory pin that was very similar. He bought it, deciding that it might do in a pinch.

"Expect it is very old," the chap who stood behind the counter declared. He seemed uneasy. Philip wondered if this could be a stolen piece, but had no way of finding out. Merely because the man had shifty eyes and grubby hands was no reason to suspect him of being a fence. On the other hand . . .

"I shall take it. My mother fancies old pins."

Back on the street, Philip tucked this pin into an inner pocket, then returned to the coaching inn where he had left Vulcan. He sat for a time, contemplating his next move while he consumed a tankard of ale and a hearty dish of steak and kidney pie. Perhaps it might be a wise thing to do a bit of shopping while he was here. He rarely came as far as Tunbridge Wells.

Once his repast finished, he sought the main street of the town and there found the jeweler he had dealt with before. He didn't rush his purchase. After all, one should always consider buying jewelry an investment, and he fully intended this to be one of long duration.

He left the pleasant shop with a feeling of great satisfaction. How nice it was to find precisely what he'd wanted, when he had been frustrated all day!

He was about to return to the inn where Vulcan was stabled when a familiar voice hailed him.

"Lord Stanhope! How marvelous to see someone we know so far from home." He stopped, turned, and saw Miss Nympha Herbert along with her mother. Mrs. Herbert looked exhausted while Miss Nympha beamed with the freshness of a summer daisy.

"How good to see you. Shopping, I suppose?" he inquired politely.

"Yes. Oh, do join us for tea. I am quite perishing for

a good cup of tea. I believe Mother is about ready to collapse unless she has one as well."

Put on the spot like that, Philip could scarce decline the invitation. "I would be pleased to join you. I think I saw a tea and pastry shop along here somewhere."

She clapped her hands with delight. "I know the very place you mean. Green's, is it not? On the upper walk of the Pantiles?" She smiled widely.

Her mother nodded permission, and walked along with them in silence, presumably too tired to talk.

When they reached the neat little shop, they found it crowded but not impossible to be served. Philip escorted the ladies to a table, and summoned the equally neat serving girl who attended them at once.

"This is the very nicest sort of surprise," Miss Nympha declared. Her face beamed with her pleasure. "Usually we shop and head for home. This makes it a special day. Do you not agree, Mama?"

"Certainly. Although we will have to depart for home immediately once the tea is finished. I agree with my daughter, sir. This tea is most welcome." She gave him a weary smile.

"A busy day shopping, I gather?" Philip hoped that they enjoyed an agreeable trip home. The roads suffered every time there was a rain, and yesterday had been a downpour.

"Mama wanted new curtains for Papa's study. We found a nice burgundy brocade that ought to please him."

They chatted a bit more before finishing the tea and tiny cakes. It was plain that Miss Nympha would like to have sat talking a while longer. He wanted to be on his way. He excused himself, but not before Miss Nympha had a last question.

"I saw you leave the jewelry shop. You bought something important, I daresay?"

"Nympha," her long-suffering mother cautioned.

"As a matter of fact, you are correct." With that, he smiled, bowed politely, then after paying for the tea, left the shop with a decisive step. Miss Nympha might be as pretty as could be, but she needed to mature.

His ride back home was not as happy as he had hoped what with no sign of the pin. Perhaps he would have to journey to London? The thief might decide it would be safer to take it there.

Something would have to be done about Mother.

The patch of wild gladiolas, once found, provided perfect examples of that flower for Harriet to paint.

Lady Lanstone spotted a yellow wagtail, and by keeping her movements small and slow to avoid startling it, she sketched and painted it in exquisite detail. It was almost as though the bird knew it was being studied and painted, for it lingered in the swamp, swinging from a low branch, inspecting a yellow flag at the edge of the shallow pond, and tarrying in general.

When Harriet saw the completed painting, she exclaimed over it with admiration. "I should think, dear ma'am, that your husband cannot fail to be impressed with this. I thought you might be able to do such detail after seeing your landscapes. I was right!"

"I confess I had trouble with the proportions at first, but since you are so patient, I finally conquered them."

"I? Patient? I am rather slow when I paint, as I strive to get each petal precisely so. I should say that in that event we make a good pair, each of us attempting accuracy. Come, let us show this to the gentlemen. I think your older son will be dazzled with your talent." Harriet grinned in shared delight.

It was late afternoon by the time they returned to Lanstone Hall. When the marchioness insisted Harriet had to join her for a light repast, Harriet accepted at once. She quite longed to learn if Lord Stanhope had any luck with finding the pin.

There was no sign of him when they entered the house. Peel ushered them into the drawing room, promising to bring the requisite refreshment at once.

The marchioness shifted about in her chair, looking

nervous. At last she said, "I cannot think what Lord Lanstone will say to this painting. Likely he will dismiss it as the daubing of an amateur, for he has books full of bird paintings." She looked on the verge of tears.

"But, my lady, this is a lovely painting of a very nice local bird by his own wife. Surely that will impress him?"

Lady Lanstone did not seem convinced in the least. "He will say I am a fool for even trying," she murmured at last.

Harriet longed to shake his insensitive lordship until his teeth rattled. She thought he was the fool, not is wife.

They both turned to face the door when they heard steps in the entryway. Harriet thought they sounded familiar. She was not too surprised when Lord Stanhope entered the room. That his father followed him was a surprise. Neither looked particularly pleased.

"How did the painting excursion go, Mother?"

Harriet could see he made an effort to be pleasant in spite of what was likely a disappointment in his hunt for the ivory dragon. She admired him for that.

Rather than reply, her ladyship rose to hand him her painting of the yellow wagtail.

"Father, will you look at this? Mother, I had no idea you could paint in such detail, still including a feeling of the area where you painted. It is exquisite."

"Hmpf." Lord Lanstone studied the painting for a time, then set it aside.

It would have given Harriet a great deal of satisfaction to clunk the man over the head with the dreadful cupid sitting on the table. How insensitive could a man be? Apparently Lord Stanhope felt much the same, for his expression could only be described as disgusted.

"Regardless, I think it wonderful and I hope you intend to paint more birds. I would like to see a collection of them mounted on the dining room wall. I have never liked that painting of the dead animals!" Philip concluded.

Harriet echoed his sentiments silently.

There was little more to be said. Tea was drunk, but Harriet had lost all her appetite. She excused herself as soon as possible and without any fuss left the house. In a short time she was headed down the avenue for her aunt's house. None the wiser as to the results of Lord Stanhope's search, true, but she suspected he had not found the pin. He would have found a way to let her know, otherwise.

As she approached Quince House, she noted the rectory gig before the front and sighed. Nympha Herbert most likely had come to pay a call.

With little enthusiasm for company after the upsetting scene she had just witnessed, Harriet entered the house, carrying her painting of the wild gladiola for her aunt.

Dumping her painting gear on the bottom step of the stairway, she joined the pair in the drawing room.

Nympha sat by her aunt. Harriet sat down in her favorite chair not far from the fireplace, first offering her painting to Aunt Cornelia.

"My dear girl, how pleased you have made me. This will go with the others to Birch House."

"That is very nice," allowed Nympha after peering over to see what had been painted. "What is it?"

"A flower," Harriet replied, somewhat abruptly.

"Oh. I was just telling Miss Quince about our trip to Tunbridge Wells."

"Lovely. Did your mother find the drapery fabric she wanted?" Harriet leaned back in the chair, suddenly feeling exhausted.

"Yes, she did. You will never guess whom we saw there. Lord Stanhope! Is that not famous? He came out of a jeweler's shop—the finest in all of Tunbridge Wells! I just wonder what he bought there!" She bestowed a triumphant smile on Harriet. "He treated Mama and me to tea and was utterly charming. Of course he would not say a word about his purchase. I think he is quite the most handsome of men." Her smile was too coy for Harriet to stomach.

It was simply too much. Harriet gave her a wan smile in return. "I am so sorry to leave you so soon, but a day in the fresh air, painting and all, has fatigued me. I am going to seek my bed at once." She rose and left the room before anyone could see the tears lurking in her eyes.

# Chapter Fourteen

It was a pity that he had been observed by the Herberts—mother and daughter—while in Tunbridge Wells. He suspected that Mrs. Herbert had not wished to intrude upon his privacy. It was Miss Nympha who hailed him and in essence begged so prettily for tea. He could not imagine Lady Harriet doing the same thing.

That Miss Herbert had noticed his foray into the jewelry shop was not in itself harmful. It was what she did with the knowledge that might prove unfortunate. That little imp was not above prating to Harriet about her tea in Tunbridge Wells, or implying more than existed. He had been around too long not to be cautious of a young miss. Lady Harriet was different. At times he had the feeling that she would as soon dump a flowerpot on his head as talk to him. The one exception was her kisses, and they had given him hope.

"Philip, attend please." Lady Lanstone admonished him with a mere frowning look.

"What is it? I fear I was woolgathering." Philip sent her an apologetic grin.

"Most unlike you, dear boy. I was saying that I do not know if I care to go painting again. Lady Harriet thought the painting might please your father. I do not think anything could please him short of a rare bird or two. He is not an easy man to satisfy."

"Where is the painting?" Philip hunted around the immediate area, then checked his mother's painting gear in the event she had replaced the painting with it.

"I believe your father took it with him."

Philip cast her a disbelieving look, then headed toward

the library. Upon opening the door, he discovered his father at his desk. A crisp sheet of watercolor paper with the unmistakable splash of yellow belonging to the yellow wagtail on it held in his hands. He sat staring at the paper as though he couldn't quite believe what he saw.

"Ahem. Sir?" Philip thought he ought to rouse him from his reverie before speaking.

"Well, what is it you want? I suppose you were in on this?" He flicked the paper with a finger. Craggy brows almost met over angry eyes as he stared at his older son.

It occurred to Philip that he could not remember when his father had looked happy. Jubilant over a new book, or a find like that yellow bunting perhaps, but never happy. For the first time in his life, he pitied the old man.

"True. I encouraged Mother to paint again. Lady Harriet thinks her very gifted." He watched his father's face to see what reaction, if any, crossed it.

"Well-done, ain't it? Why did she never tell me she could paint a bird like this?" The older man glared at Philip, a stubborn twist to his mouth. His mustache bristled more than usual.

"I suppose she was busy at first. Perhaps she thought you would think her silly to want to paint. Most young ladies paint a little, few matrons do." Philip walked around the desk so he might view the painting once again. "She has a few paintings framed in her yellow sitting room. It is easy to overlook something that is always there, if you know what I mean."

His father remained silent, simply gazing at the painting, then off into the distance.

"I wonder what Lady Harriet painted? They seem to enjoy each other's company," Philip added. He wondered what went on in his father's mind. His face gave little clue, for he habitually wore an irritable expression.

"Go away. I have some thinking to do, and you drive me mad just standing there, peering over my shoulder. I shall see you at dinner. When do the Plums depart? Telling them to leave for Derbyshire was the best day's work you have done in a long time. Can't abide Victoria. Melrose ain't much better. It's those bloody cupids of hers.

His chess sets I can tolerate, and they don't take much room. But I swear that those blasted cupids of hers are multiplying in the dark! Every time I turn around, I find another one. If she don't have them all packed up soon, I will personally throw them out of the door!" This time his glare was not so much directed at Philip as at the mere thought of the obnoxious Plums.

Philip grinned, for once in complete accord with his parent. "I know what you mean, sir. I will inform Peel that all cupids on this floor must be packed as soon as possible." Philip headed for the door.

"At once, do you hear? At once!" The marquess glanced off to the end of the room where a tarp shielded the room from any wind or rain. "When are those infernal carpenters going to finish adding on to this room? Don't know why you had to change things in here."

"Barring difficulties such as more rainstorms, or a problem with supplies, it ought to be soon. You know you need the space; your collection grows every week." He turned the knob on the door, looking back to see his father studying the painting of the yellow wagtail in deep concentration. Philip left the room without saying another word. The painting had meticulous detail that ought to delight the old man.

He sought out Peel to give him the instructions from his master. Following that, he searched for his mother. She was sitting where he had left her, looking dejected and fiddling with the silk flowers on her yellow-green bonnet.

"He is studying your painting of the yellow wagtail. Perhaps he may yet say a kind word about it?" He patted her shoulder before assisting her to her feet.

"Ours was an arranged marriage, you know," she confided. "I doubt he has ever given me much thought. I can only be grateful that he ceased chasing opera dancers ages ago to concentrate on birds."

Philip blinked, gazing down at his little mother with astounded eyes. "You knew?"

"I may well look like a twit, but that does not mean I am one." She shook off his arm and marched up the stairs in the direction of her room, a rainbow of ruffled dignity.

Philip shook his head at the departing figure. This was certainly a day for surprises. First his mother produced an incredible bird painting, and then his father reacted in such a strange manner to it. Was he a betting man, he'd not know on which side to place his bets.

He caught sight of Nick outside and left the house in favor of his brother's company. "Nick, wait up." What Nick might think of the latest family doings would be interesting.

"There," Cornelia declared with satisfaction. "That wildflower looks positively splendid once framed. I still have one or two frames remaining." She sounded hopeful.

When Harriet made no reply, her aunt gave her a sharp look, her eyes filled with concern. "You could go painting today unless you would rather write? I fear you have neglected your writing shamefully of late."

"Well, as to that, matters seem to fare no better for my heroine than they do for me. But never fear, even though I cannot write a happy ending for me, I shall for poor Edwina."

"Your heroine is named Edwina? What a lovely name. And who is your hero?"

Harriet almost replied, "Philip," but caught herself in time. "Frederico. I was going to have him as the villain of the piece, but he insisted upon being the hero instead." She smiled at her aunt's perplexed reaction.

"Let me understand this—Frederico 'told' you he wished to be the hero?" She raised her hand to touch Harriet's forehead. "Are you certain you feel all right?"

"Yes." Harriet gave her aunt an amused look. "There are times when the characters simply take over the book. All I can do is to write what they tell me."

"Of course, dear." Cornelia shook her head, clearly disbelieving.

"Are you going to pack these for your removal to Birch House? I could help if you like. Somehow I do not

feel much like writing today." Harriet took the picture,
running her fingers along the gilded edge of the frame.

"Please do help. I have found things go far faster when
there are four hands rather than two. Why do you not
wish to paint? Merely because I have no more flowers I
want—for the moment, mind you—is no reason for you
to cease painting."

"Later, perhaps. Let us find a box for all these first."

Sensing that Harriet did not wish to discuss her painting at the moment, Cornelia agreed and went off to see
about a box.

Harriet removed the paintings from the wall one by
one, neatly stacking them. When she added the last, the
painting of a fringed gentian, she held it a moment,
thinking back to when she had painted it.

The day had been rainy, she had sought refuge in the
barn, and then she had met the earl. Fallen at his feet
was more accurate. Was it proper to say one "fell" for a
gentleman? Well, in her case it was appropriate enough.

Hearing footsteps, she whirled about to say something
to her aunt. The words died on her lips, for instead of
her aunt, Lord Stanhope came up the stairs. "Hello,"
she managed to say, fearing her voice sounded a bit
strangled.

"What have you there? Your aunt said I might come
to help you." He held out a box as though he wasn't
certain what it might be for.

"She is taking these paintings with her. Cornelia dearly
loves flowers, especially wild ones."

He removed the frame Harriet clutched against her
chest to examine it. "I recall this one in particular," he
murmured. "It brings back memories."

"I imagine it isn't often that you have a girl fall at
your feet." Harriet didn't look at him, she wasn't sure
what she might see reflected in his eyes.

He had touched her ever so lightly when he took the
picture from her, brushing his fingers against her bosom.
Of course it was accidental. He could not have had the
slightest notion how it affected her. She had felt as

though a trail of fire zinged along her skin right through the sheer jaconet muslin. Glancing down, she was almost surprised that the material was not singed.

"I was astonished at the time, I admit, but as to falling at my feet, I doubt that is accurate."

At this remark, she met his gaze. "I did fall from the loft, sir." Even if she felt somewhat the fool, she could not deny the truth.

"True, you fell. It was merely an accident."

Pasting a smile on her face, Harriet took the frame back from him to place it with the others. "To be sure, an accident," she echoed.

He set the box on the floor, then began placing the paintings inside. Harriet stopped him at once.

"I believe we ought to put a bit of cushioning in with each one else the glass could break."

"Without a doubt you are right." He knelt at her side, studying her with frank appraisal. "What can we use, I wonder?"

Harriet could scarce breathe. He was far too close. His coat brushed against her arm, now amazingly sensitive. She could smell the clean scent of his linen and the aroma of his shaving soap. Lavender. Blue flecks danced in his dark eyes. Fine lines radiated from those eyes, making her think he smiled more often than she believed. And his lips? Firm, well shaped, and also too close.

"Harriet?" His whisper brushed her cheek before those lips claimed hers.

It was a brief kiss, far too brief to please her. To her shame, she wished it had gone on for minutes, ages. Once he drew away, she felt utterly bereft. Her eyes had drifted shut when he touched her lips with his, and now they remained so. Could her heart continue to beat as hard, or as loud? Could she face him again? What did he think of her to be so free with her favors? He was not to know that he was the only man she had permitted a kiss.

At last she opened her eyes, daring to discover what

she might see in his. His expression was guarded. What did he think she would do? Box his ears? She decided to pretend nothing had happened to shake her earth.

"Well? We have a box and the contents; all we need is a bit of filling." Harriet looked down and picked up the painting again, wondering what he would say or do next.

A second time he took the painting from her, again brushing her bosom with his fingers. He set the painting down before taking her hands in his. "Harriet, would you please go painting with my mother again?"

Whatever she had expected him to say, it was not this request. Harriet gave him a wary look.

"I know, I have bullied you a bit, but she likes you and I have high hopes for her bird paintings. I doubt she will venture out on her own, and she must paint another bird." His clasp was tight, yet curiously comforting. She did not feel so lost when he touched her. His thumb rubbed her hand, a sensuous caress that affected her far more than he could possibly guess. Or did he suspect how he unsettled her?

"Father was studying her painting when I left him not too long ago. This could be important—this tenuous connection between them. I believe you are right in your conjecture. He asked why she hadn't told him of her ability long ago." He paused, then beseeched, "Please, Harriet?"

What could she say when the man she loved begged for her help, particularly when it had been her idea in the first place?

"I like your mother as well. Of course I will take her painting with me. I have no idea what I can paint, certainly not a bird. While I may be able to draw a flower, I suspect my bird would look dreadful. Each artist has his or her own specialty."

"Yours seems to be charming my mother as well as painting beautiful flowers."

"Thank you." Harriet rose to her feet, pulling her hands from his clasp in the process.

"Filling," he murmured to her confusion. "Did you decide what we are to use for filling?"

Her mind still befuddled from his kiss and the request that had been couched in the most sensuous manner she could imagine, she looked about her as though the filling ought to appear from nowhere by magic.

"Harriet," her aunt called. "I found some tissue for you to use with the paintings." She appeared at the top of the steps.

How odd—Harriet had not even heard her steps on the stairway! She scolded herself for being much too entranced with a gentleman who might like her kisses, but showed no desire for her company other than to go painting with his mother.

It took but a few minutes to wrap each picture in tissue and stow it in the box. Lord Stanhope helped her. She was all thumbs and feared she would have stacked them any old way had she been on her own after the scene that had just played. Perhaps she might look on this as a means of gathering ideas for a book? She certainly ought to be able to describe her heroine's feelings on being held in the hero's arms!

Once the box was full, the earl turned his attention to Cornelia. "I trust you are placing all the things you want to take with you in one area? Perhaps one of the bedrooms? I feel certain there is a fair amount of furniture you want as well."

Cornelia nodded. "Several of the rooms at Birch House are almost bare. I intend to take all I need. Perhaps I could put them in the sitting room downstairs. I shall leave a bed for Harriet, of course."

He grinned, a beguiling, entrancing grin that tied Harriet's poor heart into knots.

"Ah, yes, Harriet must have a bed in which to sleep. I fancy you will be married soon, and that she will not have much time here before you leave for Italy."

Well, if that wasn't a splash in the face, Harriet didn't know what one was. Could he kiss her, then scarce wait for her to be gone so that he might use this house for his own purposes? It was going to be extremely difficult to be civil to Nympha Herbert after this!

"Harriet has promised to go painting with my mother.

I should like to take her away with me for a time if I may. There is something astir. I cannot say for certain what it is, but it is important for Mother to paint another bird. She will only go with Harriet—so there you are. I am spiriting her away—if she will consent to come with me."

Cornelia laughed as likely he intended. "Go! Go and paint what you want. It is good that your mother enjoys Harriet's company. I suppose it is a matter of like spirits?" She chuckled at her little pun on his words.

"Ah, yes, she is quite spirited!"

Harriet groaned, but accepted his hand when he led her down the stairs to the entry hall. Mrs. Twig appeared with Harriet's painting box. Harriet gave the earl a derisive look. "You were utterly certain, were you not?"

"I think I have come to know you a little." His smile seemed a little less confidant, she decided.

But Harriet's traitorous thoughts wondered if that kiss had been in aid of his achieving his way. Surely he would not stoop to such means? Closing her mind to more worrisome notions, she accepted his arm and left the house.

The groom walking his horse and curricle promptly brought the carriage to the front of the steps. His lordship helped her into the curricle, and they set off for Lanstone Hall.

While Lord Stanhope seemed in a good mood—and why shouldn't he after his obtaining his way so easily—Harriet was uneasy. She mulled over what had just occurred. Surely he was not such a cad as to kiss her if he was contemplating marriage to Miss Herbert? So what *did* he intend? She studied him as he guided the horse along the road wishing she could read minds.

When they passed the barn, she couldn't refrain from glancing back at it.

"That is a notable spot, is it not?" he queried, humor lightening his voice.

"Only if you say so," she joked. She had her view, and doubtless he recalled something a little different.

"Ah, my dear Harriet. I do say so, and so should you. It was where we met."

And that was his last remark until they came to the front of Lanstone Hall. Did his hands linger at her waist when he lifted her to set her on the gravel? She was too breathless to decide.

Peel opened the door to usher them inside. "Madam is in the drawing room awaiting your return. Shall I place her painting equipment with Lady Harriet's?"

"Please." The earl drew Harriet with him. "Come speak with Mother, and I can explain what is planned." Again he held out his hand to her, and she had little choice but to accept. She'd not be thought ill-mannered.

Lady Lanstone was garbed in a subdued—for her—ensemble. Cerise ribands at the neck and wrist decorated her simple blue gown. It fell straight to her feet, encased in plain blue leather boots. Harriet was impressed. She had never expected to see her ladyship dressed so sensibly.

"I hope Mother will be able to paint another bird. We depend on you for support."

"True," Lady Lanstone agreed. "I should never do this on my own, but with you along and painting as well, I believe I can manage it. I appreciate your giving me time, for I can well imagine you have much to do, what with your aunt's move and all."

"I am pleased to help." Harriet wasn't quite sure just what she was helping, but she decided not to ask—at least for the present. The earl had mentioned that something was astir, but what that might be she could only guess.

The three left the house together. Harriet observed that both of the others took care to be unusually quiet, so she made no effort to speak until they were outside.

A small hamper containing buns and a bottle of lemonade had been tucked at the foot of the curricle seat.

When Vulcan was brought forth, Harriet confronted the earl. "Surely you do not expect me to drive the curricle!"

"You handle the gig well. I doubt you will overturn this, and there isn't room for three. I thought it would save time."

His smile was disarming, but she couldn't help wonder why time was of the essence and why they had taken care to be so quiet. Perhaps she might learn later?

They returned to the low, swampy area where they had spotted the yellow wagtail. A stream flowed to one side, its bank rising sharply above it. The earl saw them settled. He departed, heading in the direction of the village.

Harriet took out her pencil with only one wistful look in his direction. And what was he to do in the village, her traitorous heart wondered.

"Be extremely still, my dear. I do believe there is a great reed warbler over there. If I am not mistaken, they rarely appear in Britain, and then only in Kent. You see, I may not collect birds, but I have made it a point to read all my husband's books when he is off hunting the poor feathered creatures."

"How clever of you, ma'am." As Harriet had thought before, her ladyship might appear silly, but she had a sound head on her dainty shoulders.

Sitting utterly still, the two women watched as the rather big warbler settled on a reed, bursting forth with an amazingly powerful song.

With fewer strokes of her pencil than Harriet would have expected, the marchioness sketched the bird. The bird's head had a somewhat crowned effect, with its back and tail a dark brown and pale below.

Fascinated, Harriet forgot she was supposed to be sketching as well. It was like watching a master, or possibly the fine teacher her mother had hired to tutor her in painting. That had been a brief, although glorious, period for Harriet.

"I do believe I matched the brown. What do you say, Lady Harriet?" Lady Lanstone held her brush in the air, giving her painting a critical look.

"Truly, I cannot imagine how it could be bettered. Do you intend to paint the reeds as well? I think it would enhance the painting, give it a touch of reality, as it were."

"You think so? Very well, I shall."

Harriet finally set her pencil to paper to record the scene of the marchioness at her painting. She worked with rapid strokes, finally adding a splash of color. It was precisely what she wanted, a mere sketch. But it revealed the charming lady intent upon her work.

A sharp *chee* note called their attention to a smart kingfisher darting its way over the water. When it settled on a branch not too distant, the marchioness flipped a page and did a quick sketch of this colorful bird. In autumn the chestnut breast would likely blend in with the foliage, but now it stood out with the green reeds behind it. Its brilliant blue back was simply beautiful.

She daren't move a muscle until the painting was done.

"There, I believe I have captured it, although I cannot put it in a case," her ladyship murmured.

Harriet remained silent, unwilling to send the kingfisher into flight again. Alas, it must have seen a little fish, for it darted off, then swooped to dip a beak into the water. Successful, it flew away with the tiny fish in its beak.

"It is gone, but not before you achieved what you wanted."

"I shall have a bun with a little lemonade before we wend our way homeward. It is later than I thought." She glanced up at the sky before taking a bun from the hamper along with the jar of lemonade. "Please help yourself. I do not believe we need stand on formality."

Harriet looked at the watch pinned to her bodice, incredulous that the time could have flown as quickly as the birds. She poured out lemonade for both of them, also helping herself to a bun. It was filled with currants, and light and tender as could be. Her stomach was most appreciative.

It didn't take long to pack up the painting equipment. Harriet stowed it neatly away, then faced the prospect of the drive home. The curricle had proven to be a little different from the gig, but she had managed on the way here. If the horse cooperated, she should be at Lanstone Hall in jig time.

She assisted Lady Lanstone into the curricle, then

joined her, but not before she observed a man on horseback coming their way. At first she had thought it the earl. It wasn't long before she realized it was his younger brother. "Lord Nicholas," she cried as he joined them.

"Thought I had better see if you had fallen into the stream. I understand you have done that on occasion." His grin was totally unrepentant that he'd brought up an embarrassing incident.

"Are you disappointed?" she teased.

He grinned but said nothing more on that matter. Harriet thought driving a bit easier with his familiar person close by as he paced his horse alongside the curricle.

When they reached Lanstone Hall, the marchioness insisted that Harriet go in with her. It was difficult to believe that lady might be nervous, but it seemed she was.

They were crossing the hall when the library door opened and the marquess stepped out to meet them. "Well?"

"We have been painting. Do show him what you did, Lady Harriet." It was such a nice command, Harriet found it impossible to refuse, although her sketch hardly merited any praise.

He made no comment at any rate. After handing the sketch to Harriet, he pierced his wife with that same intent look. "And yours, madam?"

She took a deep breath, handed him her watercolor pad, and waited while he opened it to the pages she had done.

"A great reed warbler, as I live and breathe!" He studied it a time, then turned the page. "A kingfisher? Pray tell, how did you persuade it to sit still for so long?" He gave his wife a quick glance.

"Lady Lanstone is fast, my lord. You would not believe how little time it took her to do these." Harriet swallowed with care, wondering if he was going to bark at her. For all his fierceness, she'd wager he was much nicer underneath. At the moment he almost looked as though he could smile.

"Quick and yet so accurate. Amazing." He smiled.

"Beatrice, I have long wanted to sail to Italy. I have a book telling of the birds there, but the drawings are not good at all. What do you say to a trip to Italy? We shall spend the winter painting and traveling. I promise not to stuff one bird if you will paint what we see this well."

The little lady drew herself up, offering him a hesitant smile. "I believe I should like that, Hartley."

"Come with me, and I will show you that book so that you will have an idea of what I'd like."

Harriet stood, quite stunned, as the two disappeared into the library.

"Had I not seen this, I'd never believe it." Nicholas stepped to her side.

"Nor I," Philip said from behind them. "Come, Harriet, I will drive you home. You've exceeded all my hopes and expectations."

# Chapter Fifteen

"You have exceeded all my hopes and expectations," he had said yesterday, sounding so patronizing that she could have happily dumped her paint pot on his head. It was *her* idea that his parents might be united with a mutual interest. It had also been her notion to encourage his talented mother to paint again. That his curmudgeon of a father was excessively pleased with the results had nothing to do with her, nor the earl, for that matter. Patronizing! She had seethed all the way back to Quince House in utter silence.

Perhaps it was not a good idea to remain here after her aunt left? Maybe she ought to simply write her mother to receive permission to join her new household? Yet she felt in her bones that she would be an intruder on the newly married couple. Mama was likely apt to feel she must find Harriet a husband. That had little appeal at the moment. It seemed that no matter where she lived, she became an encumbrance to someone. Perhaps if she plunged into work she could shake off her mood.

Harriet studied the growing list of things her aunt wished to move to Birch House, and sighed. Linens, china, and a goodly amount of furniture, along with various paintings she admired, were to go. Quince House would be rather empty once they were removed.

However, it was nothing to her what was taken, for those things not wanted would later be sold. Most people cleaned out the house when they moved, leaving nothing behind. At least a bed and a clothespress for her things would remain, and chairs and a table or two in the drawing room. The dining table and sideboard were excellent quality. Harriet doubted those that the major had purchased would be nearly as nice, so the dining room would be bare. She and Abby would rattle around in the house, with only a kitchen maid for company.

Lord Stanhope would have his hands full with decorating this house. She leaned back in the desk chair to contemplate what she would do in that situation. The paint was still good, although she would alter the dining room, changing the wall color to a rich, deep green. The sitting room could have pretty wallpaper, something with flowers, perhaps. The kitchen needed a new stove—one of the latest design. Since all the gorgeous Turkey rugs were to go, new ones would be required. The new Wilton or Axminster rugs might do. However, she suspected that nothing but the finest Turkey rugs would satisfy the earl.

It was rather fun to imagine redoing this house until she recalled she'd not be here to enjoy it. That realization brought her down with a thump. Pushing aside her thoughts, she rose from the desk to assist with packing up the linens.

Cornelia bustled from the rear of the house, her arms full of tablecloths. "Harriet, dear, help me with these."

Quite willing to occupy her mind with something other than this house and who would occupy it in the future, Harriet complied with haste.

By noon nearly all bed and table linens had been stowed in chests. The industrious Cornelia whirled through the rooms, indicating the paintings that were to be removed. Following that, Harriet brought her to a halt, insisting that even if Cornelia didn't need sustenance, she did.

"I vow, dearest aunt, that should you keep on like this, you will be too exhausted to enjoy your dinner."

"It is a good thing Mrs. Twig comes with me. I worry about you, Harriet. What will you do for meals?"

"Please do not trouble your head in that regard. There is the kitchen maid to help, and I am quite capable of heating a bit of ham, boiling an egg, or toasting a slice of bread. Since you intend to leave the gig with me, I shall be able to go to the village for anything I need.

Besides, I will have my own maid who has been amazingly adept at a variety of things in the past. Who knows, perhaps Miss Nympha will assist? She seems to be extremely capable. I understand the fair was an enormous success." Harriet tried to keep her feelings regarding Nympha from coloring her voice.

"There were a few pickpockets abroad, so I heard. Mrs. Twig told me that the pot boy's mother lost a treasured pin." She walked at Harriet's side to the drawing room, where the housekeeper brought a tray with tea and scones.

"I know. I was there. What do you intend to serve at your dinner?" Her aunt knew of the stolen pin, yet Harriet did not feel she ought to relate the tale of the skillful removal of that object with the compensation of the tea caddy in its place. It was not her story to tell. With the introduction of so important a topic, the conversation was drawn away from the fair.

Later, following a light nuncheon, Harriet elected to walk down near the pond. The swan and her cygnets were not to be seen, so she thought it safe. She ambled along the lawn for some time, reveling in the scents and tranquillity.

"Hello." The familiar voice brought Harriet around to face the earl as he walked across the lawn to where she paused.

"Good day, my lord," she said with the precise amount of proper respect in her voice. She would be civil to him as well as Miss Herbert if it killed her.

"How odd, I had no idea we had frost last night. You are exceedingly chilly, Lady Harriet. What did I do to deserve such treatment?" He joined her to resume strolling across the lawn to where the pretty garden could be viewed.

"Really, sir. I have not the slightest notion of what you speak." She bent over to pick a daisy that she proceeded to twirl between her fingers.

He elected to ignore her frostiness and offered affability that made her slightly ashamed of her rudeness.

"You will be pleased to know that the Plums are

nearly packed. No cupids are to be seen anywhere, and I believe they depart the day after your aunt's dinner."

"You must be pleased." She glanced sideways at him. For a morning call he was dressed extremely fine with a superb dark green coat over biscuit breeches. His boots rivaled the sun for shine.

She had never understood how a call paid at one in the afternoon could be termed a morning call, but it was and she didn't think she could change that. Best accept his presence and cope as gracefully as she could.

"Exceedingly. My parents are deep into arrangements to sail for Italy. The major has been a great help in that respect. He has an amazing fund of knowledge—from where and how to obtain the requisite documents and letters of credit as well as those of introduction. I imagine they will settle in Florence, for father liked the idea of having London newspapers as well as a local newspaper in English. There are a considerable number of English people living in Florence. He intends to be in Italy, but wants the comforts of home."

"The major said that is quite common among Englishmen so your father is not alone. Tell me," she inquired with great daring, "do you intend to travel later? Once you are married, that is?"

"That all depends," he replied.

If he chose to be evasive, she would not inquire further. "I see." It was about as noncommittal as she could possibly be.

"No, you cannot. I have said nothing." He halted, compelling her to stop as well. "I must find the pin and see it returned before I can think beyond that to my own future." He resumed walking, tucking Harriet's arm close to his side so she perforce walked with him.

Philip wished his mother had never seen that pin, or decided she simply had to have it—for whatever reason she had at the time. Complications? No one knew the half of it. He wished to devote all his spare time to courting Harriet Dane. What must he do but go haring about the country on the hunt for that elusive pin.

"You found no sign of the ivory dragon at any of the pawnbrokers?" Harriet inquired.

"None. I found a pretty ivory pin not too unlike the dragon, but not what I sought. I'll give that pin to Mother, since she was so taken with the dragon." Philip caught sight of Harriet's half smile at his pun and was encouraged. If she could still smile at his sallies, all was not lost.

"It is odd how that pin came and went and now can't be found. Aunt Cornelia says it possesses magic. I do not believe in magic, but almost she persuades me."

"I could use a touch of magic about now. I suppose I will have to go to London to inspect the pawnshops there if I cannot find the pin locally. The greater distance between the site of the theft and selling the object, the better or so I understand."

"Could Lord Nicholas help you? It seems to me that you often aid him. I should think he would wish to return the favor."

Philip agreed, but could hardly censure his brother to one outside the family. It was bad enough that she had to learn of the Plums and all their faults, not to mention the difficulties between his parents. One thing for certain, she would have no illusions regarding his family.

"He keeps busy." That was true enough. Philip scarce saw Nick of late.

"So do you. Or at least you appear to be on the go from morning to night. Did you learn anything in the village yesterday?"

"How did you know I went there?"

"You rode off in that direction."

"Nothing," he murmured, recalling how furious he had been to come home empty-handed only to see Nick standing with Harriet in the entry hall. They had been far too close to please him. Nick had leaned over to say something to her, his brown head touching her auburn curls. Why she had removed her bonnet, Philip didn't know, didn't care. But to see Nick so close, and on such seemingly intimate terms with her, while he had wanted to run his fingers through her satiny curls so many times before, was too much. He suspected she had taken umbrage at his words before he escorted her home. Any woman likely would. And there was nothing he could do or say that would erase them from her memory. He had learned she had an excellent memory.

"That is a pity. No one was approached to buy a pretty ivory dragon?"

"I nosed around, but learned nothing of use. The woman from whom we plucked the pin had complained loudly to anyone who would listen. Never mind that she had been gifted with a tea caddy. If the pin is still local, we probably will not learn of it, for now it is too well-known."

"I must return to the house. Aunt Cornelia is in a whirl to pack all she can. The major is shortly going to be inundated with boxes of linens and dishes, not to mention paintings."

"You will be all right here, alone?" Philip did not want her here on her own, but the solution to the mystery of the missing pin must be behind him before he could in good conscience ask her to marry him. If he had to search London for a duplicate to that dratted ivory dragon, he would. He would not come to Harriet with his mother's theft between them. Not that Harriet wouldn't understand. Bless her heart, she had been patience itself with his mother.

"My maid will be here, and it will not be for long. I will be able to oversee the removal of the remaining furniture, those gold draperies installed, and all. I shall be fine. Once everything is removed, I may decide to go to Birch House. I am aware that you wish to take possession of Quince House as soon as you may."

Her sturdy declaration had a touch of bravado to it. Philip resolved to have at least two of his men watch the house—perhaps stay in the stable. There had been no word of problems in the area, but it would be better to be safe.

Cornelia Quince met them at the front door as they mounted the few steps.

"Thank goodness you are here, Lord Stanhope. I need a pair of strong arms."

Harriet watched as her aunt took the earl with her to

the library. He did indeed have strong arms. She well recalled being cradled in them when he had carried her from the stream, not to forget the memorable trip up the stairs to her room when she had fallen. She drifted along behind them, watching as he maneuvered the ladder in the library. He removed his coat, so she enjoyed the sight of him in shirtsleeves, glimpsing a firmly muscled body normally concealed from view.

Shortly, he was removing books from the uppermost shelves to hand down for packing. Empty boxes littered the room, awaiting the books now shelved high and low. Excellent books, leather-bound with pages carefully cut. She had read many of them in her time spent here.

Books. That was what she must do now. She must write and write and keep her mind occupied with tales involving her imaginary characters. That way she might forget the unkind fate dealt to her. Why none of the young men in London had not appealed to her she couldn't say. Now that she had found precisely the man she could love, he appeared to be entranced with a little blond, blue-eyed chit from the rectory. Life was most unfair.

The earl looked at the clock, then informed Aunt Cornelia, "As much as I would like to continue to assist you, I must return home."

Harriet didn't blame him for dashing off. Almost anything would appeal rather than help pack books. She stepped forward. "Never mind, Aunt. I will finish packing those books for you. I fancy you want to check the supplies to make certain you have everything for your dinner."

Cornelia looked flustered that she had actually dared to ask the earl for help, and disappeared as quickly as she could after confused apologies.

"She has much on her mind, my lord," Harriet said, hoping to soothe any wounded sensibilities he might have. She waited at the bottom of the ladder, his coat in her hands. When he reached the floor, she silently offered his coat, assisting him with it, for it was a snug fit.

"You make a good valet, I believe," he quipped.

"Perhaps that is what I should do—offer myself as a gentleman's lady?" She laughed so he would see that she was not the least serious.

"I have no doubt that you will be some gentleman's lady ere long. After all, you are but twenty, I believe. You are still young with a long life before you."

"Whereas you are old and decrepit and fading fast? Nonsense. Plain nonsense. Anyone observing the ease with which you moved that ladder would put lie to that bit of silliness." Harriet had to chuckle at him. When he wished he could be so very charming. Especially to that Nympha Herbert, she reminded herself.

She saw him depart from the house, then returned to the library where she spent the next hours carefully placing books in the boxes, labeling them, and finally stacking them neatly near the door. By the end of the afternoon, the shelves were bare and she was exhausted. She was too tired to think and that suited her just fine.

At last the day came for Aunt Cornelia's grand dinner party. The major's table had been replaced with the one from Quince House, along with all the chairs. Harriet had to admire everything, for the polished wood reflected silver candleholders set with tall white tapers, a bowl of summer flowers in the center, and best of all the fine bone china her aunt had acquired in London on her last visit. The major had returned from India with a beautiful silver service, and they were to use that as well. Unless something terrible occurred, it would be a splendid party.

"How nice you look, Harriet. I do like that sea-green sarcenet you are wearing. The cream lace edging is heavenly and so tasteful. To think you were able to find matching slippers in the village. You will break a heart or two this evening," she concluded with a waggish wiggle of a finger at her niece.

"There won't be any hearts to break, dear aunt. Unless you invited a stranger?" Harriet cast her aunt a small smile, tolerant of her well-meant teasing.

Her aunt paused in her flurry of activity to stare at her niece a moment. "No, no stranger. Sometimes it is possible to overlook what is right under your nose."

Harriet left the room to her aunt's scrutiny and retreated to the major's now perfect drawing room. It had been a masculine disaster until her aunt took charge. True, the draperies needed to be changed and the sofa recovered, but all else was charming. She idly ran her fingers down the keys of the grand pianoforte. The Broadwood was polished so that it gleamed. She was certain it was perfectly tuned as well. The major would tolerate no less.

"You will play for us this evening, Harriet?" The major sauntered across the room, his limp barely noticeable. He reached the fireplace, where he leaned against the mantel.

"If you like." Her aunt had taken all the music with the piano, so there ought to be something here to play.

She was examining the music she found in the attractive canterbury when she heard the arrival of the party from the Hall. Glancing up at the door, she paused in what she was doing. Lord and Lady Lanstone entered the room, followed by both sons. Miss Nympha Herbert was with them as well. The Plums entered, looking disgruntled. Harriet remembered her vow to be civil if it killed her and wondered if she would choke on her words.

That Lord Stanhope was giving her what could only be called a significant look puzzled her, but she valiantly strove to present an unruffled facade to them.

"Lady Harriet, I see you are prepared to perform for us this evening," his lordship said, bowing low over her hand. In an aside he added, "I am sure you will find my mother's jewelry fascinating."

She offered him a frowning look before turning her attention to Lady Lanstone. Harriet almost gasped her dismay and astonishment. The ivory dragon! Lady Lanstone was wearing the ivory dragon! She had been the pickpocket!

If the sight wasn't so frightfully incredible, she would

laugh until she cried. "Good grief!" she murmured to his lordship, who seemed as stunned as she.

"*That* is putting it mildly," he muttered in reply. "Can you not imagine what went through my mind when I viewed her attire before we left?"

"I believe I can. Whatever will you do now?"

She was not to know what he had in mind because Nympha and Lord Nicholas joined them. Nympha fluttered her lashes at Lord Stanhope while Lord Nicholas watched with what appeared to be tolerant disdain.

"You will play later on, I trust, Lady Harriet," Nympha cooed. "I do admire someone who can play the pianoforte so well. Do you enjoy dancing, Lord Stanhope?"

"At times. Come, let us join the others." He ruthlessly grasped Harriet's hand to pull her with him to where his parents stood talking with the major and Miss Quince, soon to be Mrs. William Birch.

Miss Quince had invited Mr. Heron, who, as the son of a baron, was more than qualified to grace the party. To partner him she had prevailed upon another of the rector's daughters, Miss Priscilla—upon Harriet's suggestion.

Priscilla's blond curls dressed in a classical style seemed to appeal to the architect. Harriet congratulated herself on the inspiration to suggest to Priscilla that she might appear so. Even her gown suggested a Hellenic line.

It did no harm that her blue eyes echoed the blue of the Grecian sky, and that she knew one muse from another, mythology being her one strong point.

The evening promised to be interesting. Most intriguing would be Lord Stanhope's plan to snabble the pin from his mother without her awareness. Pity he couldn't just ask for it, tell her he was aware of what she had been doing, and insist that she cease. Dear, foolish man, he felt he had to be considerate of her feelings. Perhaps so, but Harriet thought she could use a bit of plain speaking once in her life. While it might be true that life had not always been kind to her, it was no excuse to take things that didn't belong to her.

"Lady Harriet? Mr. Heron was wondering if you continue with your writing?" Priscilla gently nudged Harriet from her mental musing.

"I enjoyed *The Rogue's Regret* very much. Tell me you plan to write another." Mr. Heron's smile was benign.

Harriet fought against the giggle that longed to surface when she looked at him. Perhaps she was fending off incipient hysterics? But he did resemble a heron with his tall, lean looks and that mop of shaggy blond hair.

"I am presently working on my next book, sir. It will occupy my time when my aunt and the major have left for Italy." She composed her face into a sincere pose, suitable, she figured, for an authoress.

"You think."

Harriet gave Lord Stanhope a confused look. What did he mean by saying "you think" to her? Of course she would be writing. What else had she to do with her time that would be profitable? The allowance from her father's estate was not paltry, but hardly generous, either. Soon she would need money were she to find a place to live and write. She would become like Miss Edgeworth, traveling and writing novels as she pleased. The major had said that living abroad was far cheaper than in England. Wouldn't it be amusing if she ended up in Italy as well?

The major's butler, Millet, appeared in the doorway to announce dinner in the manner of one trained in London, and at a grand home.

The earl remained by her, drawing her aside as the others surged forward in no particular precedence, other than the pairing of Lady Lanstone with the major, while Lord Lanstone walked at Aunt Cornelia's side.

"What do you mean, *you think!*" Harriet demanded in an undertone.

"One can never be certain what lies ahead. Matters may totally alter in the twinkling of an eye. How am I going to put my hands on the ivory dragon?" He placed her hand on his arm, walking slowly toward the dining room as though they discussed nothing more than the weather.

"Take it. Or you could pretend to be a highwayman and snabble it whilst they are on their way home, waving a pistol in the air." She suppressed a grin at his expression.

"I may require your help. Do you have a mask?" He leered at her.

At this, she did chuckle. "You are a wicked man, to speak so when we are in company and I may have to explain myself when I laugh, as I surely will if you persist in keeping this up."

"They will fancy I am whispering sweet nothings in your pretty little ear." He bent close to her, and to others he must have appeared romantic.

"No, is it? I had no idea." She sailed into the dining room on his arm knowing he was totally at sea.

"Harriet," he murmured in a threatening tone.

"Indeed, I am, my lord. Harriet, that is. And I confess I had no notion my ear was anything other than ordinary." She flashed him a smile intended to dazzle. It was impossible to tell what he thought, but the smile had a notable effect on him. He said not a word in reply!

It was difficult to refrain from looking at the ivory dragon. To think that they had hunted high and low, that Lord Stanhope had haunted pawnshops to find the pin that was right in his own home!

Afterward, Harriet couldn't have said what she ate. Not that she hadn't discussed the menu at great length with her aunt or anything. It was that she was so terribly aware of the man at her side, his teasing, his—oh, everything. And then the ivory dragon tended to draw her attention. She suspected that had anyone paid the slightest attention, they would have been puzzled that both the earl and Harriet kept darting looks at his mother.

The meal concluded, the women retired to the drawing room for tea and conversation.

Harriet sought refuge at the far end of the room, by the pianoforte. She had left the music in a pile on the little bench and thought she ought to replace it or at least take what she might use from it. She debated too long and saw her peace at an end.

"Lady Harriet," the marchioness said as she marched up to where Harriet now stood leaning slightly against the grand pianoforte, "I want you to know how much I appreciate all you have done to help me."

"You are quite welcome, ma'am. A talent like yours ought never be ignored. I trust you will have a wonderful trip to Italy and find many, many birds to paint. I suspect your husband will be extremely pleased with you."

"That remains to be seen," the matron replied, a hint of sarcasm in her voice.

"Well, he should be. Pleased, that is." Oh, dear, had Lord Stanhope affected her mind as well as her body?

The marchioness looked faintly mystified, but her face cleared in a bit.

Harriet couldn't help but stare at the ivory dragon.

"You notice my pin, I see."

"Yes, ma'am. Wherever did you find such a lovely thing?" Harriet wished someone else would join them. She truly did not want to discuss the pin. She just wanted it returned to the owner.

"Oh, I picked it up in the village. You like it?"

"Excessively. I think ivory dragons are charming."

"Then, you shall have it!" Before Harriet could think of anything to say in reply, Lady Lanstone had removed the pin, looked at it fondly, then stepped closer to pin it to Harriet's gown, right in the center.

"What can I say, dear lady? Thank you. Very much, indeed!" Harriet's knees were weak, and she knew her voice was shaken.

Aunt Cornelia appeared at her side, noted the pin, and said without a trace of astonishment, "How lovely. I think the ivory dragon suits Harriet to a tee. How kind of you, Lady Lanstone. I know Harriet will cherish it."

"Truly I will," Harriet agreed, thinking that correct, at least for the moment. How it would please the earl when he saw it.

The moment came sooner than she expected. The gentlemen rejoined the ladies, filtering into the room in twos, chatting as they came.

The earl immediately made his way to Harriet's side.

It took several moments before he noticed the pin. He had gazed around the room as though to assess the remainder of the evening and possible entertainment. Then he looked at Harriet, really looked.

"Your mother gave this to me," she said brightly. "Is it not lovely? I didn't even require a mask and a pistol!"

"Now the next step—we must return the pin!"

# Chapter Sixteen

"You mean to tell me that she took the ivory dragon from her son's pocket while at the fair? And that he had no idea she had?" Cornelia shook her head. "That is difficult to accept." An auburn lock slipped from under her turban as the carriage hit a bump, and she attempted in vain to tuck it neatly in place.

"Think how noisy it is at a fair, and that there are people jostling and pushing about. He would scarce be expecting his own mother would do such a thing." Harriet patted the dragon, where it gleamed from her bosom. "I did not dare give it to Lord Stanhope whilst there; I'd not wish his mother to observe that! She doesn't know that we are aware of this little dragon's recent history."

"I wonder how old it is?" Cornelia leaned over to look at the pin again, touching it lightly.

The coach pulled up before Quince House, and they went in together, Cornelia still glancing at the pin as though she couldn't quite believe all that had happened.

"Please find the little wooden box and put that pin away before some other bizarre event occurs. I would like to sail off to Italy knowing that you are not *again* hunting for that elusive ivory dragon!" Cornelia smiled to take any sting from her words, but Harriet knew she meant them.

"I agree. I'll run up to fetch it." Harriet ran up the stairs to her room, dug through her drawer, fearful that the box had also disappeared. Once found, she promptly removed the pin from her gown and tucked the little dragon into the box with great care.

She brought the dragon box with her when she joined her aunt in the drawing room. "Where can I keep this until tomorrow? Actually, I am surprised that the earl did not wish to come over to claim the pin tonight! Such a look as he gave me."

Cornelia chuckled. "I wish I could have captured his expression with pencil and paper. He was so astounded, and covered it so swiftly."

"Perhaps I might put this into your little wall safe for the night? Lord Stanhope may as well know about it, for he will be taking possession of this house before long." Harriet stroked the satiny finish of the carved box, thinking it was a shame for it to be returned to a glass case rather than to be used and enjoyed.

"It would have been there long ago if we had used our heads." Cornelia gave her niece a stern look.

"I had no notion it was so valuable," Harriet said on the defensive.

"I know dear," Cornelia admitted with a sigh. "Hindsight is always so marvelous. You know the combination. Go put the pin away, and then we may seek our beds in peace."

Harriet did as bade, then followed her aunt up the stairs. Morning could not come soon enough.

Morning brought bright sun and a slight breeze. Harriet dressed with care in a favorite straw muslin trimmed in narrow lace and having a deep green riband tied directly below the bodice. She slipped green shoes on with haste, eager for her day to begin.

Cornelia eyed her niece with favor. "I think you ought to make a fine impression. Now, eat before he comes. I'd not be surprised if he has more on his mind than returning the dragon pin to Lord Rothson. Has it been as evident to you as it has to me that he appears to be quite taken with you?"

"Well, my hopes have risen on that score, I confess."

"He is a fine man, and I could wish no better for you."

Harriet smiled, but wondered if wishes came true and how long it took.

They had scarce finished their breakfast when an urgent knock was heard on the front door.

Harriet glanced at her aunt, tossed her napkin down on the table, and hurried along the hall to answer the impatient summons. Flinging the door open, she tilted her head to give the earl an intrepid smile. "For once I know precisely why you are here. Come, I shall take you to the pin." Her brisk words were met with a lazy smile from his lordship—much to her confusion.

"Good morning, my lady." Harriet paused at the tone of his voice. Why did it reveal such warmth, almost oozing with what she thought might be sensuality? It certainly sent little shivers up her spine!

"G-good morning." She backed away from him, flustered and not a little bewildered at his behavior.

Predatory. That is what he was. He pursued her down the hall and into the library right up to the spot where the wall safe was located.

Her fingers fumbled when she tried to work the combination, but she finally succeeded in opening the little depository. "Aunt keeps a few things here." She removed the dragon box, then gestured to the neat little pile of velvet-covered boxes inside the safe before she clicked the door shut.

Why she should be so nervous she wasn't sure, but she certainly was. It was almost over. He would take the ivory dragon and be gone.

"Come over here where we can sit. We need to discuss how the box is to be returned." He placed a hand under her elbow to draw her along at his side.

Harriet swallowed with care. Why was he doing this? "You scarce need *me* to return the box. If your mother took it, you should not have the slightest trouble replacing it." He wrapped one arm about her shoulders before gently urging her to sit in a small cane-back chair near the window. She perched uneasily, eyeing him with caution as he sat on the matching chair, his gaze fixed intently upon her.

"Oh, but I do. Need you, that is."

His voice wrapped around her like warmed velvet, and

she felt as though she was melting from the heat in his eyes. This was ten in the morning! Things like this did not occur to somewhat proper spinsters at this time of day. She wrote about feelings like this in her books. She did not live them! Or was it possible that wishes truly did come true?

"I do not see why." She tore her gaze from his captivating face to stare down at her hands clenched in her lap.

"Well, our entire family was present plus several other guests at the baron's dinner. There was a certain amount of confusion as well as conversation going on at the time of the showing of his collection. I cannot go to the baron's home and request to see his collection—just like that. For one thing, I have already viewed the blasted collection. It isn't that wonderful—unless he has added to it recently."

"I still do not see why you need me." She glanced at him to note the stubborn line to his lips, the determined angle of his jaw. Oh, he was not going to give up easily. The last thing in the world she wanted to do was visit Baron Rothson. She had never met the man, for pity's sake.

"I do not know the baron," she declared in a steady voice. She was surprised at how firm she sounded, for she was quaking jelly inside.

"Easily remedied. I will write him to request a viewing of his collection. He will not deny the daughter of an earl, you see." There was a hint of laughter in his voice now, although it still had that elusive quality that made her nervous.

"Like that, is he?" Harriet compressed her lips, then nibbled on her lower lip, glancing at the earl, then back to her hands.

"Come. It will be a lark!"

"I do not see why you simply could not hand him the pin, apologize, and be on your way."

"You know that would never do."

Harriet trembled as he leaned forward to place his hand over hers. "No, I suppose not. You have your mother to think of, I know." She gave up. "Very well, I will help you. When?"

"I have to learn if the baron is in residence. I've not seen him for a week or two." He stroked her hand with a feather-light touch.

"You mean we might have to wait?" She pulled her hands from under his touch, and jumped to her feet as though fleeing a fire.

"I will keep you informed. In the meanwhile I thought perhaps we could enjoy a few drives, maybe go on a painting excursion." He rose to stand at her side, giving her that intimate smile once again.

"I think my aunt needs me," Harriet stammered. It was silly to feel panicked when she had known him all this time. They had gone painting before. So why did she feel so nervous now?

"Nonsense. She has all the servants at her beck and call. She can manage without you for an hour or two."

Oh, how she wanted to go with him, enjoy his company. But dare she? "I could take Abby with me, of course," she replied, sounding a bit weak.

"Of course." His smile was wicked, and she wondered what he had in mind. "I usually have my groom along to tend the horses. They can keep each other company."

"I see." She heard steps in the hall. A glance at the door revealed her aunt entering the library.

"Good morning, Lord Stanhope. I trust you are well? And your mother?" Aunt Cornelia swept into the room, offering a bland smile to the earl and a minatory one to Harriet. "You have the ivory dragon in your hand, I see. We will all be thankful when it is safely with Baron Rothson once again."

"I was just telling Lady Harriet that I must learn if the baron is in residence. Once I know that for certain, I will write to request a showing of his collection for Lady Harriet." His facile explanation seemed to please Cornelia.

"I fancy you clever people will figure out how to return the pin without discovery." She toyed with the handkerchief in her hands, giving the earl a questioning look.

"We haven't as yet, ma'am. I thought that perhaps were Lady Harriet to spend some time with me, we might together think of a plan. I fear my wits have gone begging."

"I sincerely doubt that, my lord. I would hazard a guess that your wits are entirely sound." Her eyes flashed with amusement. "By all means take Harriet for a drive. I have everything well in hand. She is free."

"Good. Very good. If you will fetch a bonnet, perhaps a parasol along with your gloves, we can leave at once." He took a step toward the door, placing his arm about Harriet to guide her with him.

She gave her aunt a perplexed frown, but since there was no help from that quarter, she had little choice but to do as bid.

In her room she stormed about, collecting a straw gypsy bonnet tied with wide green ribands, her gloves, and a green pagoda parasol. "I am a silly fool, meekly doing as told. Of course I want more than anything to go with him, but I should have resisted—at least a little! If he thinks he can wrap me around his finger . . . he is right. I am totally unable to resist that man."

She sauntered down the stairs, intent upon appearing cool and indifferent to him. That her heart pounded in double time and she wondered if she'd be able to speak was beside the point. She would look imperturbable.

"Ah, what beauty is mine for the afternoon! You never fail to delight me."

Again, he cupped her elbow to guide her from the house with gentle care. Instead of allowing her to climb into his curricle, he lifted her up, his hands warm at her waist and taking his own sweet time to do so. Abby stood to one side, watching silently.

A groom from Lanstone Hall came hurrying around the corner of the house. "M'lord, a moment!"

Lord Stanhope gave him an impatient glance, then went to meet him, listening to the message he'd brought. Harriet looked off into the distance, wondering what was so important that the groom had dashed over. She leaned over to speak with her maid, giving her instructions before she climbed up to the small rear-facing seat behind the main carriage seat.

In minutes, the groom hopped up behind to join Abby, and the earl climbed in to take the reins. "A surprise."

"Perhaps you would prefer to postpone our drive if something has arisen that needs your attention." Harriet shifted on the cushion as though she might get down.

"Actually, it is a good thing you are here. I just learned that the baron is home, but planning a trip to Hampshire. If we are to see him, it must be now."

"Now?" Harriet gulped. "But I, we, that is, you had no time to write to him. Did you?"

He skillfully guided his horse and the curricle along the country road, dashing toward the village at top speed.

"Is it this urgent?" She clutched at her bonnet, afraid it would go sailing along with her courage.

"I want this ivory dragon back in the baron's collection case as soon as possible. I have my reasons."

Harriet was not about to ask what they were. She clung to the side of the curricle with her free hand and hoped there were no others intent upon reaching the village at the same time.

He didn't pause when they whirled through the quiet village, but continued until they reached the baron's entrance. This time the gate stood open. Lord Stanhope slowed the curricle through this, then picked up a bit of speed as they hurried through the park, taking the avenue directly to the front door.

The groom took hold of the reins, allowing the earl to assist Harriet from the carriage at once. Abby followed discreetly behind her mistress.

"I am breathless," she whispered as he marched her up the steps.

"You may leave all talking to me if you wish. He won't expect anyone as lovely as you to have any conversation anyway."

"You wish me to pretend to be a silly, empty-headed creature?" she whispered more loudly.

"No, just be yourself." With that terse instruction, they faced the portly butler who greeted them, his wispy eyebrows flying upward at the sight of the earl and a stranger. The maid was ignored.

"I have heard the baron is planning to go away for a time and hoped that he might be persuaded to show his famous collection to Lady Harriet Dane before he leaves. Would now be possible?" The earl strolled past the astounded butler, taking Harriet with him. Abby scuttled behind, lingering in the shadows as proper.

"I, I, that is, my lord, I do not know . . ."

"Who is it, Barrows?" A tall, dark gentleman of indeterminate years came from an adjacent room. He paused, then started forward to greet the callers. "To what do I owe the pleasure of your call, Stanhope?" He looked anything but pleased, but seemed determined to be polite.

"Lady Harriet Dane is staying in the area, and she hoped to view your collection. When I learned you intend to leave shortly, I hoped we might prevail upon you for her to see it."

The baron's eyes narrowed.

Harriet figured they were sunk—what with him having accused Lord Nicholas of stealing the pin and all. What made Lord Stanhope think the baron would be willing to permit her access to his precious collection? She smiled warmly at him, hoping he might succumb to a feminine wile.

"Normally I would say no, but it is difficult to turn away such a lovely lady." He smiled at Harriet, offering her his arm.

With a backward look at the earl, pleading with him not to abandon her, Harriet went with the baron. They climbed an impressive oak stairway, then walked down a long hall until they entered a large room lit only by skylights. A servant had followed them, and proceeded to light candles to brighten the dim room.

"Have you improved your security since I was last here?" the earl inquired, attacking the matter by plunging to the heart of it.

Harriet detached her arm from the baron's grasp. She wandered along the cases, admiring the unusual collection of precious things from around the world. There was a jeweled fan from Russia, a carving of a cat that looked quite Egyptian, artifacts that had to be Greek.

"I certainly have. No one will be able to enter these cases now. There is an alarm rigged up that will frighten off the most hardened of thieves."

Lord Stanhope turned to Harriet where she leaned over one case to get a better look at a fine comb from China. "The baron had a small pin stolen about the time we were last here. Someone asked to view it more closely, and it disappeared. Is that not correct?" His look challenged the baron to disagree, which the baron wisely chose not to do. Lord Stanhope continued, "Pity, for I think you would have liked it."

Harriet smiled a bit wanly. Feeling rather dismayed at the prospect of returning the pin when the odds were so against them, she sank down on a surprisingly comfortable armchair, one of a pair set close to the fireplace. If they were not able to access the cases, how in the world would they return the pin? He had slipped it back to her just before they entered this house, giving her a pleading look. She'd had no chance to query him on that. It was up to her to find some means of replacing that ivory dragon. Apparently he was to distract the baron so she could figure out some means of doing so.

Looking about the room, she observed that all the surfaces were glass. There was no place to conceal the pin. She placed her arm on the soft leather on the chair while she considered the problem.

Suddenly it came to her. As sly as she might, she slipped the pin from her reticule, and dropped it along the space between the arm and the seat cushion. Then she pulled a small comb from her reticule and dropped it as well, this time exclaiming in presumed vexation.

"Oh, dear! My comb!" She pretended to search for the comb, but "found" the box with the ivory dragon instead. "What, pray tell, is this, sir?"

He moved to her side with amazing speed, grabbing the box from her hand with a total lack of graciousness.

"The ivory dragon! You found it there?" He gestured to the narrow spot from where she had removed the little box.

Harriet rose to stand beside the earl. "Is that the item you are missing? It must have fallen beside the cushion. Whoever dropped it failed to observe where it went and neglected to tell you. I am glad you have it back, my lord." That the baron ought to have been more careful wasn't said. To Lord Stanhope she added, "Perhaps we should leave? I have seen quite a bit, and I suspect the baron would like to return his ivory dragon to the case unobserved."

The baron recalled his manners to assure her that they were welcome to remain, but the earl took Harriet's cue and within minutes they had left the house. Abby and the groom perched behind them, quite silent.

"That was as clever a bit of work as I could imagine." He gave her a warmly approving smile before returning his attention to his driving.

"Every surface in that room was glass save for those chairs. What a blessing I was overcome and had to sit down." Harriet waited for some remark, but none was forthcoming. "Well, you did rather sweep me along with you."

"I had no idea what the baron might do. If he figured out that Mother had filched the dragon, who knows what he might have done. He has been exceedingly envious of my parents, and in particular the bird collection Father has—although why, is beyond me."

"So he created his own collection."

This time the curricle went through the village at a decorous pace, increasing speed as they headed for home. He didn't stop until they had reached the barn on the way to Quince House.

Harriet raised her brows as he handed the reins to his groom, then assisted her from the carriage. Abby and the groom remained with the carriage, seeming not the slightest surprised.

"How fortunate there is no rain in sight, sir."

"I thought we might talk." He tucked her arm close to his side, casually walking with her from the road, stepping over rocks and grassy clumps.

A flock of birds took wing in her stomach, flying madly nowhere. "Talk? We cannot talk at the house—the garden?"

He guided her past the barn with only a cursory glance at its dim interior before leading her up the path to where they had been painting.

Here he came to a halt, turning to face her. He released her arm, but took hold of her hands. "Harriet, here is where I fell in love with you. You have become dearer to me as the days have passed. I wanted to return that ivory dragon before I began to court you in earnest. It was like a cloud hanging over me."

"I cannot see . . ." Harriet was stunned by the earl's statement that here was where he had fallen in love with her. She supposed she had as well, yet she felt he could have given her a better hint!

"And now I can court you as I wish." He dropped her hands, drawing her close.

She resisted. "And what about Miss Nympha Herbert? It seems to me that you are rather fond of her, my lord."

"One-sided, to be sure—on her part." He impatiently brushed aside any attentions he had paid the rector's daughter. "I have had eyes for no one but you, my love."

"You might have said something," she pointed out logically, continuing to resist his appeal.

"I wanted to, I could not feel free until the matter of the ivory dragon was resolved. It cast a pall on all my ambitions, my hopes for our future. I wanted no impediment to our happiness, my little love."

This time Harriet did not resist him.

The touch of his lips on hers brought memories rushing back. If this was heaven, she never wanted to leave. Her bonnet slid down, landing against her back. It wasn't until later she realized where it was.

"Harriet," he murmured at long last, cradling her against his long lean body.

"What?" She clutched his arms, thinking her poor knees had definitely become very undependable.

"This cannot go on."

"What?" she cried, releasing her hold on his arms and taking a tiny step away from him. She was promptly pulled close once again.

"I mean, I cannot let you go, not for a day, a moment. Promise you will be my wife. Confess you love me as I believe you do." His dark eyes held a blazing warmth that she knew brought a blush to her cheeks.

His hands were exploring her back, and the sensations created nearly rendered her speechless. Nevertheless she managed to whisper, "I love you very much, my dear. To be your wife would be my most cherished dream come true."

"I hoped you would agree," he said, his voice deep and rich, sending tremors of desire through Harriet that surely were scandalous. She nestled against him, not wanting to ever leave his side.

"I sent for a special license—your aunt offered the information I needed. I did not know your middle name is Louisa, my dear. A very pretty name we can bestow on our first daughter. How soon can we marry?"

She gave him a cautious look. "This is very unexpected."

"It would be good to wed before your Aunt Cornelia and my parents leave for Italy. As to arrangements, we could either live at the Hall or at Quince House, once we fix it up. I daresay there is enough furniture and rugs around that we would be cozy in no time."

"You have given this a great deal of thought, haven't you?" She took a small step away from him so she could better study his face. She felt as though she was swept along on a strong wind.

"I have had little on my mind but you—other than that blasted ivory dragon." He helped himself to another leisurely kiss, which of course Harriet had to return.

"Strange, I rather like that little dragon," she managed to say when allowed to speak. "Had it not been for it, I might not have met you."

"We would have met, have no fear. You are my fate, dear heart. And I," he pronounced with a punctuating kiss, "am yours."

Harriet swallowed with care, thinking that strong wind had become a whirlwind. She was nigh dizzy with the rapidity of her emotional changes. She leaned against his chest, feeling a need for his strength.

"We will marry and soon."

"If you say so, dearest. A few more kisses, and I daresay I will marry you anytime you wish." Harriet lifted her face to his, expecting and receiving what she wanted.

"I suppose you'd wish to change gowns, although you look quite beautiful as you are this moment. I could send the groom for the rector. Or better still, we could drive to the church. It is still early in the day. Come, let us go immediately."

"What? I cannot believe what I am hearing! Tomorrow, at the earliest!" She stamped her foot on the grass.

Philip chuckled. He had shamelessly maneuvered her to agree to tomorrow when he had expected to wait a week at the very least.

"As you wish, my dear. Tomorrow."

Her look was melting, warming Philip as he ached to make her his own.

"We shall have all our tomorrows together, my dearest."

Plus a dragon or two if she had her way.